THE OLD MAN IN THE *Club*

Dear Reader:

Curtis Bunn has once again captured the mindsets of characters that will not be easy to forget. Elliott Thomas is sixty-one and feeling cheated out of time, having been unable to enjoy many of his younger years for various reasons. He is battling age and does not want to go quietly into a senior citizen home. So he does what makes him feel good: hanging out in nightclubs and dating women the same age as his adult children. Of course, everyone is not understanding and in agreement with his choices, which brings on the drama, conflict, and ultimately, redemption.

Bunn has proven himself to be a master of words, and his imagination is always on overdrive. Yet, his books pull at the heartstrings of readers since everything is so relatable—if not to them directly, to someone that they know. As always, thanks for supporting the authors of Strebor Books. We strive to bring you the most prolific authors who think outside of the norm. We appreciate the love and support.

Blessings,

Zane

Publisher
Strebor Books
www.simonandschuster.com

ZANE PRESENTS

THE OLD MAN IN THE *Club*

A NOVEL BY

CURTIS BUNN

SBI

STREBOR BOOKS

NEW YORK   LONDON   TORONTO   SYDNEY

Strebor Books
P.O. Box 6505
Largo, MD 20792
http://www.streborbooks.com

ISBN 978-1-59309-572-7
ISBN 978-1-4767-5871-8 (ebook)
LCCN 2014931185

First Strebor Books trade paperback edition June 2014

Cover design: www.mariondesigns.com
Cover photograph: © Keith Saunders Photos

10 9 8 7 6 5 4 3 2 1

Manufactured in the United States of America

For information regarding special discounts for bulk purchases, please contact Simon & Schuster Special Sales at 1-866-506-1949 or business@simonandschuster.com

The Simon & Schuster Speakers Bureau can bring authors to your live event. For more information or to book an event, contact the Simon & Schuster Speakers Bureau at 1-866-248-3049 or visit our website at www.simonspeakers.com.

To Trevor Nigel Lawrence, my childhood friend and "brother,"
who gave up clubs years ago, but is not too old
to go to them if he wanted.

Brown, Sam and Maureen Myers, Ronnie and Tarita Bagley, Tony and Raye Starks, Darryl Washington, Darryl (DJ) and Wanda Johnson, Lyle Harris, Monya M. Battle, Tony (Kilroy) and Amanda Hall, Marc Davenport, Tami Rice-Mitchell, Brad Corbin, William Mitchell, J.B. Hill, Bob & La Detra White, Kent Davis, Wayne Ferguson, Tony & Erika Sisco, Betty Roby, Leslie Leland, Kathy Brown, Venus Chapman, Monica Harris Wade, Tara Ford, Christine Beatty, Greg Willis, Al Whitney, Brian White, Ronnie Akers, Jacques Walden, Dennis Wade, Julian Jackson, Mark Webb, Kelvin Lloyd, Frank Nelson, Hayward Horton, Mark Bartlett, Marvin Burch, Derrick (Nick Lambert), Gerald Mason, Charles E. Johnson, Harry Sykes, Kim Mosley, Angela Davis, Ed (Bat) Lewis, Shelia Harrison, David A. Brown, Leslie LeGrande, Rev. Hank Davis, Susan Davis-Wigenton, Donna Richardson, Sheila Wilson, Curtis West, Bruce Lee, Val Guilford, Derek T. Dingle, Ramona Palmer, Warren Jones, Deberah (Sparkle) Williams, Leon H. Carter, Zack Withers, Kevin Davis, Sybil & Leroy Savage, Avis Easley, Demetress Graves, Anna Burch, Najah Aziz, Kevin & Hope Jones, George Hughes, Yetta Gipson, Mary Knatt, Serena Knight, Joi Edwards, Sonya Perry, Denise Taylor, Diana Joseph, Derrick (Tinee) Muldrow, Rick Eley, Marty McNeal, D.L. Cummings, Rob Parker, Cliff Brown, D. Orlando Ledbetter, Garry Howard, Stephen A. Smith, Clifford Benton, Len Burnett, Lesley Hanesworth, Sherline Tavenier, Jeri Byrom, E. Franklin Dudley, Skip Grimes, Jeff Stevenson, Stacy Gill, Lateefah Aziz, Billy Robinson, Jay Nichols, Ralph Howard, Paul Spencer, Jai Wilson, Garry Raines, Glen Robinson, Dwayne Gray, Jessica Ferguson, Carolyn Glover, David R. Squires, Kim Royster, Keela Starr, Mike Dean, Dexter Santos, John Hughes, Mark Lassiter, Tony Carter, Kimberly Frelow, Michele Ship, Michelle Lemon, Zain, Tammy Thompson,

Karen Shepherd, Carmen Carter, Erin Sherrod, Tawana Turner-Green, Marilyn Bibby, Sheryl Williams-Jones, Vonda Henderson, Danny Anderson, Keisha Hutchinson, Olivia Alston, John Hollis, Dorothy (Dot) Harrell, Aggie Nteta, Ursula Renee, Carrie Haley, Anita Wilson, Tim Lewis, Sandra Velazquez, Patricia Hale, Pam Cooper, Regina Troy, Denise Thomas, Andre Aldridge, Brenda O'Bryant, Ron Thomas, Pargeet Wright, Mike Christian, Sid Tutani, Tracie Andrews, Toni Tyrell, Tanecia Raphael, Tammy Grier, Roland Louis, April Tarver, Penny Payne, Cynthia Fields, Patricia Hale, LaToya Tokley, Dr. Yvonne Sanders-Butler, Alicia Guice, Clara LeRoy, Denise Bethea, Hadjii Hand, Petey Franklin and The Osagyefuo Amoatia Ofori Panin, King of Akyem Abuakwa Eastern Region of Ghana, West Africa.

Special thanks and love to my great alma mater, Norfolk State University (Class of 1983); the brothers of Alpha Phi Alpha (especially the Notorious E Pi of Norfolk State); Ballou High School (Class of '79), ALL of Washington, D.C., especially Southeast and the team at www.atlantablackstar.com.

I am also grateful to all the readers and wonderful book clubs that have supported my work over the years and to my literary many friends Nathan McCall, Carol Mackey, Linda Duggins, Terrie Williams, Kimberla Lawson Roby, Walter Mosley and Monica Michelle.

I'm sure I left off some names; I ask your forgiveness. If you know me you know I'm getting old. :-) I appreciate and I am grateful for you.

Peace and blessings,
CURTIS

CHAPTER 1
Age Ain't Nothing But A Number

Elliott Thomas was stuck in the bathroom. Not stuck like he could not get out, but stuck because he had to wait for his pants to dry.

He had peed on himself.

At sixty-one, Elliott's bladder wasn't what it used to be. In fact, with his prostate the size of a ripe pear, the reservoir that stored his urine was overworked. In this case, he could feel the need for a bathroom run coming on, but he was on the dance floor with a cute young prospect and could not break away in the middle of the song.

She looked even younger than her age, which made their pairing that much more noticeable. And strange. She liked to dance, and so one song became two, and three, to where Elliott began sweating. He was fighting so hard to not pee on himself right there on the dance floor.

But that was the only indicator of his distress. He smiled at the young lady, Tamara Worthington, and kept up with her moves and drew her into him. Finally, though, the urge became too strong, so he grabbed her hand and led her off the small makeshift dance area at Vanquish Lounge in midtown Atlanta.

Elliott walked her to a roped, reserved area where he had arranged bottle service for Tamara and her three friends, all of whom were in their early-to-mid-twenties with dresses so short he could see they had discarded the idea of wearing panties. It was Tamara's birthday. She turned twenty-five.

"Going to the bathroom." He leaned into Tamara's ear. His legs were pressed together as if they would serve as a levee to hold back his water. "Be back in a few. But drink up."

She looked up at him with a smile and a wink. "Don't be long."

Elliott winked back and headed to the bathroom; a man and his bladder racing against the clock. The men's room was on the other side of the space, and he maneuvered through the crowd hurriedly, trying to appear calm when inside he was panicked. The urge to go increased by the step, and so did his anxiety.

By the time he burst through the bathroom door and into a stall, the leakage had begun. The front right side of his gray trousers was soaked before he could free himself and drain his bladder into the urinal.

He looked down at the considerable wet spot and his anxiety advanced to panic. It was obvious what happened and he could not go back into the lounge, or to Tamara, looking like he'd wet himself. This was a problem he dealt with on a daily basis by keeping a foam cup in his car. He would pee into it as he drove if the urge became overwhelming, to avoid frequent stops.

In this case, he waited too late to head to the bathroom. With no other recourse and to avoid mass embarrassment, Elliott took off his pants and pressed the button on the heated hand dryer and placed the wet spot under the burst of hot air. Men entering the bathroom did double-takes, the sight of him standing there in polka dot boxers startling them.

But Elliott was unfazed. He was a determined man, and not merely when it came to pursuing young women. He learned to function with a purpose and focus, so he addressed his wet pants as he would anything else: head-on.

"Woman spilled a drink in my lap," he told a guy who asked the inevitable question. Elliott's voice was deeper than you might expect from a moderately sized man. When he wanted to, he could sound like Lou Rawls. "I would be pissed off if she wasn't so fine," he added, trying hard to be amusing.

"I got a table full of women waiting on me," he went on. "Can't go back over there with a river on my pants."

The man laughed. "I hear you, pops."

Elliott stood there for almost ten minutes in his wet drawers with his pants under the hand dryer. He could not take off his underwear, so he had to deal with that wetness up against his body. As long as the pants did not look wet, he did not care.

It was one of those moments that made him wonder why he was not at home watching old episodes of *The Honeymooners* and sipping on tea. But it was a fleeting moment. He was where he wanted to be.

The pants dried finally, Elliott put them back on, and steadied himself in front of a mirror. He tucked in his shirt and tightened his belt, and a sense of calm came over him. He was back to himself, albeit pissy.

The bathroom attendant standing at the sinks supplied soap and Elliott washed his hands as he gazed into the mirror. The image that came back was one of a handsome man whose wrinkles around his eyes and neck hardly told his story, but did indicate his advanced age.

He offset that by coloring his hair, wearing trendy clothes and keeping his body right with exercise and conscientious food choices. But what really minimized his age was his attitude and energy, which made some younger women not look at him as a father figure, but as a man who could expose them and help them to grow.

Some women could not take Elliott seriously. Others were flattered but not interested. A few laughed in his face. Enough embraced his moxie.

He was older than most at Vanquish by more than twenty years. And yet, there was a draw to the nightlife for him, a lure that was far more than about the tantalizing young girls that he kept in his world.

Being out in the night made him feel free, and for all he had experienced in his life, feeling free and alive meant a lot to him. There were many versions of the old men in the club; most of them overgrown children whose insecurities dictated that they pursue younger women. They were the proverbial "sugar daddies" that drove nice cars, flashed their credit cards and presented gifts to entice vulnerable and opportunistic young women.

It was legal prostitution, without a pimp. Essentially, they were dirty old men that could not handle an experienced woman who would challenge them or require them to make an effort. So they lured young girls with things.

That was not Elliott's *modus operandi*. He was a different kind of old man in the club. It wasn't so much that he liked it. He needed it.

It was hard to not notice the generation gap between Elliott and others at the lounge. Although Elliott was an attractive man, right around six feet with a lean body, the gray edges that shaped his chiseled face and the wrinkles around his eyes and neck were undeniable. They at least told he was older than everyone else. He was proud that he was sixty-one but kept himself together to where he was able to attract younger ladies; well, younger ladies with varying issues.

He noticed that the man in the bathroom called him "Pops," and he heard the whispers when he showed up at clubs or bars frequented by adults half his age.

And he did not care.

Women his age called him a "dirty old man" and his buddies laughed at him and wondered about his lifestyle. He did not care.

Elliott Thomas decided to live his life in a way that pleased him, which was not what could be said by most. A lot happened for him to come to this place—dark, sad, regrettable experiences that shaped the man's adult life.

He was the old man in the club, and had no qualms with it. It was a blessing to be *anywhere*. And he liked it.

What was peeing on himself to a man who, when considering the totality of his life, very well could be dead? But there he was, alive and well, and refusing to live any way other than the way he wanted.

"What's happening?" he inquired of Tamara upon his return to their reserved section.

She handed him a glass of champagne. "What took you so long?"

"Ran into a few friends," he lied. He squirmed in his seat because while his pants were dry, his polka dot underwear was wet—and uncomfortable.

"Here," he said to Tamara, pulling a gift out of the bag that rested on the table in front of them. The box was flat and wrapped in purple paper. That was her favorite color. Elliott paid attention to details like that. It was necessary as he tried to connect with much younger women. It was one of his ways of standing out among his youthful competition—young men who were not nearly as skilled in the art of dating. Or just being a gentleman. Or thoughtful. That had to be his edge in gaining younger women's affections.

"It's so light? What is it?" Tamara asked.

Elliott did not answer. He did not think an answer was necessary. And she got his point: Open the box and see. And so she did, and was surprised by its contents.

"What's *this?*" she asked with confusion in her voice and on her face.

Again, Elliott did not respond. So, Tamara moved the paper closer and adjusted it so light could shine on it.

"A passport application?" she asked. "You got me a passport application?"

"What's that?" one of her friends, Bianca, asked, from the other side of Elliott.

Tamara passed it across Elliott and to Bianca, who used the flashlight on her cell phone to read it.

"Oh, wow," she said. "This is a great gift, girl."

"An application? How?" Tamara asked.

Elliott sat between the young ladies and turned his head toward each as they spoke.

"Why?" Bianca asked. "You don't get it?"

"Get *what?*" Tamara said, sounding a bit frustrated.

"You need a passport to travel out of the country," Bianca said. "So he must be taking you on a trip. *Duh.*"

Tamara looked up at Elliott. "Really?"

"Well," he said, "we can't go where I want to go until you have a passport. So, get that taken care of and you'll get the second part of your gift."

"At least tell me where we're going."

"I'd rather surprise you when you show me your passport."

"That's not right," Tamara whined. Her cute face that did not require much makeup was scrunched, her forehead dented. She poked out her lips and, for a second or two, Elliott thought he was looking at an adolescent.

"You have about a month to coax me into telling you. That's how long it should take for you to get your passport after you submit it."

"Oh, well, I can get that news out of you before then." She placed her hand on his leg.

Elliott grinned. "I like your confidence."

They had met about six weeks before, at CineBistro, an upscale movie theater in the Buckhead section of Atlanta that had a full bar and restaurant-quality menu. Elliott noticed Tamara sitting at the bar, waiting on her date to return from the bathroom.

"I'm going to take care of that drink for you," were Elliott's first words to Tamara, who had accepted a Blue Moon beer from the bartender.

"Why would you do that?" she asked.

"Just paying it forward. Someone paid for my lunch one day when I was at Flip Burger on Howell Mill Road. Sitting at the bar like you are now. Had lunch. When it was time to go, I asked for my check. Bartender told me the woman sitting a few seats down had paid for it and gone."

"What? Really?" Tamara said.

"Yes, really." He reached into his jacket pocket to pull out a business card, then handed it to her. "So, it's my turn to return that good deed."

Tamara looked him up and down. He reminded her of a teacher she had a crush on when she was in high school. She pulled a business card out of her purse. "Well, thank you very much," she said, handing over her card.

"I'm sure you're on a date, so I'll leave you," Elliott said. "But I will call you or shoot you an e-mail to see if you have paid it forward… Enjoy your drink."

They smiled at each other and Elliott walked toward the theaters, right past Tamara's date as he made his way back from the bathroom. He turned around and saw that Tamara was looking back at him as she hugged the man.

That meeting led to an exchange of e-mails, a lunch date that Tamara did not consider a date a week later, and drinks at F&B restaurant a few days later that had the feel of a date.

By the time they arrived at Vanquish, Elliott and Tamara had seen each other seven times. Before they met that night for her birthday celebration, he made it clear his intentions, telling her, "This is a date. I like you and I have grown attracted to you. So please don't take it like I'm coming out just to support my friend. I'm trying to romance you, no matter our age difference."

He had to put it out there. Elliott did not want there to be any misconceptions.

"You don't think I'm too young for you?" she said.

"Too young to do what?" he replied.

"Hang out; there have to be women your age interested in you," Tamara said.

"Sure there are, but their interest isn't my interest. Is my age too much for you to handle?" he asked.

"I don't know. I guess that depends on your energy level."

"Excuse me?" Elliott responded.

She laughed. "Wait, that didn't sound right."

"Yeah, well, you don't have to worry about my energy level in any capacity," Elliott said.

She paused for a few seconds. "Okay, then. If you can handle it, I can handle it. And I'm talking about the age difference."

For Elliott, that meant he could help her celebrate her birthday in grand fashion. The bottle service at the Vanquish Lounge was $350 per bottle, and by 10:30, they were deep into their second bottle. And while the money did not mean anything to him, it would mean everything to Tamara on this night.

"Thank you, Elliott," she said over the loud music. "This is so much fun. And I can't wait to find out about this trip. I'm not saying I'm going on it, but I am excited to know where you picked out."

"You're going," he said so confidently that it almost came off as a boast. "And you know why? Because by the time you get your passport, you'll know me better and you'll *want* to go."

"You're pretty sure of yourself, huh?" All the drinking started to have an effect; she was looser, in mind and body. She slid to her right until her body pressed up against Elliott's. "I may be young, but I ain't crazy or silly. Don't think you're going to take advantage of me because you have more experience than me."

"Why would I want to take advantage of you?" he said. "That's not fun. Whatever we do I'd like it to be mutually agreed upon. Now that would be fun."

Tamara had not heard a man speak to her in such a fashion, and it intrigued her. Men her age were fun, but the next guy seemed like the last guy; there was no discerning them. Elliott moved her because he was different. And to get her an application for a passport as a gift...who does that? And how could she not view it as charming?

She had a unique quality for someone so young: she didn't lie to herself. She understood her strengths, admitted her weaknesses and embraced criticism, even if it came off as "hating." So, as the alcohol settled in and her inhibitions diminished, she was honest: *If Elliott doesn't mess it up, I'm gonna give him some tonight.*

She put the caveat of "if" in there, but she was pretty sure she would. He had the presence of someone in control, even in a crowd of people who looked at him and wondered why he was not at home. It was a powerful presence in a sense, one that put a woman at ease and drew her into him.

"I appreciate you letting me spend some of your birthday with you," Elliott said into Tamara's ear.

"I'm having a good time," she said. "Thank you for all this. My friends are eating this up."

Just then, a young man came and stood over Tamara. She could feel his presence. When she turned and looked up at him, she screamed in delight. It was a friend she dated right before graduating college. Their careers took them in separate cities and they had not seen each other in the four years after graduation.

Tamara hurried to her feet and she and Jacobi hugged a long time. Elliott reached for the champagne and refilled her glass as the old friends caught up, laughed and even took photos. *They are a good-looking couple*, Elliott thought. *He's more like someone she should be with*, he admitted.

They talked for up to fifteen minutes. She introduced him to her girlfriends and they shared a birthday toast. Elliott sat there, unfazed. He would not try to compete with a younger man for Tamara's attention. He would not infringe on her fun. And he did not consider it an insult that she did not introduce him. Actually, he was relieved that she did not. It would only lead to inevitable questions that would put her and him in an awkward situation:

Who's that?

Is that your father?

What's that old guy doing with you?

Neither of them wanted to hear that. Finally, Jacobi and his friends left and explored the spot and Tamara rejoined Elliott on the couch.

"Whew," she said. "That was a friend from college I haven't seen in a long time."

"It's always good to catch up with old classmates," Elliott said. "You should have offered him some champagne."

Tamara was not sure how Elliott would react to that scene, but his calm gave her reassurances about him and what she wanted to happen with him that night, when all the music stopped and the people went home.

"Can I ask you something?" She again slid up close to him.

"Only if you can accept the answer," Elliott responded.

"I like that when I ask you something I'm not sure what your answer will be," Tamara said.

Elliott smiled, and when he did that he looked exponentially younger. "Go."

"What does it feel like to be in this place with people so much younger?"

"It feels liberating, to be honest," Elliott said. "There's an energy around young people that I need. I'm where I want to be, where I *need* to be. I have an energy and appreciation for life that make me want to be places where people are living. I read somewhere that every day is a celebration of life, and that's how I live it. I don't have to be in a club or out every night. But I do have to do things that celebrate being alive because life is a gift."

Tamara put her hand on his leg, which alarmed Elliott for a second because it was the side he soiled with urine. He gathered himself quickly.

"That's a good answer, Mr. Elliott," she said.

"Oh, I'm 'Mr.' now?" he asked.

"Yes," she said. "When I call you 'Mr. Elliott,' it's a sign that I see you as an authority figure, and authority figures are very attractive to me. I never told you that you remind me of one of my old high school teachers, Mr. Nutt. What a name, right? But he was dignified and handsome and I wanted to throw myself at him."

She sipped some more champagne. "Actually, I *did* throw myself at him," she added. "But I wasn't as developed as I am now. He basically let me down easy."

"So, you like older men?" Elliott said. It was so loud that he had to virtually put his mouth to her ear, and she leaned in so close that his lips and her ear came together. It was just what Tamara wanted.

"You have soft lips," she said.

"You have a soft ear," he quipped, and they both laughed.

"I like men who can teach me something, who can add something to my life," Tamara answered. She was in Elliott's ear now, and every few words, she kissed his earlobe. "Boys my age don't do anything for me; that's why I went to my high-school prom with a college sophomore.

"And now, at twenty-five–wow, I'm a quarter of a century old— guys my age can't hold my attention. If one does, he's got about three or four other women, too. But you're a first for me. You're old enough to actually be my grandfather. But it doesn't turn me off. Most sixty-one-year-old men definitely would not hold my attention. But you, I don't know. There's something mysterious and interesting about you. You've made me very curious."

"About what? How an old man looks naked? What I can do in bed?" Elliott asked as he kissed her on her ear.

Tamara nodded her head. "Yes. Aren't you curious about me?"

"Not at all." Tamara looked confused. "But," Elliott said into her ear, "I am fascinated by you."

Tamara flashed a big smile. "I'm gonna be ready to go soon. What you wanna do when we leave here?"

"Move the party to my house. Private party."

"Just me and you?"

Elliott nodded his head. "Me, you and some candles and champagne and gourmet cheese." He picked up a champagne flute and tapped glasses with Tamara, who then moved to the other side of Elliott and told her girls she was about to leave.

"Y'all can stay," she said. "We're gonna leave in a few."

Elliott could not hear her friends' responses, but he paid the bill and asked the server to add a third bottle of Veuve Clicquot.

Tamara told Elliott she was ready. "Okay," he said, "but let your friends know I have another bottle coming. If they're going to stay, they might as well have something to sip on."

"You're so sweet." Tamara shared that information and her friends turned to Elliott and waved as they mouthed "thank you."

"I have to go to the bathroom," Tamara said. "Wanna meet me by the front door?"

"Meet you there." He made his way through the crowd and posted up near the front exit, which also was the entrance. He watched the young people come and go—a fun pastime for him. Sometimes he would go out to places in Atlanta and not say a word to anyone; he'd just watch. And that was a good night for him.

So he was not mad that Tamara had to make a bathroom run. It was his opportunity to get some sightseeing in without feeling like he might disrespect her in the process. The women came and went in impressive fashion, one young lady's skirt shorter than the next.

Tamara was gone for up to ten minutes because of the inevitable line in the women's bathroom. Right before she returned, Elliott noticed someone out of the corner of his eye approaching from the entrance. When he turned to see, he almost lost his breath.

Standing before him were Daniel and Danielle. They were twenty-one and Elliott had not seen them in almost two years. But they were not particularly happy to see him, which was evident since there were no smiles and no hugs.

"What are you doing in here?" Danielle asked, looking him over.

"Hi, Danny," he said. "Hi, Dan."

Neither responded. They looked at him with disdain.

"What are you doing here?" Daniel asked. There was anger in his voice and posture.

"I'm so glad to see you," he said. "Have you received my letters or e-mails?"

"Yeah, we got 'em," Daniel said. "And…?"

"And how are we going to get beyond all this if we don't communicate?" Elliott said. "It shouldn't be this way."

"What are you doing here?" Danielle wanted to know.

Before he could give an answer, Tamara walked up from the bathroom. "Okay, I'm ready."

Elliott looked at her and then the other two young adults.

"*Tamara?*" Danielle said.

"Danielle, I didn't even see you," she responded. They hugged.

"You know Elliott?" Tamara asked.

"You're leaving?" Daniel said to Tamara. "We came here for your party. And how do *you* know *him?*"

The awkwardness was palpable, and Tamara sensed it.

"Everyone is still at our section over there," she said, pointing. "There's another bottle coming. But I've been here a long time, so we're leaving."

"How do you know him?" Daniel asked again.

Tamara was confused. Daniel's and Danielle's reactions was more than about the age difference. It was something else.

"What's going on?" she asked.

"Nothing," Elliott said. He clutched her hand and started toward the exit. "Let's go."

Daniel grabbed Danielle's hand and pulled her in the opposite direction.

"Are you dating him?" Danielle yelled.

"Why does it matter?" Tamara asked.

"Don't worry about it," Daniel said. He pulled Danielle into the crowd.

Elliott stood there looking in their direction as Tamara looked up at him.

"What was that about?" she asked.

He continued to look off in the distance.

"*Elliott…*" Tamara said.

He turned to her and had a look on his face she had not seen, a look of humiliation, which was big because he seemed to be impervious to embarrassment.

"That was my son and daughter," he said.

CHAPTER TWO
Life, As He Knows It

"What? Danny and Danielle are your children?" Tamara asked as they walked past the line of people outside that extended along Peachtree Street to Eleventh Street. "I went to college with them."

And that fact shook her. It was one thing to cavort with Elliott around people who did not know him. It was quite another for her to know his kids. It was a connection she did not embrace.

Neither did Elliott. He placed his hand on the small of Tamara's back and guided her across Eleventh Street and into Café Intermezzo, a light-night dessert place that was an after-party haven.

"I thought we were going to your house?" Tamara asked.

Elliott responded without looking at her: "We should talk first… and then see if you still want to go."

She nodded her head as they were led to a table on the patio that ran along Peachtree Street. Tamara decided she would not say anything and let Elliott take the lead. She was frustrated that the events had diminished her birthday buzz.

"How about some champagne?" Elliott surveyed the extended menu.

"More champagne?" Tamara asked. "What are we celebrating?"

"It's still your birthday."

"Yeah, but it's not like what happened didn't just happen."

"I'm glad it did, in a way."

Tamara gave him a look.

"I haven't seen them in two years," he said. "That's not the good part. They looked good, didn't they?"

"You know how crazy this whole thing is for me?" Tamara asked. "How can I look them in the face again?"

"Easy," Elliott said. "What you and I do is none of their business."

"That might make sense for you," she responded. "But it's bigger than that for me. Danielle and I are friends. And I know Danny. And I'm running around with her dad?"

"When you put it that way, it doesn't sound so inviting for me, either," Elliott said.

"Let's get to the real point then," Tamara said. "I like you. I do. You're very intriguing. The fact that you're older—much older—has not bothered me that much, until now. I need to know: what do you want from me? I mean, what do you *really* want from me? No bullshit. Why are you pursuing someone close to your daughter's age?"

Elliott ordered champagne, and then he got right down to it.

"What do I want with you?" he started. "Sex. Fun—"

"Did you say *sex?*" Tamara jumped in, sounding insulted.

"If you're going to be in a grown-up situation, you can't be surprised that a man wants to engage in sex with you," Elliott said. "I'm not trying to be your mentor on relationships or anything. We both have something to offer each other. But if you think I'm not interested in sex with you, then you're being naïve. You're pretty, sexy, smart, fun…why wouldn't I want to have sex with you?"

At twenty-five, Tamara's relationship experiences were far less than Elliott's, but she had never heard a man (or boy) admit his sexual intentions. The funny part was that it turned her on. His candor justified why she believed guys her age were not ready for her. She wanted something different from her girlfriends, something that would open her up and enlighten her. Grow her.

She wanted the truth.

Tamara shook her head while staring into his eyes. "I can't figure you out."

"No need to try," Elliott responded. "We're all more complicated than we realize. Figuring me out would only confuse you."

Tamara smiled.

"What I was going to say," Elliott continued, "was that besides sex, I want fun times, interesting conversation. I want to be taken out of my comfort zone, to have new experiences. I don't want to feel my age or do things people my age do. That, for me, is living my life."

"So what have you been doing up to this point?" Tamara asked. "Sleeping?"

"Sleepwalking," Elliott said. "In some cases sleepwalking, in some cases, struggling…Where do you want me to begin?"

"You know what? Can we save this conversation for your house? I get the feeling you're about to go in, and we should be chillin' at your spot instead of around all these people."

"I'm about to 'go in.' Is that what you said?"

"Yes. It means, in this case, to get really deep," she explained.

"See, this is what I'm talking about," Elliott said. "You can keep me up-to-date and I can show you old-fashioned things. Balance. I'm not young and hip, but I like to be around young and hip people."

"But why?" Tamara asked.

"Because it keeps my spirit young," he said.

Tamara had no response, and after several minutes of chatter about passersby and her birthday, they made their way to Elliott's car and took the five-minute drive to his high-rise condo in the W Hotel in downtown Atlanta.

"You live *here*, at the hotel?" she said, trying but failing to conceal her amazement.

"There is a resident portion to this place, too," he said, trying and succeeding at sounding unimpressed with his digs.

They took the elevator up to the twenty-seventh floor, where Elliott opened the door to his condo that had a breathtaking view of the Atlanta skyline, and beyond, via floor-to-ceiling windows. Tamara was mesmerized.

Elliott threw the keys on a table and offered her a drink.

"Whatever you have will be fine," she said.

He lit some scented candles that rested on a pair of shelves next to photos of family members. "Make yourself comfortable." He turned on some music. "You can get what you want. I've got to take a shower. Take off your shoes. Relax. Be right back."

Elliott disappeared to the right of the kitchen into his bedroom, eager to discard his urine-stained pants and freshen his body. Tamara slipped off her heels and took in the majestic view of his place and the city. She opened the sliding glass door and stepped onto the balcony. A breeze cooled the summer night air and added to her calm.

She looked down at the traffic flowing on Interstate 85 and out at the buildings that illuminated the sky. She was a long way from her hometown of Waycross, Georgia, which was closer to Florida than it was to Atlanta. It was a friendly place, a wonderful place to grow up—but a place one had to escape to truly grow. At least that's how she felt.

Because her family had relatives in Detroit, Tamara's father insisted she look at schools in Michigan. It was a major point of discord between her parents, her mother preferring that their only daughter stay close.

But Tamara saw beyond life in Waycross and told her mother a month before her senior high school year: "Daddy is right. What is there here for me? I love it here. But for me to not resent it, I have to get away."

Her mom, even in her disappointment, considered that a mature approach and eventually acquiesced. Tamara received a partial academic scholarship to Michigan State, where she met Elliott's kids in her junior year. After graduating with a degree in political science, she volunteered on Barack Obama's 2008 presidential campaign and later earned a job in the Atlanta mayor's office.

Tamara was ecstatic about her professional life. But she was tortured by her family life. Her dad had developed dementia. One summer during a visit from college he was as he always had been: soft-spoken but firm, funny and sentimental about his daughter. The next summer, he hardly could be trusted alone. His memory deteriorated and he went in and out of awareness more and more frequently. He attended her younger brother's high school graduation, but no one was sure how much he actually absorbed or remembered.

Seeing him that way pained Tamara, who had always been held up by her father's strength. She admired him more than anyone. And he was a girl's daddy. The only time she saw him at conflict with her mother was when he stood up for her in the face of her mom's overprotection. Thinking about her dad on Elliott's balcony brought tears to her eyes.

"It's nice out here, isn't it?" Elliott said from behind her. He startled Tamara, who wiped the corners of her eyes.

"Beautiful out here," she said, turning around. "Can we sit out here for a while?"

Instead of answering, Elliott pulled a chair closer to the one Tamara sat down in and retrieved a candle from inside and placed it on the table in front of them.

"I'm into creating a nice atmosphere," he said.

"No complaints here," Tamara responded.

Both looked off at the view for a moment. Tamara broke the silence.

"So, what's up with you, Mr. Thomas? You're old enough to be my father or maybe even my grandfather. Why do you like hanging out at spots around young people? What's your story?"

"What's my story?" he repeated. "It's a mystery, a drama, a tragedy, a comedy, in some cases. And, I guess I'm trying to get it to be a fantasy."

"You said a lot but you didn't say much," Tamara said, "if you know what I mean."

She was young, but smart, which made Elliott interested. He had dated many twenty-somethings. Only a few of them held his interest.

"You mean you want specifics," Elliott said. "Okay, in general, I'll explain it this way: I have no interest in being a senior citizen. I'm not at that age yet and I don't like what it seems to mean, which is you're old and, therefore, have to live a lifestyle that consists of a rocking chair, a sweater even when it's hot outside, and watching old Westerns.

"I remember my father when he was my age and he seemed to think that meant watching Johnny Carson and going to bed. Well, not me. I always had this sadness about my dad, like he was missing out on life. He never went anywhere. My recollection of him is that he was always this old man. Even when I was a kid he seemed old and settled and not quite like life was treating him right.

"The reality is that life doesn't treat you; you get out of life what you want out of it. There is too much available in the world, especially nowadays, to be this old man who has his place.

"I don't have one place. I have a lot of interests and a lot of opportunities and I'm making it happen for myself. Does it look crazy to some, seeing me at sixty-one years old in a club full of youngsters my children's age? I guess so. A guy called me 'the old man in the club' tonight. Guess what? It didn't faze me. It was true. I wasn't offended.

"When you live the life I have lived, you are thankful for each day more than most people. I missed out on my twenties. I didn't get to be young and carefree and enjoy life.

"Well, I have that chance now. I'm angry about some of the things that happened to me. But I am here; I'm still here. So I'm going to do what I damn please. And I don't care what anyone thinks about it."

Tamara did not interject when Elliott paused. She was not sure if he was done. But after several seconds, she figured he had said his peace—or all he wanted to up to that point.

"I see you're really passionate about this," she said. "What happened to you?"

"I can't tell you everything at once; it'd be too much for you to handle," he said. "But I will tell you about what happened with my children, why they weren't exactly happy to see me tonight."

"Let me guess," Tamara said. "You cheated."

"I could be insulted," Elliott said, "but I'm going to let it go because you don't really know me yet. But—"

"That's right," Tamara interrupted, "and you said you want to have sex with me, even though you admitted you don't know me."

"I said that you don't know me; I *know* you," Elliott said.

"Now how can that be?" she responded. "Never mind—don't even answer that now… Go ahead."

Elliott smiled and poured Tamara a glass of the champagne he brought to the balcony.

"Maybe you should go." He looked away from her.

"Why? I don't want to go."

"We'll see about that," Elliott said, and the way he said it made Tamara uneasy, but not scared.

"I'm here because I want to be here, Elliott. What happened?"

"You notice that when we talk during the day, I am always out walking?"

"I did notice that. Why?"

"I'm always out walking because all of my twenties and some of my thirties—almost twelve years in total—I was confined. Prison. I had a limited space I could travel. So walking wherever I want confirms that I am free."

He delivered every word while looking directly into her eyes. He was searching for her emotion.

"What?" Tamara asked. "Why? What happened?"

"They said I raped and killed a woman in Virginia." Elliott was looking away now, toward the darkened sky, as if it was an enormous movie screen and he could see that part of his life playing out in front of him.

Tamara, meanwhile, was stunned—and scared so much that she was frozen in her seat and speechless.

"You still want to be here?" Elliott asked with sarcasm.

Tamara said nothing.

"I was in my last year of college, at home working in Woodbridge,

Virginia at a car dealership for the summer," Elliott began. "This woman who had come to do a test drive with me earlier that day was found raped and murdered near her home around the time I got off work that evening.

"I was driving back to my parents' house in D.C. The route took me past the woman's home. Before I could get to Interstate 95, police sprung up from every angle, with their guns drawn. Scared me so much I was afraid to pull my hands off the steering wheel to roll down the window or open the door. Before I knew it, I was snatched out of my car, on the ground, roughed up and in the back of a police car. I thought I was dreaming."

Tamara's fear eased. She was not sure why, but it did. "Why did they think you did it?"

Her question pleased Elliott. She could have asked, as another young lady had, "Did you do it?" Asking the question Tamara did sent the message that she hadn't judged him.

"It was crazy," he said. "When her body was found, sometime before I left the dealership, this woman said she saw a man drive away in a yellowish car. I had a yellow 1969 Duster and—"

"A what?" Tamara asked.

"Oh, wow," Elliott said. "There was a car at that time called a Duster. It was made by Dodge. This was 1971. They haven't made them for a while now. You're so young.

"But anyway, they said my car matched this witness' description of the car leaving where the body was found.

"So I'm in jail and not sure what the hell is going on; no one said anything to me about this crime. So, finally a detective comes in and shows me a photo of the lady's driver's license picture. He asked if I knew her. I looked at the photo and said I didn't. She didn't look familiar.

"They then questioned me over and over about why I was in that area, where was I going, I mean, just about anything they could think of, they asked me. I left out something, though: I had stopped at this little area that was off the beaten path, not far from the job, down by a lake. I went there to smoke a joint. I got high back in those days. It was a long week and I would do the same thing every Friday—go to this place, loosen my tie and smoke a joint while sitting there in my car, listening to music.

"Well, they finally tell me that the woman in the photo was dead—and that they knew I had killed her after raping her because she was jogging in that same area where I had my joint.

"I'm sitting there looking at them like they were crazy. I stood up and told them I didn't do it, wouldn't do it and couldn't do it. They didn't believe me. After taking my mug shot and fingerprints and making me feel like a criminal, I was put in a cell and given an arraignment date. My parents, my whole family, was scared and angry.

"But why did they think it was you?" Tamara wanted to know.

"A crazy list of coincidences," Elliott said. "The lady in the picture was a woman I had gone on a test drive of a car with earlier that day. She had told her girlfriend that she had visited the dealership, and when they checked with my boss, the records showed that I took her on the test drive. But she didn't look like the photo on her license, which I did not see at the dealership when she had the test drive because an office assistant made the copy of it. Her hair was different and she wore glasses. I didn't recognize her. And I just did not recall her name.

"But they said I was lying about that, and if I was lying, that meant I was hiding something.

"And they found my fingerprints on her car door. They were

there because I walked her to her car when she was leaving the dealership and opened her door for her. They didn't believe that. They said I opened the door while she was in the car and pulled her out.

"They also said someone saw my car at the lake and saw me sitting in the car as the woman jogged past me. I didn't remember her. But because I didn't tell them that I stopped to smoke a joint, they used that against me, saying I knew that if I had told them that I was there, they would link me to being where the woman was.

"It was crazy. My family went broke paying for lawyers to defend me. They lost their house. My father even lost his job because it was a horrific crime. The woman was white, a mother of a young boy, and by all accounts a great lady. I remember feeling that way about her during that ten-minute test drive. She was very pleasant. Anyway, the people on my dad's job associated my charges with him and didn't want him around the office anymore. It was a total mess."

Tamara sat there listening intently, as if she were hearing a story-teller weave an intriguing drama. Only it was Elliott's life.

"And although so much money was spent and because the crime was so horrible—the woman's head was bashed in with a tree branch—they had to find somebody guilty of it. And that somebody was me."

Elliott turned to Tamara and looked into her eyes, eyes that expressed confusion and empathy at the same time. "Do you know what it's like to stand before a courthouse full of people and be called guilty, knowing you did nothing?" he asked, his voice much softer and poignant. It was as if telling the story pained him.

"I was a total mess. It was unreal, unbelievable. In the newspaper the reporter in the courtroom wrote about me pinching myself after the verdict was announced. I thought I was dreaming and I needed to pinch myself to see if I was awake. I kept doing it, hoping I wouldn't feel it, but I did. And I started crying. I looked at my family and friends and they were all so upset. It was crazy."

"Elliott," Tamara said with sorrow in her voice, "I'm so sorry. I don't even know what else to say."

"Your empathy says a lot," Elliott responded. "I appreciate that more than you know."

He looked away and took a deep breath. He had not told this part of his story in some time, but with each sharing of it came pain and anger that was so intense he could almost touch it. He was not the most fun person to be around when he was that way. He was sensitive and quick to lose his temper, even thirty years later. But Tamara made it more tolerable because she did not look at him with judgmental eyes and shared no doubting comments or body language.

In fact, she rose from her chair and went over to Elliott and kneeled down in front of him. She rested her arms on his knees.

"I am so sorry you went through that," she said.

He hugged her, and they remained embraced for a few minutes, neither of them saying another word.

CHAPTER THREE:
Kicking It Up A Notch

The next morning, as the sun peaked above the Atlanta sky-line, Elliott awoke to the sound of the shower. He was slightly disoriented and it wasn't until he grabbed his glasses from the nightstand and put them on that Tamara's dress came into focus, sprawled over a chair in the corner.

He pulled the sheets up to cover his body. He was in fantastic shape, considering his age, with still-muscular arms. But the slightly protruding belly bothered him. He was not the Adonis he once was; he was a stereotypical prisoner in one way: He buffed up while behind bars. But over time, his workout regimen waned. He was conscious of his body because he figured Tamara was used to twenty-something physiques with low body fat.

The more he sat there, the more the night came back to him. He recalled that they left the balcony and Tamara was not interested in spending time in the living room.

"Why sit in here?" Tamara said. "It's late. Let's go to bed."

"Makes sense to me," Elliott said. That morning, he had taken the pill Cialis, which enhances a man's sexual potency. Just in case. He had no idea if Tamara would end up in his bed, but if she did, he wanted to be ready. Elliott was not impotent, but he was not the sexual dynamo he was a decade before. With the younger women that attracted him, he wanted to be up to the task.

And yet, the details of the night were blurry. Images flashed in his head, but they were sketchy. He needed coffee. And just as he got up to retrieve his robe, Tamara emerged from the bathroom.

They stood there looking at each other, naked.

"I thought you were in the shower; the water is still running," Elliott said. He did not consider covering himself up; it would have signaled weakness at best, insecurity at worst. Tamara was proud of her body that was fit and curvy; she stood in the nude with her hands on her hips, her perky 32B breasts sitting up as if on a perch.

"I let the water run because I was about to clean up the shower," she said. "But I can turn it off."

She turned to go into the bathroom.

"Wait; don't move," Elliott said. "I like what I see and I'm not finished looking."

Tamara smiled and began to put on a show, offering Elliott seductive poses.

He smiled at her. "I see you're feeling good this morning," he offered.

"How can I not, after what you did to me last night? I wasn't sure what to expect from you. But I'll be damned if you didn't make a statement for senior citizens."

Elliott smiled. He felt proud, but he would have felt better if he could remember the stream of events, not just pieces. He stared at Tamara's naked body, and it helped him recall how it felt to caress her.

"What are we doing, Elliott?" Tamara asked.

"We're going to have breakfast." He slipped into his robe. "Don't take this the wrong way, but don't be a typical woman right now. We're still in the moment. Let's let it last a little longer before it turns into something else."

Tamara loved that position. Elliott slowed her down and taught her about being a woman, not a typical woman.

"I don't know what to expect from you," she answered. "I told you that I like that about you... Okay, breakfast it is. And I'm cooking."

Tamara attempted to walk past Elliott on his way to the bathroom. He clutched her wrist and pulled her into his body. "There's a lot I like about you, too," he said into her ear. He kissed her on her neck. "A lot."

Her infatuation with Elliott grew, especially when he smacked her on her ass as she walked away. She took that to mean he was in charge, and she liked that.

Tamara's last boyfriend was a twenty-six-year-old sales manager for Coca-Cola. He doted on her, treated her like a fragile piece of jewelry. It was exactly what she did not want. She thought she felt that way before her night with Elliott; she *knew* it afterward.

Elliott was delicate with her, but aggressive, too. He was forceful in his sexual moves and in control of the lovemaking. When it was clear Tamara wanted sex, he pulled her hands away from her dress and took over, pulling it over her head. He stood over her as she sat on the side of the bed and undressed while she boiled inside over his confidence.

The way he kissed her—deep and sensual, sloppy and intoxicating—made her head light. He laid her on her back and explored her body with his mouth and tongue, giving Tamara the feeling that he was in control of her pleasure and in command of the night. She was vulnerable to his desires...exactly what she had desired in a partner.

Age did not matter in that moment. Elliott adjusted her body to different positions and pounded her with forceful thrusts, making her feel free to express her pleasure in primal screams. At a heightened point of passion, she looked back at Elliott, who, with a firm grasp onto her hips, thrust into her in rapid-fire succession. Tamara had to make sure it was sixty-one-year-old Elliott laying it on her like he was.

Her body felt achy-good in the morning, and over breakfast—orange juice, coffee, oatmeal, turkey bacon and English muffin—Tamara told Elliott how pleasantly pleased she was with their session. "I just had to cook for you this morning. I had to do *something*."

He smiled and actually blushed. Her recollection of the night jarred his memory, and the events started to come together in his head. He remembered thinking as they entered his bedroom that he was going to go for it.

Elliott had twenty-somethings before; two others, in fact, and a pair of ladies in their early thirties. He kept a ledger in his iPhone. Tamara was No. 5. He liked her, and yet he knew there was no real future with her—not that he was seeking a future with anyone. Although sixty-one, Elliott considered himself twelve years younger for the time he was locked away.

"What are your plans for the rest of the day?" she asked Elliott as she cleared the table.

"I'm going to walk and come back home to watch the NBA playoffs; the Lakers and Kobe Bryant play today. Gotta see the closest thing to Michael Jordan," he said. "But mostly relaxing until tonight. I have a party to attend tonight at Compound."

"Compound?" Tamara said. "I haven't even been there yet. So you really are the old man in the club? I watched you last night. You were in your element. This is what you do? Go out and chase young girls?"

There was outrage in her voice but mostly disappointment.

"Don't get righteous on me," he said. "I'm just living my life."

"But you don't think it's a little strange that you're sixty-one with kids twenty-one and yet you're seeking women their age?" she asked. "There's nothing strange about that to you?"

"I'm doing what any or most men my age *wish* they could," he said. "One of my friends who is my age—actually, he's two years younger than me—said I'm living the dream. And I told him, 'I'm just living *my* life.' And that's how I look at it, no matter how strange it is for you or other people. You've heard this before but it might not resonate with you because you're so young, but here goes anyway: Life is short. I prefer to live mine doing the things that fulfill me."

Tamara flopped down in her chair and laid her head in her hands, exasperated.

"I have a question for you," Elliott said. "It's an innocent question, so don't take it the wrong way."

Tamara raised her head to look at him.

"If it's strange that I like young women," he said, "isn't it strange that you are here with me when I'm thirty-six years older than you?"

"It's different," she said after a moment of contemplation. "I didn't seek you out; you approached me. I don't, as a rule, date senior citizens. I just don't. Being here right now is freaking me out. It's not what I expected but I admit that I was curious about you. But I was only curious about you because of the person you are. Other older men have hit on me before but they seemed creepy.

"I'm comfortable with you and I feel confident that you're a good person. And learning a little about your life and the arrest and everything…it made me feel closer to you."

"You mean sorry for me?" he asked.

"In a way, at first, yes," she said. "But I looked at how you carry yourself, where you live, how happy you seem to be. I feel like you overcame it all. There's no reason to feel sorry for you. I feel sorry it happened to you. But you're still standing, with your head up. When I processed all that, it was a turn-on."

"I appreciate you being honest," Elliott said. "That's one thing I have to have in a friend—honesty. At the same time, I'm not judging you, so it would be nice if you didn't judge me. Going to a party or liking young women doesn't make me a bad man. It doesn't make me a dirty old man. It makes me a man who knows what he likes and who lives the life he wants to live. After what has happened to me, that's exactly what I'm going to do because I know probably better than most that life is a gift.

"What I told you last night about my past, I haven't told many people. I told you because you deserve to know and I didn't believe you would judge me or hold it against me. But I told you about it because I wanted you to get a look into my head and see why it's important that I live the life I do—not the way anyone else believes I should live because of my age."

Tamara wanted to ask Elliott more questions, but she was cutting it close for a shopping spree with her mom at the Premium Outlets up north off of Highway 400. So, she headed to the bedroom to put on her dress and make her way home so she would not keep her mom waiting.

Elliott took a quick shower and threw on a pair of jeans and a T-shirt and took her home to her townhouse in Avondale Estates, a small, mixed community a few minutes east of Atlanta. The conversation was light on the ride there.

"Should I write down my sizes?" he said. "Just in case you get an urge to buy something for me."

"If I get an urge for you," she said, getting out of the car, "it won't be about buying you something."

She smiled and winked and was on her way.

CHAPTER FOUR
Party Over Here

Elliott walked almost every day—to stay youthful, to build his stamina, to stay healthy, to feel free. Three of his friends around his age had died in the previous five years, two of a heart attack, one from a stroke. In either case, it was about an unhealthy lifestyle. He committed to himself that he would not have an avoidable demise.

At the first funeral, he was especially shaken because Danette Patterson was a close friend and former lover who looked and seemed healthy. Her heart valves were clogged from terrible eating habits; although strong genes gave her the appearance of a healthy, fit woman.

He traveled to Chicago for her services that spring. Witnessing her lay in her coffin sparked remembrances of many conversations they had about love and life. Danette spoke often about living without regrets, how she married a man she *hoped* would be good for her but who turned out to be exactly who he showed himself to be.

"You can say what you want, but you have a second chance at life, Elliott," he recalled her saying. "If you want to ride jet skis or try out for the Chicago Bears, do it. I spent twenty-seven years in a marriage that wasn't meant for me. That's a lot of time wasted. The worst part is that I could have done something about it a long time ago. So, I say don't live with regrets. Do the things that make you happy."

Those words and seeing Danette lying in a casket pushed Elliott face-to-face with his mortality. And his life. He and Danette were the same age, fifty-five, when she died. If ever there was a singular time he chose to live on his own terms, that was it. That's when the idea of sucking in as much youthful air as he could emerged. Danette's death charged him to change his life, starting with keeping his health up to par.

So, after dropping off Tamara, he switched into shorts and went for a walk that took him down Ivan Allen Boulevard, up toward and through Centennial Olympic Park, past CNN and down Spring Street, passing the Apparel Mart and the American Cancer Society before arriving back to the W. It was one of the routes he took to get in his exercise, to keep his heart valves clear, to maintain his weight and, above all, to express his freedom.

And almost every time he walked, he thought of Danette. His relationship with her was the last one he had had with a woman in his age range before his ex-wife. Had she not died, he would not have made the turn he did to maintaining good health and eventually seeking younger women. She was special to him.

Danette pulled him through the hard-to-describe phase of being free after nearly a dozen years in prison for crimes he did not commit. He shared with her the extremes he went through to prevent from being raped; the constant fear that hovered above him for four thousand, two hundred and six days; the immense fear of freedom after so many years of incarceration.

They met, as it would happen, at a traffic light. She almost hit Elliott as he stepped into the crosswalk in downtown D.C. less than three months after DNA evidence showed he was not the criminal the jury convicted. Family and friends had turned on him and the wicked system had not provided him with any resources to reemerge into society. So he did what he knew, which was to search tirelessly for a job.

He was walking, head down, reading *The Washington Post* Jobs section when he heard Danette's horn at the corner of F and Twelfth streets. She stopped about two feet from hitting him. He was so alarmed by the horn and sight of the car so close to him that he threw the paper into the air as he jumped back.

Danette was alarmed, too, and thought she had hit him. She jumped out of the car and ran to his side. She grabbed him by the arm and he looked down at her hand. A woman had not touched him in twelve years.

"Did I hit you? Are you okay?" she asked.

"I'm fine," Elliott said. "I was reading…trying to find a job. I'm sorry. It was my fault."

"What kind of job are you looking for?"

"One that pays."

"Let me pull my car out of the street. I might be able to help you."

"What? Are you serious? If that's true, then it would have been okay for you to run me over. I would take getting hit by a car if it meant a job."

Danette smiled and moved her car into a loading zone on 12th Street.

"I gotta tell you," Elliott said, "I haven't worked in twelve years. I have a bad story."

"Even better—if you're okay now," she said. "What's your story?"

He explained his wrongful conviction. He didn't mean to get in to so much detail, but he found talking to her easy. She was attentive and interested and mortified, all at the same time. But she also felt a need to help.

"I started my own headhunting firm, a job-placement company," she said.

"I know what a headhunter is," Elliott interjected. "Before all this I was a good student in college. And I read everything I could get my hands on in prison, to stay sharp."

"I wasn't trying to offend you. There two ways I could likely help. In the three years since I started this business, I've built relationships with companies that might hire you on my recommendation, despite your lack of experience. Also, there is this pilot program they started at the Georgetown University Law School that offers a handful of jobs to paroled inmates. I'm not sure if you qualify because you technically were not paroled. But it's worth a try."

"I have one question," Elliott said. "Why would you do this for me? You don't know me."

Danette smiled. She was waiting for that question. "Three years ago," she began, "when I quit my safe job I hated with the Interior Department, I struggled to make ends meet. I didn't do it as some people do it—save up a lot of money and have a nest egg to fall back on. I just went for it. I'm spontaneous like that a lot of times. One day I decided that Friday would be my last day, and that was that.

"I love a good steak and I sat at the bar at Ruth's Chris one night after a bad day. I was on the phone with my mom, telling her I was going to get a salad because I was too afraid to spend the money on the rib eye that I wanted, that I *needed*. I needed some comfort food in the worst way. But I ordered a salad and water with lemon and I looked around at all the people there talking and laughing and eating and it made me depressed.

"So, about ten, fifteen minutes later, my order comes. The guy has a rib eye with baked potato and the salad. I said, 'No, this isn't mine. I just ordered the salad.' He said, 'The gentleman who was standing right here ordered this for you and already paid for it.'

"I was shocked. I looked over to where he pointed, but the man was gone. I vaguely recalled someone next to me, but I was in my own pitiful world, talking to my mother. But he heard my conversation and ordered the meal I needed. Can you believe that?

"The waiter said, 'He ordered it medium well. I hope that's okay.' It was exactly how I would have ordered it. How did he know that? Who was he? It was an act of kindness that I carry with me every day. He had no clue who I was and yet he did something for me—a stranger—to make me feel better.

"So that's why I'm willing to help you, even as we have only just met. I know what it felt like to be helped by a stranger. I know what it *means*. That, to this day, was the best steak I have ever had. And it was not all about how it tasted. It went down good. And guess what: The next day—the very next day—I placed three clients in jobs and I have not had that feeling of desperation I had before that man did that for me. Coincidence? Maybe. I like to think it was way more than that."

Elliott shook his head. He almost got emotional. "Whatever comes of this, this is the best day I have had since I got out of Lorton Reformatory," he said. "To know there is someone out here like you—and that man who helped you—gives me hope."

By the end of the week, Elliott had a job at Georgetown University. And his friendship with Danette continued over the years and lasted through his marriage to his children's mom and heightened the last years of her life.

She was as influential over him as anyone, and her words of living the life he desired brought him to live the life he missed out on when he was locked up. That was a reason he sought younger women; he didn't get to do it when he was their age.

"I understand the motivation, as you explain it," Dr. Nottingham, his therapist, said when he told her of his intentions. "But you cannot get back the years lost in prison, no matter how unjust your conviction was. Life goes on and you have to travel with it."

"Are you saying, doctor, that I'm wrong for wanting to live the life that was taken away from me?"

"I'm saying you *can't* live the life that was taken away from you," she answered. "It's gone. No matter what you do, how many young women you have relationships with, it does not mitigate the fact that those years are gone and that you cannot get them back."

Elliott trusted his therapist—she kept him sane when he struggled to regain his life—but he was not so sure about her position.

"Elliott," she said, "could this all be about feeding your ego? In many cases when men feel the need to spread themselves among many women, they are nourishing an insecurity or an ego that they believe needs that kind of attention."

"I don't know, Dr. Nottingham; maybe so," he answered. "But what I do know is that it feels good. I feel younger. I feel like I'm getting back on the system that ruined my life. I'm not living in the past. But I'm capturing a piece of it that was lost. I don't see anything wrong with that."

"I'll leave it at that for today," she said. "As long as you're trying to get back at the system that ruined your life, you're not completely letting go and moving on with your life. And that's my concern, that you go on and live a productive life. I'm so proud of you. You've shown amazing strength to persevere over the years. I don't want you to sabotage your gains by trying to live a bygone time of your life."

Dr. Nottingham's points were taken into serious consideration. In Elliott's quiet moments, he contemplated what he was doing. He remained doused in anger and bitterness about his conviction. It was not overwhelming—Dr. Nottingham and others before her talked him through that phase—but it was there, it was real. He knew it would always be there. But he felt something when engaging young women like Tamara. He felt outside of his body and away from his recent past, and he could see himself as a twenty-something sitting there in the scene. That's what kept him on course, despite Dr. Nottingham's cogent perspective.

That's what he needed to feel like his time in prison was not a total waste.

"Thank you for a nice time, Mr. Thomas. #SuperSeniorCitizen"

That was the text message Tamara sent to Elliott's cell phone not long after he returned from his walk. He smiled and texted her back: "4 years before I'm a senior citizen. So get me while I'm young."

It was Tamara's time to smile. She was smitten and surprised: A man older than her father would have been was her new lover. She never would have expected that, but she felt more at ease and comfortable with him than she ever had with a man in her age range.

After shopping with her mom and while watching recorded episodes of *Love & Hip Hop*, Tamara tried to figure out how she went out with Elliott, let alone bedded him. The answers did not come easy and, really, only added to her confusion.

"What does this say about me?" she said aloud.

Family members had told her growing up that she was an "old soul," that she had "been here before" and that she was "ahead of her time." At family reunions, instead of hanging with the preteens when she was twelve or with the young adults when she was a teenager, she always lingered with her much older aunts and uncles. And they allowed her to hang with them because she was comfortable and contributed interesting elements to conversations.

Tamara never told anyone about her attraction to teachers in school or professors in college. She played along when her friends talked admirably about the school's athletes or the cute guys. But she never fully bought in. The man with a little gray hair and a lot of experiences piqued her curiosity. A lot.

Around 9 p.m., when Elliott had just awakened from a nap before going to the club, Tamara sent him a text message. Inadvertently, her mom influenced her to contact him. While shopping, Tamara told her mother about Elliott. Tamara did not share that Elliott was older than her mom, but she did say enough for her mom to endorse him.

"His name is Elliott and I feel much more mature when I'm with him," she said as they looked at dresses in the DKNY store. "His energy is different. He's not all over the place like guys I have dated. He's calm and assured and comforting. I've never felt that way with a man."

"I think you should focus on your career," her mother said. "But who am I fooling? You don't listen to me."

Mother and daughter laughed.

"Really, though, when you can feel secure and like you're growing with a man, then that's a good thing. A rare thing," she said. "Trust me, I know. Your father had the same effect on me when we met. Now don't take that to mean you should marry this man. I'm just saying embrace him but take it slowly. Let everything play out naturally. Don't go trying to force anything."

"No, that's not me, Ma," Tamara said.

"So when are you going to see him again?" her mother asked.

"I wanted to see him tonight. But he said he has to go to a party."

"And you left it at?" her mother asked. "If you want to see him, you should let him know. Maybe he would pass on the party. Why let him go out to a party and meet someone else when you're really interested in him? I'm not pushing you to be aggressive. I'm just saying don't be too lackadaisical."

The advice her mom gave ricocheted in Tamara's head, leading to her text message: "Do you have to go to that party?"

Elliott received the message as he was about to start shaving. He put down the razor to respond.

"Have to go? No. I want to go. But why?" he responded.

"I was thinking I would come over and hang out with you."

Elliott smiled and shook his head upon reading the text. Then he said aloud: "I see. Well, look at this."

He wanted to cancel his plans and tell her to come over. But Elliott analyzed women up and down, and he deduced that seeing her on back-to-back nights would convey the wrong message. So he texted her: "That sounds good. But I committed to being there and I don't want to be a no-show."

"U can text ur friend now and let them no something came up," Tamara shot back. The more he refused to give in to her, the more eager she became to get her way.

On the other end, Elliott was tired of texting. He knew he had to with the generation of women he desired; it was their way. But after about two in succession, he had enough.

And instead of texting back, he called her.

"Hi, Elliott," she said with excitement in her voice. "I wasn't expecting you to call."

"You want to give me arthritis with all the texting?" he joked. "You just learned something about me. After about three, maybe four texts in a row, I'm done. If it's going to go beyond that, we need to talk."

"Don't you enjoy the anticipation of what the response is going to be when you receive texts?" Tamara asked. "It's fun. It's a real important way in how we communicate now."

She paused for a second. "I'm sorry," Tamara said. "I didn't mean to sound like I was schooling you. I was trying to make a point."

"It's okay; I'm good," Elliott said. "And I understand your position. I get to the point sometimes where talking is the best way to go."

"I understand," Tamara said. "In my texts, I was trying to say that you'd have way more fun with me than you would at any party."

She sipped on the glass of Sauvignon Blanc that helped her get more daring. "Don't you agree?"

Elliott got her drift, but his near obsession with frequenting the Atlanta nightlife overwhelmed him. He wanted to answer her, "I don't know." Instead, he said, "Of course. But I can't cancel on them at this late point. I'm getting dressed. And why do you want to see me anyway?"

He threw in that last question not only as a way of gathering information, but also to take her mind off of why he didn't want her to come over.

"Well, hold on," she said. Tamara took the remaining half glass of her wine in one gulp. And she even burped after downing it. "I'm sorry," she said. "I had to finish my wine before I gave you my answer."

"Which is…?

Tamara blushed.

"My mother told me to," she started.

"Your *mother?*" Elliott said. "You told your *mother* about me?"

"Not really, not specifically," she answered. "I told her that you make me feel mature and she gave a little speech about how wonderful it is that a man could do that. And later she told me to assert myself and to keep you from going out to meet other women."

Elliott said, "How do you and your peers put it? 'It's not that serious.'"

"But that's the problem," Tamara said. "I think it might be that serious. I didn't give you the full picture on how I felt about us being intimate last night. The truth is, it was wonderful. I wasn't trying to compare you to men I have slept with, younger men. But I couldn't help it. It's impossible not to. And it was made more impossible to notice because it was so different."

Ellliott had not received any complaints from the other two twenty-somethings he had slept with, and he was proud of his performance with her.

"I thought the men I had slept with were doing something," she said. "I enjoyed it with them, but they were really jumping up and down in me, showing off how long they could go or how big they were—and all of them weren't that big. And there weren't that many, either, so don't get any bad ideas about me."

Elliott did not respond. He listened. And even in that he was impressed.

"See what I'm saying?" Tamara said. "A younger guy would have had a bunch of questions and interrupted me. You are listening. I love it. Thank you. But anyway, what I was getting at is that younger men basically fucked me. Excuse my language, but it's the truth. They made sure they got theirs. They either were not concerned about pleasing me or didn't know how.

"The worst part is that I was okay with that. I didn't know any better—until last night. In your mind, you probably fucked me, too. But the way it felt on my end was loving and careful but strong and attentive. You caressed me and admired my body with your hands and kissed me delicately on my neck and shoulders and made me feel like a woman, like you cared about how I felt.

"You enjoyed yourself; I could tell. But it wasn't only about you being pleased. You wanted to please me. And experiencing that made me wet, made me feel alive and made me want to make sure you were pleased. Through you, I experienced for the first time what making love really means. I would never have expected that. But now I want more."

Elliott smiled. "See, how long would it have taken you to text all that?" he joked.

Tamara laughed. "What can I say? I'd like to believe at some point I would have said, 'Let's just talk about it.' But you beat me to that."

"Well, thank you for all those words that will always mean something to me," Elliott said. "I'm not sure what to say after that except making love to you felt wonderful. Your body is soft and made for caressing. And I want to feel it again."

Still, he was not going to miss the party. So he came up with a solution. "How about I leave a key for you downstairs and you meet me here around twelve-thirty, one. That'll give me some time to show my face, mingle and get back to you."

"You have to go to that party, huh?" Tamara asked.

"I made a promise that I would be there and I'm trying to make a compromise with you," Elliott said. "I had these plans for about three weeks. I'm willing to cut my night short to accommodate you."

Tamara had a moment where her age showed. "Don't do me any favors," she snapped.

"Is that what you really want to say to me?" He had vowed to not get overly reactionary to a woman's flippant remarks. *She's just being a woman*, was his thought process, chauvinistic as it might have sounded.

"You're right. I'm sorry," Tamara said. "I shouldn't have tried to get you to break up your plans. Thank you for meeting me half-way on this. I will get there around midnight and pick up the key. But I will text you when I'm on my way."

She smiled as she said those last words because she had already planned to give Elliott a memorable greeting when he returned home that night.

And that's how they left it, which was good for both sides. Elliott knew he had a fun evening ahead of him even if the party was a dud. Tamara was excited about a chance to feel Elliott's loving again.

CHAPTER FIVE
To Compound Matters...

R&B star Melanie Fiona and hip-hop star Chris Brown were performing at Compound, which was the reason Elliott was so determined to go to the club. He liked Melanie Fiona, but was totally unaware of any Chris Brown song. But he believed that the entertainment would bring out a bevy of young beauties for him to peruse.

It would be a much different crowd from Vanquish, though. At Vanquish, while it was mostly a younger group of people, there were much older patrons, too, up into the fifties. At Compound, it would be women mostly in their twenties with some up to their mid-thirties. And because the crowd would be so young, he had to switch up his look.

At Vanquish, he let the gray on the edges of his sides and other parts of his head show. At Compound, he figured a younger look would prevent him from standing out more than normal. So, he pulled out his Just For Men after he spoke to Tamara and carefully, meticulously colored the edges of his hair, eliminating most of the gray. Doing so took off about ten years in his appearance.

Then he put on a pair of fashionable Sean John jeans and a pullover shirt that was fitted and showed off his strong arms over a man's version of Spanks to minimize the small protrusion of his stomach. He also put in a diamond stud earring.

It took him but ten minutes to get to the club. He handed the valet guy a twenty-dollar bill to keep his car up front. Last thing he wanted to do was have to wait for his car when he was ready to leave.

Compound was, indeed, a compound, a unique and fabulous venue that spanned several acres. It was like a park or a military base, with lounge areas around lagoons outside and separate buildings that, in essence, housed different parties. It was west of downtown and you could see the Atlanta skyline in the distance. The place could hold more than a thousand people and it looked like it was well on its way to capacity when Elliott arrived right before ten.

A vodka company sponsored one party in the first building, where a deejay spun old-school hip-hop music. The room was dark with a strobe light making it feel like the building was moving. At least that's how it felt to Elliott. By how the younger partygoers moved about, the strobe light did not faze them.

He made his way through the thick crowd to the bar, where, after five minutes in line, he was able to secure the complimentary promotional cocktail. But the music was too loud and the lighting too busy for Elliott to stay there. As much as he desired to be the old man in the club, he was, indeed, old—the noise bothered him as well as the lighting.

So, with drink in hand, he immediately headed to the exit to escape the thumping music and visit another area of the expansive space. He at times said aloud but to know one in particular, "Damn," as he marveled over the young ladies' skimpy outfits that magnified the shape of their bodies.

Elliott would not want his woman to dress so revealingly, but he sure enjoyed watching women who did.

"How do you like this drink?" he asked a young lady who was sipping on the same cocktail as Elliott while sitting outside.

"It's too sweet, actually," she said. "I don't like sweet drinks. They taste like calories. At least give me the illusion of not being fattening."

Elliott flashed a broad smile. "That's funny. My name is Elliott and I'm probably too old for you. But I'd still like to get you a drink that is not too sweet."

"How do you know I'm not too old for *you?*" she said.

"Oh, I can tell," Elliott said. "But I see you ain't scared."

"Of what?" she asked. "You? I would get my girls if I needed them, but I think I can take you."

"I get it now," Elliot said. "You're drunk."

"A little, yeah," she said, smiling. "But I would call it a little tipsy. Still, my uncle used to say, 'Being a little drunk is like being a little pregnant. You either are or you aren't.' What do you think?"

"I think you are drunk—I mean, tipsy—and I think your uncle is right," he said.

"That's probably true," she said. "But I'm still a lady. I'm not sloppy or anything. I'm still looking cute. I still have my wits about me. I'm not slurring my speech. And if I didn't tell you, you wouldn't have known I was tipsy. Right?"

Elliott smiled. "In this big place, they might have somewhere I can get you some coffee." He studied the young lady as he spoke to her. She was attractive, with beautiful locs in her hair, wearing a dress that was about four inches above her knees, exposing a shapely pair of legs. She smiled in a sort of devilish way, like Phylicia Rashad would to Bill Cosby on *The Cosby Show*.

"Coffee? It's June, about eighty degrees," she said. "What will you suggest next? A sweater?"

"What's your name?" Elliott asked.

"Wouldn't you like to know?"

"Only if you want to tell me. If not, I'll just have to make up a name for you."

"Really? And what would that be?"

"Let's see," Elliott said. "Maybe I'll call you Supernova."

"Now why couldn't you just say, 'Tina' or 'Precious' or even 'Pumpkin?' Super... Super what?"

"Supernova."

"What does that even mean? Or is it a made-up name, like Shaneskaterra?"

"Supernova means a star that gets so hot that it explodes into this brilliant burst of light. That's what I see in you—this really special illumination. You project that."

The woman looked at Elliott for several seconds, making him feel awkward.

"What?" he asked.

"My boyfriend—my ex-boyfriend—told me I was a dark cloud," she said. "He tried to make me believe I was this evil spirit that cast darkness upon him. I knew he was wrong, but you can't help but remember what someone who used to be important to you says about you. This was about a month ago, but I was talking to my girlfriend about it yesterday.

"Her hating-ass said, 'Well, he had his reasons for saying what he said.' She's my friend and I love her but I was so pissed that she said that. And then here you come along. We talk for three or four minutes and you say I'm a brilliant burst of light. A supernova. Wow.

"I really needed that. Thank you? Can I hug you?"

"If I can hug you back," Elliott said, and they embraced.

"My name is Nicole. But you can call me Nikki."

They separated. "Nicole, if I'm not mistaken, means victorious people. So, you're a winner," Elliott said.

"Oh, my God," Nikki said. "Do you know that he also said I was a loser because I wanted to break up with him? He said it more than once. And I never even knew that my name means 'winner.' This is a trip.

"I'm glad I met you…what did you say your name was? I'm sorry."

"Elliott."

"And what does it mean?" Nikki wanted to know.

"It means 'The Lord is my God,'" Elliott explained.

"Interesting," she said. "So you've memorized what people's names mean?"

"I learn the meaning of the names of the people close to me," he said. "Just so happens that my sister's name is Nicole."

"Well, I'll be damned."

"No, you won't. At least not over you and my sister having the same name."

She smiled at him and he smiled inside. He had her. His strength was getting women to listen to him. He almost surely would have a different, fresh approach that would disarm them, make them forget about his age and inspire them to focus on what he said.

"Since you said I'm too young for you, why are you talking to me?" Nikki said.

"I didn't say that. I said I'm probably too old for *you*," he answered. "That's different from you being too young for me."

"How young do you think I am?"

"Too old for R. Kelly," Elliott said, and they laughed.

"For right now, I'm not even going to ask why you like young women," she said. "I'm going to guess you're at least fifty. Everyone in here is in their twenties and early thirties. Don't you feel old?"

"The only time I feel old is when I ride my stationary bike too long," Elliott said, "and even then, it's just my butt feeling old. Not my body."

"Who are you here with?" Nikki asked.

"You," Elliott responded without hesitation.

"Sir, you're old enough to be my father," she said. "In fact, you probably would really like my father. He can't sit still, either. Always chasing. For that reason, I'm glad my mom isn't around to see him."

"You lost your mom?" Elliott asked.

"Yes," Nikki said. "Lost her to a rich African."

They laughed.

"She got remarried and moved to Ghana three years ago," she continued. "I talk to her and we Skype. But I haven't seen her in person since she left.

"But that's beside the point. You're too old for me. You mess around and get hurt."

Elliott said, "Age matters only when you allow it to matter."

"Hmmm," Nikki said. "I like the way you put that."

"You'll like a lot more once you get to know me," Elliott said.

"You're definitely confident," she said. "Older men have come on to me many times before. But they always tried to offer me money or to pay my bills or buy me stuff. What's your angle? Why should I get to know a man probably twenty or twenty-five years older than me?"

"I'm offering you me," Elliott said.

"Yeah, but who are you?" Nikki asked.

"Someone told me a few minutes ago: that's for me to know and for you to find out."

Nikki laughed and shook her head. "So what do you suppose I do now?"

"You certainly shouldn't leave that up to me."

"You know what I mean."

"Let's go have a drink and talk some more and after that, if you don't want to communicate with me, no problem. But I'm having a drink. You probably should have water."

"Look at you, being noble. Most men would have tried to fill me up with drinks."

"I hope that's not true."

"I can tell you some stories."

"I'd rather hear about you."

Her cell phone that she glanced at often vibrated. "Excuse me a minute," she said while reading and then sending a text message.

"My friends are in there for the concert. They said Chris Brown just got on stage."

"Don't let me stop you from enjoying the show," Elliott said.

"You're not going in?"

"I was, but it's going to be too loud in there for me. Plus, I don't know any of his music. Now, if it were the Isley Brothers, that would be something different."

"Well, maybe I'll stay out here with you. I've seen Chris Brown before. He puts on a good show. But I don't have to see him again."

"You'd pass up Chris Brown for me?" Elliott asked, smiling.

"I wouldn't put it that way," she answered. "But let's go get that drink…I mean water."

They went into the building where Chris Brown was performing and Elliott asked Nikki to wait on him as he went to the bathroom. When he came out, he maneuvered his way to the front of the bar and handed the bartender a five-dollar bill as he asked for two cups of water.

With the cups in hand, he returned to Nikki, who was confronted by a guy who liked what he saw. She seemed uncomfortable as the young man moved closer to her. He seemed drunk and overly aggressive.

Elliott stepped in. He said, "Here you go, honey," as he handed her the water. "Sorry it took so long. It's crazy at the bar."

The guy stepped back and looked hard at Elliott. "This is your man?" he asked Nikki.

Before she could answer, Elliott said while giving the man a stern look, "Her bodyguard."

The guy looked back at Elliott, but detected something in his look that said he was in danger. In his time in prison, Elliott became a master at defending himself and intimidating people without saying a word.

"Her bodyguard?" the young man said, shaking his head. "Yeah, right."

"I appreciate you keeping her company for me," Elliott said, again staring deep into the man's eyes.

The guy looked Elliott up and down and finally turned and walked away.

"See, you need me around," Elliott said.

"You might be right," she said.

They went back outside and found a bench and sat there and talked for forty minutes. It was difficult for Elliott to stay focused on Nikki because he was often distracted by the constant passing of attractive young women.

He thought he was being discreet.

"Would you like some Visine?" she said with sarcasm.

"Sure," Elliott said. "It'll help my eyes. I don't want to miss anything."

"So you admit to staring at every woman that passes while sitting here with me?"

"I'm people-watching. Nothing more, nothing less."

He wanted to tell her that more than a decade in prison had engrained in him the importance of watching his back, of understanding who was around him and figuring out where trouble could come. He was perpetually concerned about someone having an angle on him, who was around him. Without that paranoia, he believed he would not have made it in prison. Sharing this with Nikki having just met her would have been too much.

"A lot of times I go out and I don't say anything to anyone," he went on. "I watch people, how they interact, what they do, how guys accept rejection, how women deal with men constantly approaching them. It's very interesting."

"You ain't slick, Mr. Elliott. People-watching? You mean girl-watching."

"Can't put anything past you, huh? Would you rather I watch men?"

"There's enough of that going on in Atlanta without you joining the madness. It's so rampant—I'm speaking about the number of gay men here—that it makes you scared to date. You don't know who's who."

"Well, I have a story to tell you about that subject."

"I'm listening."

"Well, it's too long and I'm about to go," Elliott said. He wanted to stay but Tamara had texted him while he was in the bathroom letting him know she would be leaving shortly to head to his place. He did not want her there without him for too long, but he did want her there long enough to feel comfortable and to get comfortable.

"This isn't a trick to get your number; I really would like to tell you about this situation," he said. "But I have to leave."

"It's not that late," Nikki said. "But then again, you're old."

They laughed. "I'll let you get away with that…for now," Elliott said. "How about I give you my number and you call me if you'd like to hear my story and/or get together again?"

"You'd better take my number," Nikki said. "I'm old school. My mom and dad taught me that the man should pursue you and should make the first phone call. I'm a woman of today in most instances. But in some ways I'm 1950s."

"Well, that's my era, so I can relate and respect that point of view," Elliott said, pulling out his cell phone. She recited her number and he programmed it in his phone.

"Do me a favor and text me to let me know you made it home safely tonight. I will text you my number now. Is that too forward of you, to let me know you're safe? It doesn't matter what time it is."

"Oh, wow, you're a gentleman, I see. I gotta watch out for you."

CHAPTER SIX
Beyond Her Years

On the ride home, Elliott called one of his closest friends, Henry. They met when Elliott was released from prison and moved to Atlanta. Both were at the Division of Driver Services and struck up a conversation during the endless wait, and became friends. They shared a passion for women, golf and long drives.

"I met another one," Elliott said when Henry answered the phone.

"Yeah, hello to you, too," Henry said.

"Oh, my mistake," Elliott said. "Just had to tell you before I got home about this girl."

"How old is she and where did you meet her?" Henry asked. Those were always his first two questions.

"I'm not sure about her age; she wouldn't say," Elliott said. "I'm guessing she's thirty or early thirties."

"Oh, a seasoned woman by your standards," Henry cracked.

"She looks about twenty-five. But she has a good spirit about her. Great conversation. It shows you can still get a good conversation out of a young woman."

"I'm sure that's not what you're really looking to get from her."

"No, but I will take it. I'm leaving Compound. This place is crazy."

"Yeah, I've been there. Nice. But what are you going to do about all these women you keep meeting? I'm just saying. You can't go on this way forever. You'll be sixty-two in a few months. I think that's when you should retire, find one that you like and settle down."

"That sounds nice…like a fairy tale. Meanwhile, in the real world, I'm pulling up to my garage. Upstairs there is a young lady who turned twenty-five yesterday, waiting on me. Remind me to tell you about that tomorrow."

"Yeah, let's meet for lunch. Call me."

They hung up and Elliott made his way through the garage and up to his apartment. He opened the door and found a scented candle burning on the coffee table, near her purse, but no Tamara. There was music playing on the iPod. He peeked into his room and the second bedroom and she was not there.

Only place left for her was the balcony, and there he found her leaning on the rail, looking over the city with a glass of wine in her hand…totally naked.

Elliott looked around and was glad his balcony wrapped around the apartment and had no connecting balcony.

"You should see your face," she said.

"I see your everything," he said. "And it looks damn good."

"I feel so free," she said, raising her arms above her head and spilling some Pinot Noir on her shoulder. "Totally liberated."

"Shit, seeing you like that out here makes me feel liberated—and I still have my clothes on."

"Not for long, I hope," Tamara said.

Elliott went over to her and they embraced. "It's a nice night to be nude on the balcony," he said into her ear. "I'll be right back."

A few minutes later, he returned dressed in a silk robe, holding a glass of Glenfiddich on the rocks.

"You need to take that off," Tamara said. "It's not the same."

Elliott did not resist. He handed her his glass, slipped out of the robe and tossed it on the chair alongside hers. She handed him his Scotch and Elliott made a toast.

"To being naked on the balcony," he said.

"And to feeling totally free," she added. And they tapped glasses.

"My neighbors…"

"What about them?"

He scanned her tight body. "Too bad they don't have the same view I have."

"I feel so good." She placed her forearms on the railing and looked north toward the Buckhead section of Atlanta. Elliott sidled close to her and did the same.

"Thank you for cutting your evening short for me," she said, her eyes transfixed on the images in front of her.

"I had a good time," he said. "But I knew a better time was awaiting me here."

"On my way here, I thought about it," Tamara said. "What makes you tick? What really can you see in me; I'm so much younger than you? There can't be a future with us. How can I be friends with Danielle and Daniel? They're your children. What am I doing here?"

Elliott sipped his drink. "Wow, you had quite a drive over here," he said. "I'm surprised you didn't smash into the back of someone's car. My head would explode with that many thoughts rushing through it on a fifteen-minute drive."

"I'm serious," Tamara said.

"I know you are, and that's the problem right there," he said. "There's a time for being serious and this doesn't seem to be one of those times. We're out here Butterball turkey naked on the balcony, a beautiful night, sipping on drinks…and you want to talk about questions that can be answered at another time—or can't be answered at all?"

"I want it on the record, even as I stand out here in my birthday suit—hey, that's right, technically, it's still my birthday because women celebrate all month or at least all week. Anyway, I want it on the record that I had stuff on my mind."

"Duly noted," Elliott said. "We will get to those questions, I promise you that. I don't want you having any doubts or questions or discomfort."

Tamara looked at him with admiration in her eyes. That alarmed Elliott, but he dismissed it. There was a lot going on at that moment, and his hang-up about women needed to go somewhere.

"How was the party at Compound?" she asked, helping Elliott's thoughts move on.

"That place is nice. Huge," he said. "It was like a campus of clubs on the grounds. I had fun. Met some good people."

"By that you mean women, don't you?" Tamara tried to sound casual about it, but she didn't succeed.

"Of course I met women; men, too," he said. "That's what socializing is all about. But mostly I people-watched."

"Do you have a girlfriend?" She wanted an answer before sleeping with him the night before, but the moment escaped her to ask. She knew that was a big mistake to not inquire before sex.

"This was one of those questions you pondered on your way over here, wasn't it?" Elliott responded.

"No. This was a question I had on my mind last night, but you got fresh with me and made me forget," she said, smiling.

"I don't have a girlfriend," Elliott said. "I date. But even with that, I only date women I feel good about. I don't date for the sake of dating."

"I didn't think that," she said.

"Well, I wanted to put that out there. The assumption has been made to me that because I go out a lot—or not even a lot but that I go out to places with much younger people—that I'm on the prowl. Well, I'm on the prowl for a good time. That's it. Whatever happens in the course of that, well, that's okay, too."

"You told me last night that you wanted sex with me," Tamara said.

"I also told you I wanted a whole lot of other things, too," Elliott said. "And the other things I said were just as important as sex. But you choose to ignore that."

"I might be young but I'm not dumb," Tamara said. "Sex is more important than the other things you said you wanted because of what's involved. I don't just have sex with anyone. I hope you don't think that."

"I have no reason to believe that," Elliott said.

Tamara said, "I slept with you last night—"

"Because you wanted to sleep with me," Elliott interrupted. "There's no other reason. You wanted sex and you got it. You either like me or were curious about me because I'm so much older or you were horny and I was around…whatever the case may be. But you wanted sex."

Tamara wanted to say she was insulted, but she couldn't because he was right. So she sipped more of her wine and Elliott went on.

"And there's nothing wrong with you wanting sex," he said. "In general, you're right: Sex is more important than the other things I mentioned. But for me, for my life and what I have gone through, I need more than that. I'm not Denzel or that guy Idris whatever his name is, but I can get sex if that's all I wanted.

"But my dick has eyes—and a conscience. I need more than physical beauty in a person to desire sex."

The combination of the wine, the night air, being naked and Elliott's words made Tamara wet.

"Your dick has eyes?" she said. "Well, let me see."

She set her glass on the balcony floor and sat on her robe on the chair. "Mr. Thomas, you and your dick with eyes are needed over here."

Elliott did not hesitate. He stood before her with his manhood dangling in the breeze. "Let me see about these eyes," she said as she clutched and stroked his instant erection. "I see only one eye, and it's dripping a little something."

Then she covered his erection with her mouth as he stood there, sipping his Scotch. She had one hand between her legs and the other on his third leg, beating it as she went up and down on it in a fury. Elliott was surprised; he did not expect this oral gift from Tamara, but he enjoyed it.

He used his free hand to push her head down so he could go deeper into her mouth. Tamara did not back down. She took as much as she could. After several minutes she stopped, but only to take Elliott's drink from his hand and pour some of it on his throbbing meat. He flinched.

"You're trying to turn me out, huh?" he said between groans.

She looked up at him while bobbing down on his manhood. She winked. Elliott shook his head. He liked Tamara more than he expected.

She stopped sucking but kept stroking. "I want you to cum."

"Where?" he asked.

"You decide," Tamara answered and went back to providing oral pleasure.

Elliott sipped his Glenfiddich and looked to his left at the skyline. He wanted to savor the event. Finally, he could feel an explosion coming, and grabbed hold of Tamara's hair and thrust his hips forward. Elliott let out a loud gasp, and felt the energy in his body release with his semen. Tamara kept sucking.

"You're amazing," he said. "You're too young to be that good at that."

She reached up for his Scotch again, this time taking a swig as she swallowed his juices.

"The best Scotch I've ever had," she said, leaning back in the chair.

Elliott, who prided himself on having a response to most everything, had nothing to offer. He placed his robe in the other chair and sat down across from Tamara.

"You're ahead of your time," he said.

"Actually, I'm behind time; I've got to go," she said.

"What? Go where?" Elliott said.

"Home, then church."

Tamara was a faithful attendee of her church, and was scheduled to be an usher at the 6 a.m. service.

"I'm sorry, but I have to be there at five-thirty," she said. "It's almost two o'clock now. I've got to get my uniform ready and get at least a little sleep."

"So why did you come over here then?" Elliott asked.

"I did what I came to do," Tamara said as she walked inside. She grabbed her clothes and a small toiletry bag and went to the bathroom, where she brushed her teeth, gargled and freshened up.

"You really are far more advanced than your age," he said as they rode the elevator down to the garage, where her car was parked.

"Why? Because you think I got skills?" she asked.

"No, because you were not concerned about pleasing yourself," he said. "Younger women usually haven't learned enough to be selfless. And to leave after pleasing me, that's a very mature thing. Most younger women—or most women, period—would need to stay just to not feel like they sold themselves short."

"I see what you're saying, but doesn't that speak to their insecurities?" Tamara asked.

"Exactly," Elliott said. "Clearly, you're as secure as they come."

At her car, he hugged and kissed her before she got in. "Maybe one day you'll take me to your church," he said.

"You have to slow down; I don't play when it comes to church," she said, rolling down her window and putting the car in reverse. "You come to my church, then that means we're serious—and we know you don't want that. Besides, your kids go to my church."

She backed out of the parking space and drove off as Elliott watched, unsure if he should feel great about having been pleased as he was or down about the lack of relationship with his kids.

CHAPTER SEVEN
The Future Has A Past

Elliott did as he was supposed to do on Sunday: he called Tamara. No matter how mature she seemed, she would be upset if he did not call her the day after sex. Any woman would be upset.

"Good to hear from you, mister," she said when he called her in the afternoon. "If you hadn't called me, you would have had a problem."

"I solve problems, not create them," Elliott said.

"I bet you do," Tamara said. They chatted for a few more minutes and then hung up. Elliott then called his friend Henry and cancelled lunch. He was tired. Although he was in solid condition, especially considering his age, Elliott at times just felt run down.

The doctors did not say, but Elliott attributed his occasional fatigue to a difficult bout with cancer. It took three years to overcome prostate surgery, a blood clot that almost killed him and a return of the cancer two years later before finally beating it. He was seven years cancer-free, but underneath his bravado and confidence was an intense fear that it would return.

He was not sure what was harder to conquer: almost twelve years in prison for a crime he did not commit or three years battling cancer. Few people had been tested with that combination of challenges.

A few years after his release from prison—DNA evidence showed his specimen was not inside the victim and an investigation found that police officers deliberately withheld information that would have dismissed him as a suspect—Elliott met his ex-wife and mother of his children, Lucy. They attended the same S.W. Atlanta church. Elliott had moved from the D.C. area to start fresh. Being in the area reminded him of a part of his life he wanted to forget.

The equivalent to what today is called a "Singles Ministry" hosted a meet and greet one night and Lucy complimented Elliott on his black and gold cardigan sweater. Elliott had not noticed Lucy in church, but she enthralled him the moment she said, "That sweater looks good on you."

"Oh, thanks," he said. They smiled at each other. "I'm Elliott Thomas," he added, extending his hand.

"Lucy Dancer," she said.

That basic introduction was the start of their courtship. Lucy was from a small town called Whitakers, N.C. She moved to Atlanta to escape a troubled past, too. Lucy was a social worker who was inspired to do her job after a personal tragedy. Their first date was lunch at a quaint restaurant in the west end of Atlanta on Ralph D. Abernathy Road. He told her at the table, "We're going to make some beautiful babies."

"You're way ahead of yourself, don't you think?" Lucy responded. "I'm not sure I even like you."

At that first date, over roasted chicken, mashed potatoes and string beans, Elliott shared with Lucy his traumatic story of prison. He had never told anyone that he did not know intimately, but there was something about Lucy that drew him in and his story out.

He was almost shocked when she said, "You can trust me, Elliott. Already I see who you are and you're not what they said you were.

Don't let them win by thinking for a second that you are. You know that God knows who you are."

He was shocked because she connected with him enough to know that being accused and convicted of something he did not do made him wary of most people. So many people had to distrust him to believe he would rape and kill a woman, and he found it hard to trust that anyone would see him for who he really was.

"I appreciate that," he said. If he had said more, he would have cried. So, he kept it short and ate his food.

A year later, they were married. Their connection was sorrowfully ironic. She empathized and sympathized with Elliott in a way no one else had when he told her of his wrongful conviction. And he was a strong support system when she told of having been raped and her assailant was arrested but later freed on a technicality.

She, in fact, had not told any man of her horrific experience. But with Elliott's transparency came a trust in him that she could open up. It took her seven months to tell Elliott. She waited until she was sure they were in a serious relationship.

He cried when she told him. Then he hugged her tightly, securely. "I'm so sorry," he said. "You didn't deserve that."

The next day, he proposed. "Why are you doing this now?" she asked.

"I cried yesterday when you told me what happened to you," he said. "After prison, I thought I had lost all emotion about anything or anyone other than myself. But immediately my emotions came forward because I love you. My love for you opened up emotions in me that were dead."

He was thirty-four and Lucy was twenty-six when they wed. And it turned out that in their marriage they served as quasi-counselors to each other. They talked about how their experiences affected their lives and how they looked at relationships and even their dreams. Each had separate psychologists that they visited. But their therapy extended to home.

"We have been through something very similar," Elliott told Lucy the night she accepted his proposal, as they lay in bed after celebratory sex. "I can relate to being violated as you were. When you were…you know—"

"You can say 'rape'; I've gotten beyond hearing the word," Lucy said.

Elliott went on. "Well, I know something was taken away from you that night. I will always remember the violation against me, the shock, the hurt, the emotional trauma. You will never be the same. I know this. You will be all right; you *are* all right. But, inside, the violation never leaves you. Am I right?"

"You are," Lucy said. "I went through some serious counseling and some serious soul-searching. In the beginning, I tried blaming myself. I said I put myself in a position by what I was wearing and where I was at the time. I had on a dress that was kinda short and tight and I stopped in this neighborhood I was unfamiliar with in a town called Enfield, trying to get a pack of cigarettes. Yes, I smoked in those days.

"It was about midnight, close to it. I had gone to a party and wasn't feeling it because a guy I used to date was there. So, I left. Figured I could get home, get some rest and go to church in the morning. But I stopped at a store to satisfy that cigarette urge. I saw the guy come out of the store as I was going in. I saw him.

"When I came out, instead of getting into my car, I started opening the pack of Kools right there by the road. All of a sudden, I could sense someone behind me. Before I could really react, he had me in a headlock and pulled me behind the building. You know how things are like a dream and you truly don't believe they are happening? That's how this was.

"I was breathless. I pushed him and yelled, but he punched me and said, 'If you scream again, I'm gonna kill your ass.' The look on his face... I was so scared. I tried to close my eyes, but I couldn't. He raped me and I was mentally taking notes. I looked into his face. I noticed the cloud and stars in the sky. I heard cars drive by. And before I knew it, he was gone. I laid there almost in shock.

"My nose was bleeding, and my lip. It was warm outside, but I got really cold. I was shivering. I wanted someone to come find me, to help me. I was too scared to scream; I was scared he might be nearby. Finally, I got up. I pulled myself together and drove to the hospital.

"I never cried that night. My mind was blown. And I was too angry to cry. Too shocked. It wasn't until the next day, at home alone, that I realized the violation, as you put it. That animal took something from me that I could never get back, and that hurt."

After those initial days following the attack, Lucy had not spoken about that night to anyone outside of the authorities. When the rapist was caught but eventually released because of a so-called improper search of his home, Lucy was devastated. The violation was magnified, and talking about it was even more difficult.

But Elliott's openness and their closeness as a couple allowed her to share with him.

"It wasn't until I really talked to God—and listened to Him—that I realized it wasn't my fault," Lucy said. "I should—we all should—be able to wear whatever we want to wear and go wherever we want to go without being raped. I wasn't wrong; he was an animal. A sick animal. It's a simple thing, it would seem, right?

Why believe you did something to yourself when something was done to you? When I came to really understand that—that God put me here to live my life and not blame myself for something I did not do—I was able to move on with my life."

Elliott related to Lucy like no other man. They both were twenty when each respective life-changing event happened. And they happened in the same month. He connected with her and understood her emotional swings in a way few people could because he experienced them, too.

"My violation was different, but still a violation that will never leave me," Elliott said. "I avoided being physically raped in prison, but I had already been raped by the judicial system. I remember being in court and feeling like, 'I'll be glad when this is all over so I can go home and back to school.' I was naïve, I guess. I believed that the truth would prevail. Innocent people don't go to prison. That's what I thought.

"You did good to not cry; I cried like a baby," he added. "I was supposed to be entering my senior year of college. Instead I was sentenced to life in prison. *Life*. They tried to take my life away from me. Actually, they did take it away. It was a miracle that I was able to get it back."

DNA testing emerged in the early 1980s, as Elliott was going into his twelfth year at notorious Lorton Reformatory, about twenty miles south of D.C. It was a place of mayhem that broke Elliott's spirit.

He had dreamed of owning a business. His work at the car dealership made him feel like it was an area he would like to pursue. But all that evaporated. His ambition became staying alive and not being raped, which he managed by staying away from prison politics, drugs and being a stellar basketball player that many inmates admired.

But he spent almost every waking moment afraid or paranoid at best. He lived among criminals, some of them *real* rapists and murderers. When he spoke of his conviction in prison, which was rare, he spoke of the murder charge. To speak of being convicted of rape would enhance his chances of being brutalized.

A family friend read about DNA testing in *The Washington Post* and how each human has a genetic makeup that was unique from anyone else. Those distinguishing chromosomes would be a part of evidence in a rape case. The family located a lawyer at the Innocence Project in New York, which found a DNA expert who had the evidence tested to determine that it was not Elliott who committed the crime.

At thirty-one, and with little fanfare—certainly far less than the media horde that covered his trial—Elliot was released from prison. "May 22nd, 1983—that's my 'rebirth day,'" he told Lucy. "That's when I got out. I celebrate that day more than I celebrate the day I was born."

After meeting Danette, who placed him in a job, Elliott slowly but painfully reimmersed himself back into society. His "friends" had long since eased away before he was released. He walked Hains Point on the Potomac River and Rock Creek Park as a way of expressing his freedom. He could go anywhere he wanted. But he was angry and bitter that the years he should have been partying and traveling and being carefree and finding himself were spent in the most vile place on earth among mostly crazy men. So he moved to Atlanta to separate himself from it all. Didn't know anyone there, but heard enough about the Southern way of life, the abundance of professional women and reasonable cost of living to pick up and give it a try. And he loved it.

But just when he found his footing, the doctor told him he had cancer.

"Couldn't catch a break," he told Lucy a month into knowing her.

"Are you serious? Oh, my God," she said. "You've got to be the strongest man I've ever met."

"Depends on how you look at it," he said. "I felt like I was the unluckiest man in the world—but meeting you seems to have changed that."

"I feel the same way," Lucy said. "I feel like I have finally met someone who really connects with me and understands that I'm going to have my moments and can relate to them."

They could not afford an elaborate wedding or an exotic honeymoon. They went to the justice of the peace and drove to Myrtle Beach for three days for their honeymoon. And they were as happy as any couple around.

"If money is going to determine our happiness," Lucy said, "then where does our love come in?"

That's how Lucy liked to talk. She'd pose a question and leave it up to Elliott to figure it out. When he asked her why she did that, she said, "Because questions make you think."

All he could do was smile.

Two years after their wedding, Lucy got pregnant. Elliott wept when she shared the news. "Why are you crying, baby?" she asked her husband.

"Not that long ago I was in prison, and I could not see this for myself," he said. "I was done. My life was over. And now here I am, a few years later, with you and now you're telling me we have a child on the way. This might be normal stuff to the next man. But to me, it's amazing."

When the doctor told them a few months before delivery that they were having twins, he thought he was dreaming. Danielle came out first. Lucy was happy it was a girl. Daniel came six minutes later. Elliott was proud to have a son to raise into a man.

They agreed on Daniel's name because in The Bible he was a young man of strong convictions, someone who understood the ways of God and who studied the law. Elliott found those attributes important. "And even when he was held captive into Babylon," he told Lucy, "he remained pure and unfazed by all the drama. And God ended up entrusting him with the ability to understand and interpret dreams and visions.

"I want that for my son," Elliott added. "Not literally interpreting dreams or visions, but being able to see the life he wants and to do what's necessary to live it."

Lucy was charged with the girl's name and she chose Danielle because it meant "God is my judge."

"If we have a girl and she lives her life understanding that, then she will be inclined to do the right thing," Lucy said. "And that's all I ask of her—to do the right thing understanding God is watching."

They were not prepared for two children, but they adapted quickly. Elliott was unaware of how to handle an infant, much less raise one, but he was a fast and eager learner. He treated his kids like the treasures they were. Danielle owned his heart, while he saw toughness in Daniel as early as one year old.

"He's the youngest, but he will protect his sister," Elliott said. "He has that spirit already."

They represented a happy family, navigating their way through minor crises, enduring financial concerns and growing together. When Elliott was awarded $2.4 million in a settlement in his wrongful conviction, their lives were made. Then it all came crashing down when the kids came home while in the eleventh grade to find their parents in the midst of a fight.

There had been arguments before that the kids heard, but the tone in this one was more volatile. They could only hear fragments, but it was perfectly clear when Lucy screamed, "Just leave, Elliott!"

Then there was silence. Daniel and Danielle looked at each other. "It's gonna be okay," Daniel reassured his sister.

Daniel was wrong. A few minutes later, Elliott stormed out of the house, a suitcase on wheels carrying some of his belongings.

Fear ran through the children. Some of their friends had divorced parents. They felt sorry for them. That evening they could see that would be their fate, too.

CHAPTER EIGHT
Kids Will Be Kids

Elliott could afford to live in the residential section of the W Hotel because he had money from the civil suit.

He hardly told anyone about his triumph. He took care of his family and the few who stuck with him while he was in prison. He invested in two small auto dealerships that flourished. He also purchased a few properties that he managed. Much of his money was in interest-bearing accounts.

Financial concerns were not a part of his life. But that fight with his wife started a dissent that led to divorce. And his kids blamed him.

When they asked their mother what happened, Lucy said, "I don't want to talk about it. Ask your father."

When they asked Elliott, he said, "I love you guys. You know I do. But this is between your mother and me. It has nothing to do with you and I don't think it's a conversation we should have."

"It has everything to do with us," Daniel said. "Aren't we a part of this family?"

"I'm saying that the problems your mom and I have do not have anything to do with you," Elliott said.

"I know what that means," Daniel said.

"You do? What does that mean?" Elliott asked his son.

"That you cheated on Mom," he said. "We have money. So why

else would she ask you to leave the house? If it wasn't true, you'd say so. But you're giving us this bullshit about it's between you and Mom."

"Hey, listen, boy, don't you ever curse at me again," he said. "I don't care if you're seventeen. I'll kick your ass."

Daniel started to talk back, but Danielle jumped in. "Daddy, this is messed up," she said. "Please tell me, did you cheat on Mom?"

"Honey, don't ask me that," he said.

The look on her face pained Elliott. It told of her disappointment in her father, the man she admired the most.

She got up from the couch, crying as she went into her room. Daniel and Elliott sat there. Finally, Daniel said, "You broke up this family. I hope you're proud of yourself."

"You don't know what you're talking about, Danny," he said. "I understand you're hurt."

"If you didn't do something, why would she tell you to leave?" Daniel asked. "There's only one reason she would do that."

Elliott wanted to talk, but he could not bring himself to do so. Instead, he rose from his seat and put his hand on the shoulder of his son, whose head was hung. "One day you'll understand," he said as he walked out of the house.

"No, I won't," Daniel said.

"Daddy," Danielle said. She had come back into the living room.

Elliott turned to his daughter, his pride and joy. They looked at each other for a moment before she walked over to him. They hugged.

Daniel came over and pulled his sister from their father's arms. "Come on, Danielle," he said. "Let him go. Let him get out of here. Let's go check on Mom."

That was among the last extensive conversations he'd had with his children. Daniel insisted he and Danielle limit their contact with him. Danielle did not want to go along with her brother, but she did because she sensed the pain her mom suffered. She felt it would be a betrayal of Lucy, the victim in the marriage, to maintain close contact with Elliott, the destroyer of the marriage.

At their high school graduation, the kids were cordial to their father but not warm. He was proud and he was hurt. "Lucy, this is killing me," he said.

Daniel heard him and told his sister. "He's over there begging Mom to forgive him, talking about 'This is killing me.'"

"Maybe it really is killing him, Daniel," Danielle said. "You know he loves her. You know he loves us."

"If he loved us, he wouldn't have had an affair and they wouldn't be divorced," Daniel said. "Look, it's graduation. I don't want to talk about this."

That summer, before going to Michigan State, Elliott asked to take out Lucy and their kids. They agreed, mostly because Lucy insisted. At Paschal's Restaurant on Northside Drive, they ordered soul food and talked about each other's lives.

"So, Michigan State, huh?" Elliott said. "The Spartans. Great basketball program. I'm really glad you all are staying together in college."

"Yeah, me, too, Daddy," Danielle said. "Daniel gets on my last nerves sometimes, but I'm not ready to separate from him yet."

"Well, your mother and I started saving for your education when you were born," Elliott said. "Since you all earned scholarships that's taking care of tuition, I'm going to take care of room and board. And you can use that money we saved for your incidentals: fun, food, clothes, whatever you want."

"Don't do us any favors," Daniel said.

"What's your problem, son?" Elliott said.

"Daddy, don't listen to him," Danielle said. "I love the idea. Thank you. Thank you both."

"It was your father's idea and it's a good one," Lucy said. "We're so proud of you both."

"Don't try to make him look good, Mom," Daniel said.

"Daniel—" Elliott started.

"Wait," Lucy jumped in. "Daniel, I want you to stop being so angry. We're sitting here having dinner as a family. There is no need for you to be rude to your father. Why would you do that?"

She did Daniel as she had many times before done Elliott: She made him think.

After a long pause, Daniel said, "I don't know. It just feels right."

"That's a child's answer," Lucy said. "You're a young man; a smart young man at that. Unless you can express yourself better than that, I say you let go of your hostility and enjoy this family time. You two are going to college in two weeks. I'm sad to see you go. But I'm glad to see you go. It's your time to grow up."

"I miss you all, and you haven't even gone yet," Elliott said. "I know it was a busy summer, but I really wish we had seen each other more."

Everyone braced for Daniel to fire off an angry response. Instead, he said, "Dad, thank you for the room and board."

It was the first comment to Elliott that was not angry in the year-and-a-half since the divorce. "Sure, son," Elliott said.

"You don't plan on coming to visit us at school, do you?" Daniel asked.

"Actually, I do," he answered.

"Well, I'm sure I'll be busy when you come," Daniel snapped.

"Well, you can hang out with me, Daddy," Danielle said.

"No, he can't; you'll be with me," Daniel said.

"Listen here, Daniel, enough is enough," Lucy said. "Let me tell you what happened."

"No, you're not," Elliott jumped in.

"Look," Daniel said. "He doesn't want us to know what he did."

"I told you before," Elliott said, looking around to make sure no other patrons were listening to their conversation, "this was none of your business. Lucy, we agreed that we would deal with this ourselves. The children should not be in the middle of it."

"You act like we're kids or something," Daniel said. "Shoot, we know the truth anyway."

"We're going to continue our meal talking about pleasant stuff, if that's okay with you, Daniel," Elliott said. "If it's not, then too bad."

Danielle snickered. "That's funny to you?" Daniel asked.

"This is your last warning," Lucy said. "You hear me, Daniel?"

"I hear you, Mom," he said, staring at his father.

There was no more drama the rest of the meal, but the animosity Daniel—and to a lesser degree, Danielle—felt grew over time. Elliott went on with his life, occasionally speaking to his daughter, who did not relay to her brother that she was in touch with their dad.

It ate at him that his relationship with his children was less than great. It was important to him. Elliott had a close relationship with his father. But the toll of his arrest and conviction wore heavily on Walter Thomas, and his health faded slowly and then rapidly while his son was incarcerated.

By the time Elliott was released, his father was a fraction of the active, jovial man he had been. Depression led to physical breakdowns that doomed him, no matter how many letters Elliott sent him from prison insisting that everything would be all right.

His dad's death was a landmark event in his life. It not only riddled him with guilt because he believed his father would have been fine if he did not get convicted, but it also reinforced the idea that life was short and to live each day as if it were your last.

"Obviously, there is truth to that," his therapist said to him the week before he saw his kids at Vanquish. "But could it be that you're using that as an excuse to live this lifestyle of a younger man?"

"Maybe I am," Elliott conceded. "I don't know. I just know it feels like the thing for me to do right now. Maybe it will help me relate better to my kids and can help me rebuild our relationship."

"What I can say for sure is that you're not going to rebuild the relationship *hoping* to rebuild it," Dr. Nottingham said. "Nothing happens without action. So, the question becomes: What are you going to do?"

Elliott was stumped. "You're always asking me questions," he said. "I come here for answers."

"I just gave you an answer," she said. "Do something. If it were me, I would call my kids together and tell them what they want to hear."

"And what's that?" Elliott said.

"Do I really need to tell you that?"

"There you go again with the questions," he responded.

Dr. Nottingham looked at him.

Finally, Elliott said, "There are a lot of things I want to say to them. But then my son gets so angry and disrespectful."

"He's only angry because he loves you," she said.

"What?" Elliott asked.

"He cannot express his love because he's angry. But through his anger he's expressing his love," she said. "He could not be so mad at you if he didn't care about you as he does."

"His sister is mad at me, too, but she's very respectful and available to me," Elliott said.

"Your daughter is spoiled and the female extension of you," Dr.

Nottingham said. "The doting father to a daughter is almost more valuable than anything she could ever receive. At the same time, her brother is her twin and that connection is usually unbreakable. It's natural for her to go with him, even if her heart is telling her something else.

"For Daniel, his mother is the symbol of life for him, and the older he gets, the more responsibility to protect and defend her he takes on, especially after a divorce. He feels like he's protecting and defending her by being angry with you."

Elliott left his session convinced he would have to take the lead to end the contentious relationship with his children. He thought he would invite them over for dinner and have a heart-to-heart. But before he made the call, he ran into them at the lounge while with their college friend, Tamara.

He went on that night and the next to have nice times with Tamara, but he was saddled with the thought of what his kids thought of him. He did not feel like meeting Henry for lunch or doing much of anything—sudden fatigue he attributed to post-cancer trials. But it really was mental. He was drained from his lack of a relationship with Daniel and Danielle, and Friday night's encounter only magnified the rift.

Worse, he was embarrassed. It was one thing to philander with women less than half his age. It was another that his kids knew it—*and* were college classmates of Tamara. Caught up in the moment, he pushed aside the awkwardness of the situation. With quiet time to think about it, he was panicked.

He sat on his balcony sipping on an Arnold Palmer and lamented his plight. This was far from the relationship he expected to have with his children. He called Lucy, who lived in Southwest Atlanta, to see if she could offer advice. He had spoken to her on this subject many times over the years.

"I don't know if you have a different solution now," he said, "but I just want this to get better."

"Well, Elliott, from what I was told yesterday, it got worse," Lucy said. "Daniel called."

He knew his son had told his mother that Elliott was with Tamara. Elliott felt weak.

"Is it true, Elliott?" Lucy asked. "You're dating one of their friends? No, don't answer. I already know. I have heard things from some of your so-called friends over the last year or so about you hanging out at nightclubs, like you're twenty-five or something. So this only makes sense. And it's disgusting."

"Lucy, I didn't call you to make you upset," he started.

"You can do whatever you want to do," she snapped. "Just keep my kids out of it."

"Oh, now they're *your* kids?" Elliott said. "All I have ever done since this marriage fell apart was protect them. And you know that."

"I didn't ask you to try to protect them," Lucy said. "I have said all along to tell them the truth about why we got divorced. They deserve that. It's been *you* that has insisted they don't know."

"That's not why I called you," he said. "I called to see if you had any idea how I could make some headway with *our* kids."

"Don't date their friends," Lucy said. "That's one way."

Understanding she would provide little help, Elliott said, "Okay, thanks. Take care," and hung up.

He had learned how to deal with anger over the years, which was hard to do coming out of prison when he should not have been there. He developed his own method, which required him sitting back with his eyes closed and praying. He thanked God for protecting him and sparing him and asked for patience.

After that call with Lucy, he put down his drink. He leaned back in the chair, clasped his hands together on his lap and closed his eyes.

"God, bring calm over me now," he prayed. "Protect me from myself, from my past, from my flaws. Deliver me to a place of peace. Quiet the noise in me. Settle my emotions…"

He remained in that posture for several minutes. It was only broken by his need to go to the bathroom. But he had unburdened himself. Praying always worked for him. He stopped praying for what he called "big things" after he was freed from prison. "God has done more than enough for me," he told Danette. "I used up my 'big things,' and that's all right. It would seem selfish to ask for big things after he protected me in that place and got me out."

He quickly learned that the "little things" are needed more often than the "big things," and so calling on God was a frequent thing. This prayer made him feel more at ease, more focused.

He was eager to get to Dr. Nottingham for some advice on how to proceed. He had an appointment in two days, Tuesday, so after he had some time to mull it all over, Elliott decided to go with his original plan: To have them over for dinner before they went back to college to let them know how important it was to be a family and for them to communicate better and more frequently.

Elliott knew he could handle that part of an evening with his children. But as soon as one of them asked, "Are you dating Tamara?" the potential for reconciliation would evaporate like rain under an incendiary sun.

He had to prepare an answer that was not a lie, but one that also did not portray him as an old man hanging out in clubs seeking young women. He was good with words and had a good mind— he read more than two hundred books while in prison. He called his boy, Henry, who deceived the mother of his young son for years before finally telling her the truth of his multiple affairs, which ended their relationship.

"You have experience with crisis management and deception— I'm sorry, I can't think of another word right now," Elliott said. "How do I bring my kids back into my life without getting into dating younger women? Is that even possible?"

"You're asking the wrong guy," Henry said. "I was the guy, re- member, who came clean, who aired all my laundry to get that burden off of me. It cost me my marriage, but that's what I needed to stop feeling like a hypocrite—and to do right by my wife."

"Well, I just thought that because you deceived her for so long you could help me with that," Elliott said. He knew it sounded crazy seconds after he said it.

"Let me back up," he said, trying to clean it up. "I need you to help me figure out the best way to get my relationship with my kids back on course."

"You don't want to hear this, but the best bet probably is to tell them what they want to know—the truth about why you got divorced," Henry said. "You said that's what your son continues to harp on. Maybe if you came clean, they would accept things and move on."

"That might be the answer," Elliott said, "or it might cause more problems. They might start asking for specifics and that opens up more wounds."

"Your kids are twenty; they aren't eight," Henry said. "At some point you have to trust that they will deal with stuff as adults. Maybe they'll say, 'Thanks, Dad,' hug you and move on. Think about me being up front with you and how you received that."

Henry gave Elliott something to consider. He had given up on worrying after his long prison stint and instead focused on the beauty of life, the beauty of freedom. But he worried about his kids and his relationship with them. The longer the rift went on, the wider the gap would grow.

Elliott called his daughter. She was upset with him, but she also held a soft spot for her daddy. She could be the key in a reconciliation. But she did not answer her phone, so he left a message:

"Danielle, sweetheart, it's your dad. Please call me as soon as you get this message. It's important."

A few minutes later, he received a text message from his son, Daniel. It read: "Do us a favor and leave us alone."

Elliott's heart sunk. But then he got angry. He called Daniel. "Let me tell you something, boy, I don't care how angry you think you are at me, that'd better be the last time you get out of line with me."

"I wasn't out of line," Daniel said. "I was just saying what we want."

"I didn't text you; I called your sister," Elliott said. "If you want to be that way, then be that way. But don't corrupt your sister. She can think for herself."

"You broke up our family," Daniel said. "She knows that much and she's not happy about it."

"So you're her spokesperson now?" Elliott said. "Son, there's no way you can go on with all this anger in your heart. It's not healthy and it's not right. I love our family more than you can know—"

"So why did you mess it up by cheating?" Daniel asked.

"There's so much I want to say right now, but it is all beside the real point," Elliott said. "Here's the real point: I love you. I raised you and we were close. To be as we are now does not make sense. You know my story. You know what I overcame. Life is short. Do you want to spend it mad at your father?"

"You're giving me answers, Dad, but they aren't the answers we need," Daniel said.

"I want to see you two before you go back to school," Elliott said. "We have to talk."

"We'll see," Daniel said.

"No, you won't see," Elliott said. "It's happening. And I will let you know when. The kid gloves are off. I've tried to ease my way around this with you. No more. I'm the father and I don't care how old you are, you do what I say."

"That sounds good in theory," Daniel responded. "But you can't make me do anything anymore. The day you walked out of our house was the day you ended that privilege."

"I didn't stop being your father, so it didn't end and it will never end," Elliott said. "You talk this trash, but you're certainly taking my money for room and board and my money that's in your pockets. So, I don't want to hear you talking like you're this grown, independent person because if I pulled the plug on your housing and money, what would you do then?"

Daniel didn't respond.

"See you and Danielle at my house this Saturday at eight o'clock," Elliott said. "Come hungry because I'm cooking."

Then he hung up the phone and smiled to himself.

CHAPTER NINE
Watching People, Being Watched

Elliott regained his energy over the course of a few days and was excited about going out to Del Frisco's Grill in Buckhead for drinks on Thursday. He'd learned through the many e-mail promotions he subscribed to that there would be an event there featuring one of the *Real Housewives of Atlanta*.

He found the show to be silly and mind-numbing, but he knew the event would attract a crowd. He counted that he had been dealing consistently with four women and sleeping with two (Tamara and a thirty-two-year-old named Rita) but decided he had room for more. He always sought more.

Elliott called one of his peers, fifty-eight-year-old Vincent, a mechanic originally from outside of Birmingham, to join him at the event. "Man, I told you I'm not messing with those young girls," he said. "All they looking for is someone to buy them dinner and drinks. I ain't got it like that."

"I'll pay for the drinks," Elliott said. "Just come out and do something different."

"You tryna turn me into you?" Vincent said. "Ain't but one you, that I know of. When you want to go to Ellery's or some place like that, you let me know. I'm all in."

Ellery's was a down-home place in Southwest Atlanta where folks had a good time and did not wear airs. They were real and fun and most of them dropped the sophistication at the door, if they had it at all. Elliott was a regular there years back, but when his interest turned to younger women, he needed to be somewhere else.

So, Elliott went to Del Frisco's alone. He executed his plan ideally: got there early enough to commandeer a seat at the head of the downstairs bar, which would give him a view of both sides of the room and everyone who entered the restaurant. Also, there was an area where most people gathered to talk near the bar, and he was right there, too.

He gave up heavy drinking decades before, so he took to the wine list and decided on an Oregon Pinot Noir called Alexana. By heavy drinking, he meant consuming so much that he was sloppy drunk and unable to remember much of the night. He'd have an occasional Scotch, but turned to wine on most occasions.

Elliott watched as the people came in, one-by-one, and he was in total bliss. He truly loved to people-watch. Although he had been released from prison twenty-nine years earlier, remnants of it remained in him, in one fashion or another, and he fought to counter them.

In this case, one of the ways to affirm his freedom was to sit back and watch people function as free people. For twelve years, he watched people move and do as they were told. "Those kinds of limitations stick with you," he told his therapist. "So I have to do things that take me away from that time and place."

His bar seat was the place to be that night. The crowd flowed like late-night traffic, and Elliott was in the middle of it all. He had his eyes on the hostess, a tall and sexy woman named Mary. They chatted briefly on a few occasions, and her sophistication and genuine nature attracted him. It did help, too, that she had a captivating body that worked well with her short-short natural haircut and infectious smile.

But Mary was working, so his attention spanned the room. Television cameras and photographers came in and captured the so-called celebrities that came through. The crowd had to shift to make room for that scene, which pushed Stacy literally up against Elliott.

"I'm sorry," she said as she bumped into him. "It got crowded in here so fast."

"It's okay," Elliott said. In a nanosecond he surveyed her body. That's all it took. He learned in prison that staring was not a good thing, so he taught himself to process whatever was in front of him in an instant, almost like speed reading.

Stacy had dark eyes and a smile that spoke to you. It said, "I'm here." Her breasts were plump and round in the deep-cut top she wore, and the large dangling earrings accentuated her roundish face and short hair with streaks of blond that indicated she was bold and daring.

"Your smile woke me up," Elliott told her. "I wasn't actually falling asleep. But it gave me energy."

"Oh, yeah?" Stacy said. "Well, what can I say? Energy is my middle name. My first name is Stacy."

"I'm Elliott," he said, extending his hand. "I bet you like margaritas, Stacy, and mojitos. And martinis. I see you on a beach, with sunglasses on, relaxing with something cold and refreshing in your hand."

"I like how you see things," she said.

"I'm ordering another glass of wine," he said. "What can I get you?"

Before she could answer, Elliott rose from his seat.

"You should have a seat," he said.

"Being a gentleman can get you places," she said.

"That's a good thing," he said.

He ordered their drinks and a flatbread. As the crowd loudly socialized around them, Elliott and Stacy shared in their own world.

"You remind me of someone," Stacy said.

"Please don't say your father or your uncle," Elliott said.

"Why not? They're good men," she responded.

"You think that about me and you put me in a box," he answered. "A box that limits where I can go with you."

"Well, I was going to say you remind me of a politician or CEO," she said. "You have a presence."

"Well, I appreciate that," he said. "I'm the CEO of me, that's for sure."

"I hear you," she said. "What brings you out here tonight? This doesn't look like your crowd."

"No, it's my crowd," he said. "Any crowd where people are out, enjoying each other and life is my kind of crowd."

"How old are you?" Stacy asked, and Elliott liked that. His position was: You want to know, ask.

"I'll be sixty-two in a few months," he said. "Was that what you were thinking?"

"Honestly, I didn't know, but I felt around fifty or so," Stacy said. "You've taken good care of yourself."

"If I don't, who will?" he said. "But thank you. I get my cardio in and try to eat right. I want to enjoy my life as a healthy man, not someone limited because I didn't do what was right for me."

Before Stacy could respond, her friend, Sophia, emerged from the crowd. She was the anti-Stacy—attractive but pompous, self-centered and demanding.

Stacy introduced them. Sophia said, "Hi," to Elliott and turned her back to him.

"Come here, Stace," she said.

Stacy turned around in her barstool. "What's up?"

"Why are you wasting your time talking to this grandfather?" Sophia asked.

Stacy said, "He's a nice man. Don't hate."

"Hate? Please," Sophia said. "Get him to buy me a drink."

"What? No," Stacy said. "What do you want? I'll buy it."

"Let him get it," Sophia insisted. "That's the least he can do."

"I'm not doing that," she said. "What do you want?"

Elliott heard Stacy and interjected. "I'll be glad to put it on my tab."

"Thank you…whatever your name is," Sophia said.

"Whatever my name is?" Elliott responded. "Excuse me, but that's pretty rude, Sophia."

"It's not rude; I don't know your name," she said. "I didn't hear Stacy when she said it. You can't blame me because it's loud in here."

"Well, you're right; it's loud in here," Elliott said. "Not sure how that has anything with you being rude."

"We were having a nice conversation," Stacy jumped in. "I'd like to get back to that."

"Well, are you going to get my drink so I can leave you back to your nice conversation?" she asked Elliott.

"If they had class by the bottle I would order one for you," Elliott said. "But since they don't—that's something that you either have or you don't—no, I'm not getting you a drink."

"See what I mean," Sophia said, turning to Stacy. "Loser."

"No, I can't let you say that, Sophia," Stacy said. "He's been a perfect gentleman—and he offered you a drink. Instead of being grateful, you insulted the man. I know other men who would have had some nasty words for you."

"I would have respected that more than him trying to be cool about it," Sophia countered. "Trying to impress you. He's about seventy years old. Damn shame you're even out. Don't you need to be in bed?"

"What did you say?" Elliott said, acting as if he did not hear Sophia. "You need me to go to bed with you? I'd rather not. Thanks for asking, though."

"Wait, wait," Stacy said. "Let's stop this now. This is a fun time. What's going on?"

"You should respect your elders," Elliott said to Sophia. "I'm sure you know better."

"How many drinks did you have over there?" Stacy asked.

"As many as that guy was buying," she answered.

"Then you've had enough," Stacy said. "I'm getting you some water."

"Thanks, anyway," Sophia said. "I know who will buy me a drink." And she walked away from them.

"I'm sorry, Elliott," Stacy said. "She's really a nice person. But when she drinks…"

"Yeah, well, I hope she's not driving," he said.

"She's riding with me," Stacy said. "Hopefully, she'll calm down. I can't believe how rude she was."

"You can only be responsible for you," Elliott said. "Anyway, before she came over, you were talking about how glad you are that we met."

"Funny that I don't remember that conversation," Stacy said, smiling. "I think you're remembering what you want to remember. Or is it an early sign of dementia?"

Elliott laughed. "That makes us getting together as soon as possible more important," he said. "With dementia setting in, I might not remember you if we wait too long," he cracked.

She laughed. Then she said, "I'm unforgettable." And she said it in a way that could be perceived as flirting. Elliott was not sure how to take it; he liked to err on the side of caution. But he processed quickly that she stood up for him with Sophia and, beyond that, was sitting there engaging him.

"Confidence is attractive," Elliott said.

She finished a second margarita. "So what's your deal? Really," she said. "You told me you're sixty-one. I'm thirty-two. What could you possibly want with someone my age? Better yet, what would I want with someone *your* age? I'm not being rude. I'm just being real."

"I've dated women younger than you," Elliott said. "That's not to impress or turn you off; it's a fact. I like the energy of younger women. And I'm not talking physical energy because, believe it or not, there is very little difference in that department if the older woman has taken care of herself. I'm talking about the spirit, the liveliness, the zest for life and feeling that the world is in front of you.

"Having that mindset makes you project a different energy, a different vibe. My friends my age, well…we're on the other side. We've lived longer than the years we have left. And there's a resignation that comes with that. People get more conservative, more responsible. I promise you I'm not saying there's something wrong with that. I'm saying dealing with that regularly does not inspire me."

Stacy got the attention of the bartender and ordered another round of drinks. "These are on me," she said. "That's the least that I can do after that answer. Wow. I hear you. My uncle Charles, he likes to chase young women. When I was little I was too afraid to ask him why. When I did, he said, 'I just like young girls.' That was it. He had no real reason. And then you tell me all that…"

"Everyone is different, you know?" Elliott said. "You also asked me why you would have an interest in me."

"You have an answer for that, too?" Stacy asked.

"No. You do," he answered. "But if the only reason you wouldn't is the age difference, then…well."

"Well, what?" she said.

"Then you don't really have a reason," Elliott said.

"That *is* a reason," Stacy countered.

"Is it?" he said. "I'm not trying to convince you of anything. But we got along great here. There was definitely some chemistry. If I were your age, you'd be interested. If I were white, you might be interested."

"I don't do white boys," she shot back.

"Why? Because of what your friends and others would think?" Elliott said. "That's my point here. You could have been anywhere else in this place tonight. There are young men your age all over. But you're here and you have had a good time and there is a spark—don't deny it—and yet you don't see a need for us to get closer?"

"You might be right about all that," Stacy said. "But whether it's next week or next year or in five years, the age would matter. The gap is too big. I can't get into you—and I know we just met, but women think ahead; that's how we are—when there is such a gap in who we are."

"As I said, I don't want to seem like I'm trying to change your mind," he said. "But you don't really know if there's a gap in who we are, what we like, how we like to live. It could be that we're kindred spirits. But we'll never know, I guess."

"We can be friends," Stacy said. "Let's exchange numbers. We can have a drink sometime. I'm glad we met. I don't reject good people in my life. But…"

Elliott considered exchanging numbers a way of Stacy subtly

keeping open the chance of something. That was a case of him massaging his ego. But he was intent on not pushing. Young women had rejected him in the past. That tweaked his ego, but sparked his determination more.

They punched in each other's numbers in their cell phones and engaged in small talk before Elliott excused himself to go to the bathroom. On the way and back, he marveled at the legion of attractive young women who pranced about seemingly without a care in the world. The sights energized him.

"I'm not sure how much longer I'm going to stay," Elliott said to Stacy when he returned to the bar. "I can only stand rejection from you for so long."

"You can't handle the truth," Stacy said.

"I can handle far more than you know," he responded.

They smiled at each other as Elliott felt someone behind him. When he turned, there was Tamara, looking as elegant as he'd ever seen her.

"So this is why you didn't want to have dinner with me?" she said. There was no attitude in her voice.

Elliott did not answer her. Instead, he hugged her. "Hi, Tam," he said. "I'm glad to see you."

Stacy looked on, curious. Tamara looked younger than her and yet it was clear Elliott had something with her that was more than friendship.

He introduced the ladies and was upfront with Stacy about his connection with Tamara. He was accomplishing two things: Easing Tamara's mind and luring in Stacy. Men found it puzzling that many women found a man more attractive by the female company he kept.

More than twice Elliott met women primarily on the strength

of them having seen him with attractive women. He talked to other men about that phenomenon, and they came to the conclusion that women thought: "If she's with him, and she's pretty, he *must* be about something." And so they were interested in him, too. Elliott figured with Tamara looking so wonderful, it would have to have an impact on Stacy.

"I've had a good time, Stacy; this is my friend, Tamara," he said.

The ladies exchanged greetings. "So, who are you with?" Elliott asked.

"I'm with you now," Tamara answered.

Elliott played it as nonchalantly as possible, while Stacy, her straightforwardness increased by the margaritas, was not delicate.

"So you two date?" she asked.

Elliott smiled at Tamara, who said, "Yes, we do. He didn't tell you?"

"Actually, he did say he dates women younger than me," Stacy said. "I guess he was talking about you."

Elliott hugged Tamara again. In that moment, he had to make a decision, and he chose to make Tamara feel totally comfortable. If it helped attract Stacy, fine. But he could not risk putting off Tamara for the unknown that was Stacy.

"You want to order a drink?" Stacy said to Tamara.

"Well, it looks like you all have had a few. I guess I have to play catch-up," she answered.

"I'm going to let you sit here," Stacy said, rising from the barstool. "Here's the money for the drinks I bought. I had a good time, Elliott. Nice to meet you. And nice to meet you, too, Tamara."

She and Elliott shook hands and she went off to find her friend, Sophia.

"So you out picking up women again, I see," Tamara said, getting settled in the seat. "Can't leave you by yourself for a minute."

"You know me," Elliott said. "I'm a people person."

"A people person?" she asked. The bartender came over and she ordered a glass of wine for each of them. "A people person? Tell me, how many men have you met when you go out? I can answer that. None. So, no, you're not a people person. You love women."

Elliott was in no mood to lie or even cushion the truth. The wine opened him more than usual. "Anything wrong with that? I mean, I am a man, right?" he said. "I like feeling free to do what I want more than I like women."

"I can't even imagine, even though I have tried, what it was like to go through what you have," she said.

"People are out having a good time. You look incredible. We're sipping wine," Elliott said. "This is no time for sad talk. Let's have fun."

"I'm good at that," Tamara said.

"Me, too," Elliott added.

CHAPTER NINE
A Friend In Kneed

On their way out of Del Frisco's Grill, a woman who was coming into the restaurant recognized Elliott.

"Hi. You remember me?" she said.

Tamara was tipsy and was not in the mood for another woman infringing on her space.

"Hi, I'm Tam," she jumped in.

"Yes, I remember you, but I don't remember your name," he said.

"I'm Rochelle," the woman said. "I'm a friend of Henry's. We met at that party at Ventanna's last year."

"Oh, yeah," he said. "Tamara, you haven't met Henry yet. He's my closest friend here in Atlanta."

"How is he?" Rochelle asked.

"You haven't talked to him in a while?" Elliott responded.

"I haven't, but I'd like to catch up with him. A really nice guy," she said.

"I will tell him I saw you and to reach out," Elliott said.

"Please do," she said. "We had some unfinished business."

"Wow, she's trying to be down with your boy," Tamara said.

"Yeah, well, she might as well cool it off," Elliott said.

"Why? He's married or something?" Tamara asked.

"Or something," Elliott said.

The valet pulled up Tamara's car with Elliott's behind hers. He tipped the valets and they hugged and he kissed her on her neck and shoulder. "See, you know I have to go to work in the morning," she said. "Don't get me started."

"This weekend," Elliott said. "Maybe we can start *and* finish. Your place. Dinner. Saturday."

"I'll call you," Tamara said.

Elliott jumped in his car and cruised down Peachtree Road. He did not play music or the radio. He wanted to spend the drive home in quiet. But then his cell phone rang.

"What do you mean, 'Or something'?" Tamara said on the other end.

"Huh?"

"You said that when I asked about your friend, Henry," she reminded him.

"Yeah, I did," Elliott said. "I should have just let it go."

"Why? What is he, a womanizer?" she asked.

"Not exactly," he responded.

"So what's the deal then? Why are you being so cryptic?"

"Look at you, using big words on me," Elliott said.

"Don't try to avoid the question," Tamara said.

"I'm pulling into my garage, so I'm going to lose you. I'll call you when I get upstairs," he said.

"Whatever, old man," she said.

Elliott had about ten minutes to decide if he was going to sully his boy's reputation or lie. He elected to not call Tamara. Maybe she would get home and forget about it.

But just as he was beginning to feel he would not hear from her, she called him.

"Oh, hey," he said. "I dozed off."

"I was just letting you know I made it home like you asked me to," she said.

"Glad you did," Elliott said. "Sleep well. Call you tomorrow about Saturday night."

Tamara said good night and Elliott did not have to get into the question about Henry. But as he sat with his feet up in his living room, he thought about his friend and their unique relationship.

About six months earlier, Elliott learned that Henry was gay.

They had chased women together, gone on double-dates, plotted on how to get into women's panties, shared stories of conquests... and one day, Henry—as calmly as one might give directions— told Elliott that he was attracted to men.

It was a Sunday in late spring, and they were sitting outside at Strip at Atlantic Station, a shopping and eating area in Midtown Atlanta that became a popular hangout spot. They liked to have lunch out on the patio because they could watch women pass by in the courtyard. It was Henry's idea.

"So what's up with you?" Elliott said to Henry. "Haven't seen you about a month."

"You know how it is," he said. "Work. I'm just forty-two; can't think about retiring yet."

He was a real estate agent who survived the housing downturn and was flourishing in its upswing. But he was burdened.

"Man, I haven't felt right about something, and I need to get right about it," Henry started.

"Yeah? What's up?" Elliott asked.

"I haven't told many people this," Henry said. "And I'm only telling you because we're close. We're close, right?"

"You're my boy," Elliott answered him, but he became nervous. It had to be bad news; he wouldn't hesitate or preface anything if it were good news. He immediately thought of health concerns. Henry was a workout fiend, but Elliott knew muscles could hide internal issues.

"You okay, Henry?" he added. "You're making me nervous. I can't lie."

"I'm good," he said. "I need to tell you something about me."

Elliott did not respond. Henry fidgeted, looked away and finally said it. "I'm gay."

Elliott flinched. He leaned back. The surprise on his face was plastered there, like a tattoo. A man who always had a comeback had nothing.

Henry did not know what to say. He was so relieved to get it out. The weight of carrying his revelation was enormous. He worked hard to conceal his true sexuality. He dated women to prevent any inkling of his interest in men. He boasted of his conquests to Elliott and initiated nights out at strip clubs and bars to give the appearance of pursuing women.

He talked about sports and smoked cigars. He did everything he thought would be considered "manly" to hide his real desires. He did this for decades. Finally, he could not handle the lying, the deceit, the fraud. The reward of telling Elliott would be great—if Elliott accepted Henry for the man he truly was instead of the man he pretended to be. The risk was even greater—he could lose a friendship that had become invaluable. But he had to unburden himself.

"What are you talking about?" Elliott finally asked. "You're gay? How?"

"How?" Henry responded. "I don't think 'how' is the right question."

"What are you talking about? How can you be gay when all I've ever seen you with or heard you talk about is women?" Elliott said.

"Elliott, I'm the same person," he said. "I just don't have an interest in women."

He could tell Henry was serious. And in that moment, Elliott took it as a personal affront. The magnitude of what Henry revealed overtook the shock of it. And he got angry.

"So you're a faggot?" he said. "I'll be damned. You think telling me that was going to accomplish what? I was going to say, 'Oh, really?' It's okay because you're my boy? Hell, no. I don't play that. I don't roll like that."

"So, because of my sexuality, you're not my friend anymore?" Henry said. "Is that what you're saying?"

"Wake up," Elliott said so loudly that people at other tables turned their way. "You think I would run around town with a fag? Hell, no. Not me."

"Why not? That's what you've been doing for years and years, Elliott," he said. "You just didn't know it."

"Well, knowing it makes all the difference in the world," Elliott said. "And what about this? I really want to hear your answer to this: How could you have a child as a gay man? How could you deceive these women you dated over the years? That's some bitch-ass shit if you ask me."

"I'm not gonna say anything about you calling me a 'faggot' because you're upset, but it's disrespectful," Henry said.

"Like I give a fuck," Elliot countered.

"Anyway," Henry went on, "those are legitimate questions. And the truth is that I was trying to fool myself to be what everyone wanted me to be; what I even thought I should be. So, yes, I dated women and I have a son, a son that you love and who loves you. What, you're not going to be his godfather anymore?"

"This isn't about Jarrod," Elliott said. "But I wonder what you're going to tell him. How do you think he's going to react to knowing his father likes dick?"

"Don't mistake me for not being able to kick your ass," Henry said.

"You mean scratch my eyes out, don't you, or beat me with your pink purse," Elliott said.

Now, both men were furious and glaring at each other with death stares. The server arrived to take their orders and Elliott got up.

"Get him some quiche—and sprinkle some fairy dust on it," he said, and stormed out of the restaurant.

Elliott did not want to tell Tamara that story. He didn't want to tell her because he was ashamed of his initial reaction to Henry's brave revelation. For the next several months, he separated himself from his closest friend. He took Henry's number out of his cell phone, as if that would help him forget about how close they were.

Henry was his Sunday sports bar partner during football season. Elliott was such the Washington Redskins fan that he converted Henry, who liked the local Falcons. Henry was the first person Elliott shared news with, good or bad. When he told Henry of his wrongful incarceration, his friend empathized with him and made him feel free enough to share his story in detail.

When Henry revealed he was gay, the biases in Elliott emerged as if shot out of a paintball gun: They splattered everywhere. His time in prison gave him a perspective on homosexuality that influenced his anger and pain and disappointment.

In prison, he witnessed men having sex—some of their own will, some forced. Either way disgusted Elliott. He committed himself to killing the man who would attempt to violate him in that way. And he looked at the man who would have sex with another man as less than human.

Eight months after that lunch with Henry, he received a phone call from LaWanda, the mother of Henry's son. Elliott was just headed to his car after a round at Wolf Creek Golf Club near the Atlanta airport. He didn't recognize the number, so he thought it was a woman he had met at Bar One a few nights before.

Reflectively, without even thinking, he hurried to Grady Memorial Hospital: Henry's fourteen-year-old son, Jarrod, had been hit by a car. The driver was an eighty-two-year-old man who lost consciousness behind the wheel. The car veered off the street, jumped the curb on Glenwood Avenue and Second Avenue and slammed into Jarrod.

Through LaWanda's hysteria, Elliott was able to make out that the trauma was severe. He was airlifted to the hospital.

He had taken a measure of relief that he never entered the doors of Grady Hospital, the city's premier trauma facility. If you were sent to Grady, you were in bad shape.

The ride to Grady was spent praying for Jarrod and thinking about how he was he going to deal with seeing Henry for the first time in eight months. He remained incensed and disappointed in his former friend, and was even embarrassed that they had been friends. He also stretched his brain to figure out how he could not have detected that Henry was gay. He angered himself more when he recounted the intimate details of his life that he shared with Henry, the golf trips they took together, the women he introduced to him.

Replaying all that made him mad all over again. Elliott entered the hospital's emergency room with his pent-up emotions bubbling over. He was directed to the waiting area, where he found Henry sitting with his head buried in his hands.

He walked over to him, intent on getting information about his son and walking away. He had nothing to say to him. But when Henry raised his head, he revealed eyes that were stop-sign red and the overall look of a broken man. Tears streamed down his face. His lips quivered.

And immediately, all the animosity and anger and disappointment Elliott felt for Henry disappeared. In that moment, he realized his sexuality was of no significance.

He was a man who was crestfallen about his son, just like any other man would be, just as Elliott would be.

Elliott realized right away that he had been an insensitive homophobic jerk and, worst, disloyal friend. He had judged Henry when his friend never judged him about his suspect behavior with young women or his difficult past.

He sat down next to Henry and put his arm around his shoulder. Henry's body involuntarily shook, from pain and from the comfort of his friend. "He died, my son is gone," Henry said in a low voice.

"Oh, God. I'm sorry," Elliott said. He was talking about his behavior as much as Henry's loss.

Then he shocked himself when he grabbed Henry's hand and said a prayer.

"God, please let Jarrod's soul rest in peace. You brought him into Your arms and we know there is no better place for any of us. Please God, bless my friend Henry and his family. Give us all the strength, understanding and will to move forward carrying so much grief and sorrow. In Your name we pray, Amen."

Then, for the next five minutes, Elliott sat there with his arm around his friend and cried.

CHAPTER TEN
Small World

On his Friday walk, Elliott realized he had asked Tamara to cook dinner for him Saturday night but also had asked his kids to visit him for dinner. Not good.

"I have to cancel dinner tomorrow," he said to Tamara while on his daily walk. "I forgot I had made plans. I'm sorry. Can we do it tonight or Sunday?"

"I put up with you turning me down because you'd made plans to go out to some club or party," Tamara said. "But you asked me to cook for you on Saturday, and I went grocery shopping and cleared my schedule for you. And now you're cancelling on me, after you picked the day? Are you serious?"

"I know, I know," he said. "I wish I didn't have to cancel. I have some people coming over. It's important."

"People?" Tamara said. "Who?"

"I don't want to get into explaining myself too much," Elliott said. "You should trust that if I say it's important that it is really important."

"I don't deserve to know why you're cancelling on me?" she responded. Elliott detected tension in her voice.

"First of all, calm down," he said. "Second, I told you why I have to cancel. Please don't make this a big deal. I will make it up to you. Just trust me. Please."

"I don't get it," she said. "Last Saturday, when I wanted to come over, you told me that you had to go to Compound for a party. So you can tell me last week what your plans are but you can't tell me now? What are you hiding?"

"I don't have to hide anything and I don't have to explain anything," Elliott said. "I'm sorry. I guess I shouldn't have told you my plans last week. I don't want to get into the habit of having to explain what I'm doing."

"Why? What's wrong with that?" she said.

"Tamara, can we get together tonight?" he asked. "Come over for dinner. I'll cook a great meal for you. I don't want you to be upset. There's no reason to be upset. I promise you, there isn't."

"I'm busy tonight," she said. "I have a date."

"I understand," Elliott said. "Let's do Sunday then."

"I'm busy Sunday," she said. "You know how many men would change their plans for me?"

"I don't know, but I can imagine most," he responded. "Just not me, not in this case. I talked to you last week about not being a typical woman."

"Don't try to teach me some lesson about being a woman," Tamara shouted. "Because you're older than me doesn't mean you know everything."

Elliott remained calm. "Please let me know when you're available and I will make myself available."

"I'm available tomorrow," she said.

"Give me any other day and I'm in," Elliott assured. "I cannot do tomorrow."

"Well, I've got to go, Elliott," she said. "Have a nice weekend."

And she hung up, before Elliott could respond. He was not happy about that, but he went on with his walk and thought of what he would prepare for his children the next night.

He walked along Peachtree Street, past the Hard Rock Café, Hooters and the Ritz-Carlton and cut west and then north, back toward his place. He was floating more than he was walking. Getting Danielle and Daniel to come to his home for dinner was monumental in his step toward reconciliation. He was not sure how he would quell his son's animosity, but the twins were close. So he figured if he could get Danielle to let go and move forward, her position would move her brother off his stance.

Getting Danielle to embrace him again would be easier, but not easy. She and her mom were close and grew to be like sisters as she got older. Seeing her mother so distraught when Elliott moved out scared Danielle. Lucy was strong and confident. Watching her husband leave the house, she looked weak and insecure.

And Danielle cursed her father for making her mother cry, for breaking up the family and for forcing her to lose some respect for him. The thought of her father being unfaithful to her mother sickened her when she was younger. As she got older, she came to realize that it happens, and so she was less sick than she was disappointed.

Her disappointment was heightened by the knowledge that her mother accepted Elliott despite his twelve years in prison. Although he was wrongfully convicted, he was locked up, meaning he adopted some prison ways that the family helped him break.

For instance, in prison inmates had a short window to eat and they ate at the same time every day. Elliott had become conditioned to have breakfast at 6 a.m., lunch at 11 a.m. and dinner at 5 p.m. And even though he could eat whenever he liked as a free man, he had to eat at those designated times because his body had become regimented. It took him more than seven years to comfortably dine at different times of the day.

Not only that, but because they were forced to finish their meals in fifteen minutes, inmates packed their mouths with food, their cheeks filling up like squirrels storing nuts. Twenty years after his exoneration, Elliott finally broke that habit—and it took much chiding from Lucy and their kids to make him aware he was doing it.

In other words, his family helped him adjust to the free world, and Danielle was particularly proud of that. She was her father's daughter, even looked like him more than her twin brother, Daniel. She considered pre-law with the idea of going to law school and eventually working with the Innocence Project, the firm headquartered in New York that presented DNA evidence that freed her father, but later switched to economics. Still, she was connected to her dad. So, the divide between them really pained her.

Elliott knew that because he was equally pained. That being the case, he figured Danielle needed a reason to forgive him and she would again embrace him.

He had not cooked dinner for his kids in years. Since he last did, he created a cooking experience that he believed they would enjoy. His idea was to paint himself as a regular guy, someone who is the same person they grew up with and adored.

He was confident listening to him and spending time around him would garner him some points in their good graces. But there was the problem of Tamara. How was he going to explain being out with their twenty-five-year-old friend?

He thought about that the rest of the day—all the way to Happy Hour at the Lobby Bar at the 12 Hotel in Atlantic Station—and he still came up with no answers. Nikki, the young lady he met at Compound, was to meet him there for drinks. It was a summer Friday night in Atlanta, and Elliott could not bear to stay home.

"You look nice," he said when she arrived. She wore jeans with heels and a top that was sexy but not too revealing. "You want to sit at the bar?"

"Yes, I like sitting at the bar sometimes," Nikki said.

They ordered drinks: Nikki had a peach martini and Elliott a glass of Malbec.

"So why aren't you on a date tonight?" he asked her.

"I am," she said.

"I like that," Elliott said. "You like this place?"

"I do," she said. "I haven't been here in years, back when Friday nights used to be packed. Live music with Quinn and his band. People everywhere. It was a good time."

"Yeah, it's nice like this, too," Elliott said. "Not so many people. And I don't have to scream into your ear for you to hear me."

"So why did you say you wanted to meet for a drink or two and then go home?" Nikki asked. "Somebody there waiting on you?"

"Nah," Elliott answered. "I'm having my son and daughter over for dinner tomorrow and I have some preparing to do. Haven't cooked for them in a long time, so I want it to be nice."

"That's nice," she said. "They're lucky to have their dad around. I lost mine when I was in high school. Still miss him."

"I bet," Elliott said. "I haven't hung out with my kids in a while. They're in college in Michigan."

"You haven't? Why?" Nikki wanted to know.

"Basically, their mom and I got a divorce and they never forgave me for it," he said. "That's what it comes down to. They feel like I broke up the family."

"That's tough; sorry to hear that," Nikki said. "I hope you all figure it out."

"I'm trying to figure you out right now," Elliott said.

"How so?"

"Well, two things on two different subjects," he said. "One, I'm probably twenty years older than you. Why would you be out with me? The other one is why haven't you gone to Ghana to see your mother?"

"Wow, you remember I said that to you?" Nikki asked. "Do you know I have friends I've been knowing for a long time, good friends, who never asked that—or anything about my mother. Wow. Anyway, I haven't gone to Africa because she hasn't asked me to come.

"And I will admit that bothers me."

"Why don't you tell her you want to visit her?" Elliott suggested. "My situation is not good with my kids, but I know one thing: I'm going to tell them what I want. If I don't, I will never know where I stand."

The drinks came.

"That makes sense," Nikki said. "I don't know; I guess I just need an invitation from her to feel like she wants to see me."

"You're scared of what her answer might be," Elliott said. "Not if she says yes, but if she says no."

Nikki looked at Elliott. "You're psycho-analyzing me?"

He smiled. "Just call me Dr. E."

"Okay, Dr. E, to the second part of your question," Nikki said, "I'm here with you because I really enjoyed my conversation with you Saturday night. It was interesting and fun, and, if you didn't know, getting that these days is not that easy."

"What about the age gap?" Elliott asked.

"What age gap?" she answered. "You don't know how old I am. I don't know how old you are. If we never tell each other our age, then there's no gap to overcome."

Elliott laughed. "That's a first," he said. "I have dated younger women in the last couple of years. It's been fun. It's been interesting. It's been needed."

"Needed? Why?" she asked.

"I'm regressing," he said, laughing. "What was that movie when the guy started off old and got younger?"

"*The Curious Case of Benjamin Button*," Nikki answered.

"That's it. That's me," Elliott said. "I've had some things happen in my life that made me decide to live my life. Don't talk about living it or daydream about living it. Live it. So, younger people have more energy and an attitude that I like."

"Well, in my case, I've never dated an older man," Nikki said. "I don't have any real hang-ups about age. But I have girlfriends who have dated older men, white men, younger men. They talk all the time about it being about the person and not anything else. I guess hearing it enough has worn off on me."

"Why is it so difficult to get a good conversation from a man?" Elliott said.

"You're asking me?" Nikki said. "I was hoping you could tell me."

"I don't date men, so I can't say," he said. "You should be telling me."

"Well, my theory is that the men—especially in cities like Atlanta where there are so many women—don't have to really engage you. To engage someone takes time and effort. But the men I have met—I don't want to generalize and say *all* men—have been sort of like, 'If you're interested, let me know now so I can move on to someone else if you aren't.'

"I really feel that. They have become arrogant because so many women are so desperate that they will tell them they are interested even though they don't really know them. So when they come across a woman like me, who is not desperate and who insists on getting to know someone before sleeping with them, they'd just rather move on than actually engage me."

"Wow, if that's true, then that's sad," Elliott said. "I really enjoy getting to know women. That's the fun part. Hearing opinions, learning about people's lives, feeling someone's presence."

"See, I'm like that, too," Nikki said. "I'm a people person and I like to meet people. I'll talk to almost anyone in a social setting. You can learn a lot just through talking to people."

With that, she excused herself and went to the bathroom. Elliott pulled out his iPhone and sent Tamara a text message: "I hope you're having a good date."

He also ordered another round of drinks after checking his watch. It was only twenty minutes to nine. He figured after another forty-five minutes with Nikki, he would head to Publix to purchase items for the dinner he would prepare for his kids.

When she returned, she leaned into his ear. "You have an admirer," Nikki said.

"Plenty," Elliott said.

"I mean here, right now," she said. "In the bathroom, this woman comes in and says to me; 'Is your father married? I noticed he wasn't wearing a ring.' I was, like, 'Excuse me. Father? Who?' She said, 'That's not your father you're sitting with at the bar?' I said, 'No, not my father. We're friends.'

"So she goes, 'Well, can you introduce him to me? Or let him know I'd like to buy him a drink.' I told her I would, and so I am."

"Who was the woman?" Elliott asked.

"She's attractive. Might be too old for you, though," Nikki said. "She looks to be in her mid-to-late forties. That's her over there. But you probably consider that Bingo game material, huh?"

Elliott looked to his left and saw the woman in the distance. She was attractive and smiling. Classy. "You're right; she's too old," he said to Nikki.

"Are you serious? That's a mature woman, Elliott," Nikki said.

"She is," Elliott said. "But I'm here with you and interested in you. I'm surprised you would even tell me about it."

"Well, it only seemed the right thing to do," Nikki said. "You should at least go over and say hello to her. Her name is Darlene."

"Nikki, you're taking nice too far," Elliott said. "How do I look leaving you here to go meet another woman?"

"We don't have anything going," she said. "We're out having a drink."

"That may be true and that woman may be cute, but I can't do that," Elliott said. He was showing restraint he did not know he had. The more he glanced at the woman, the better she looked and the more curious he got.

But he did not move from his seat. He dismissed it with enough conviction for Nikki to let it go.

"I appreciate the way you handled that situation," Nikki said as they waited out front for their cars to come up from valet.

"I like you, Elliott—a lot," Nikki said. "But we should be friends. The age difference is real and you probably have a bunch of women—young women—you're dating. I'm intrigued. But I won't do that to myself."

"I respect that," Elliott said. He was disappointed. Nikki looked better the second time he saw her and her mind interested him. But he made a rule of never overpursuing.

"You're doing yourself a disservice, but okay," he said.

"A disservice?" Nikki said. "I don't want to do that. We can be friends."

"That works for me," Elliott said.

They hugged and Nikki jumped into her Jeep and drove off. Elliott headed to the Publix near Georgia Tech to grocery shop for what he considered one of the most important evenings of his life. He wanted to regain his good standing in the lives of his children, and he hoped having them over for dinner would be a significant step toward his family uniting.

In the store, which was filled with college students, Elliott took his time shopping, watching the coeds as much as he was scanning the shelves. He thought of Nikki for a moment and then Tamara and finally he pushed the cart up the aisles with thoughts of what to prepare for dinner.

He remembered his kids' favorite meals, and decided on them: Cornish hens with macaroni and cheese, steamed broccoli and warm bread. His son loved Elliott's homemade cheesecake with strawberry topping, so he picked up the necessary items to bake that, too.

The more he shopped, the more excited he got about seeing his kids in his home. *The way to a man's heart is through his stomach*, he thought. *I hope that works for a man's children, too.*

The shopping experience was uneventful until his cell phone chimed, indicating he had a text message. It was from Tamara, responding to his earlier text.

"I see you were at the 12 Hotel on a date. Just can't sit home, can you? SMH"

Elliott was miffed. *How could she know I met Nikki at the hotel? Was she there, too?* He had looked around and would have seen Tamara because there was one way in and one way out. And he was quite observant.

"How do you know where I was?" he texted in return.

He waited for a response as he checked out, but received none.

So, he carried on, but frequently checked his phone. After unpacking the bags—leaving out the materials to bake the cheesecake—Elliott sent text messages to Daniel and Danielle.

"Just came from shopping. Excited about spending time and cooking dinner tomorrow. See you at 8."

Danielle responded almost immediately: "See you then."

But there was no response from Daniel. It was approaching 11 p.m., but Elliott sent a text to his ex-wife, Lucy, anyway. Instead of responding, she called him.

"What's going on?" she said when he answered the phone.

"I'm—again—trying to get right with the kids," he said. "They're coming over for dinner tomorrow, and I wondered if you had some thoughts on how I can get us back together."

"I have told you from the beginning," Lucy said. "Tell them the truth. That's what they want to hear. Tell them the truth and let them deal with it."

"I can't do that and you know why," he said. "There's a limit to what they should be informed about our marriage. You agreed with me and promised to not say anything. That's what I need from you; to keep your promise."

"I have kept the promise, Elliott," she said. "As much as I don't want to, I have. On one hand, I agree with you about it really not being their business and that them knowing specifics could be something they don't want to hear. But I also think it's the best way for you to restore your relationship."

"I'm worried about Daniel," he said. "With Danielle, she's following her brother's lead. She wants us to be right again; she does. But she does not want to be disloyal to Daniel, which I respect."

"Maybe you should focus on Danielle then," Lucy said. "I know you think Daniel has a hold over her. But, really, she has the influence over him that even she doesn't understand. If you won't tell them the truth, then getting Danielle to move on might be the easier route to go. Daniel is stubborn, much like his mother, I admit."

Then she said something that shocked Elliott. "What if I came over for dinner, too?"

"Excuse me?" he answered.

"Just think about it: If the kids see that we are okay, then that has to make them feel like they should be okay with things, too," she explained.

"I don't know, Lucy," Elliott said. "It might make them more upset that we're not together as a family anymore. And that would make things worse."

That was the fastest logical answer he could create without notice. The additional reason was that he was not sure how he would handle being around Lucy again after so long apart. He wanted them to work out the marriage, to go to counseling and figure out a resolution that could keep the family together. She wanted no part of it. Above all that, he still loved her.

"It was just an idea," she said.

Elliott moved on to Daniel to minimize the awkwardness. "Have you talked to him? How do I make inroads with him?"

"Talk about you, your life, what you've overcome," she said. "He needs to know the man you are and not the man he thinks you are. Once that happens, he'll lighten up. He's definitely stubborn, but he's not mean."

"I don't like talking about that too much, especially to the kids."

"You asked me and I told you my opinion," she said. "Up to you how you actually go about it."

He thanked his ex-wife and ended the call. He then got dressed in some loungewear, turned the radio to WCLK, the Clark

Atlanta University jazz station, and turned up the volume. Then he went into the kitchen to make the cheesecake.

Elliott became a master of prison cell cooking, fashioning tasty offerings of Oodles of Noodles and other meals that required little fanfare because prison was no place for a wide array of food or seasonings. But when he was released, Elliott pursued cooking and became stellar in the kitchen.

When he cooked, he made it an experience and fun, for himself if no one else. His kids loved his theatrics, and he planned to use them when they got to his house. But first came the cheesecake; he wanted it prepared the night before so it would be completely settled and cool for the next day.

So, with nice jazz playing, Elliott took to the kitchen. He pulled the covering off a Keebler graham cracker crust. He unloaded eleven ounces of cream cheese into a mixing bowl and covered that with a half-cup of heavy whipping cream and three-quarters cup of sugar in the raw. He cracked an egg and added it. Finally, he dropped in a splash of vanilla extract.

He turned on the mixing bowl and let the contents come together over less than ten minutes, until it formed into a smooth, fluid mix that he poured neatly into the graham cracker crust. He admired its pristine look while enjoying the remnants that clung to the side of the bowl with his fingers.

That made Elliot smile. He used to let his kids finish off the bowl of cheesecake with their fingers when they were small children. He hoped cooking for the kids while at his house would make them feel nostalgic, too.

As he waited over twenty minutes for the cheesecake to bake, he received a text message response from Tamara. "Facebook" was her reply.

Elliott was confused. He had asked how she knew he was at the

12 Hotel. *What does she mean, Facebook?* he asked himself. Then he recalled that he had set up an account on the popular social media site, but hardly visited it. Tamara was one of his "friends" on Facebook.

Before responding, he fired up his laptop. It took a minute to see that Nikki had "checked in" at the 12 Hotel with the note, "Drinks with Elliott Thomas."

He was confused. He was not "friends" with Nikki; they hadn't even discussed Facebook. But when he visited her page, he noticed that she was "friends" with Tamara. His mouth flew open.

He had heard younger men who really engaged in the Atlanta social scene talking about how the city "could close in on you." This was the first case where someone he dated knew someone else he dated—or *tried* to date.

Elliott did not attempt to run from the situation. "How do you know Nikki?" he texted back. "And why are you texting me? I thought you were on a date."

He put his feet up on the coffee table and waited for a response. It did not come, and he drifted off to sleep and dreamed of the days when he was still married and his family was intact. It felt good to see the four of them smiling and enjoying each other, even if it was in his dream.

The ring of the oven timer interrupted the joyous moment. The cheesecake was ready. Elliott placed it on the granite counter-top, where it would reside for a half-hour, at which time he set it in the refrigerator to chill overnight. When he first learned how to make the cheesecake, he was less patient and would place it in the freezer for an hour or so to indulge in right away.

His patience improved through occasional yoga classes and plain effort and discipline. He had been patient in allowing his kids to drift away from him—too patient, in fact. Elliott thought allowing them to vent and to separate themselves from him would give them the space they needed to see things clearly over time. Instead of them gravitating back to their father, they—especially Daniel— grew to hold strong animosity toward him.

Elliott went to sleep with that on his mind and awoke with it there the next morning, too. And that made him nervous. He was nervous about spending quality time with his kids for the first time in a few years. The occasion seemed like a make-or-break, the more he thought about it. He played the "What if?" game with himself: *What if they are coming here to tell me they hate me? What if they say they will never forgive me? What if I lose my patience and tell them off?*

After a breakfast of oatmeal mixed with blueberries and straw- berries and a cup of coffee, Elliott went on his walk. It usually served as the antidote to a clogged head. This walk worked, too. He took a different route, up to Peachtree Street, where he turned left toward Midtown instead of toward downtown. When he approached Gladys Knight's & Ron Winan's Chicken & Waffles, he slowed down; there was the usual crowd of people waiting out- side to be seated.

To his surprise among the people milling about was Tamara, who gave him a pleasant look at first, but quickly turned it to the evil eye. As soon as he saw her he remembered that she had spoken of that being her Saturday morning breakfast spot. Still, he was amazed that he had run into her for a second time in three days.

Elliott could not tell if she was with the guy standing nearby or the woman to her left. So, he smiled at her and said, "Good morn- ing," as he kept walking. Tamara stepped out of the crowd, toward Elliott.

"How was your date last night?" she said.

"It wasn't quite a date, but it was good," he answered, looking over her shoulder to see if the young man was watching. "How do you know Nikki?"

"Don't worry about it."

"Why would I worry about it? Just asking."

"So that's your girlfriend?" Tamara asked.

"Don't have a girlfriend," Elliott answered. "Don't do girlfriends."

"Really? So what am I? A piece of ass?" she said.

"Is that how I made you feel?" he responded. "Come here for a second."

He moved farther away from the crowd. "Tamara, you don't have to get crazy with me. You know how I regard you."

"What I know is that you were out on a date with a friend of mine last night and tonight you have another date," she answered. "What am I supposed to think about how you regard me?"

Elliott's impatience rose up, but he quieted himself by smiling and taking a deep breath.

"What are you grinning about?" she asked.

"I'm glad to see you," he said. "I'd love to connect with you tomorrow. I have a spot I want to take you to."

"I'm busy tomorrow, but free tonight," she said.

He slowly nodded his head and looked away from her, up Peachtree Street toward prodigious buildings. When he looked back at Tamara, her face held an exasperated expression.

"Well, I understand," he said. "Let me know when you are available and I would love to see you."

He leaned in for a hug, but she took a step back. Elliott smiled again, turned and walked away. He did not bother to look back.

CHAPTER ELEVEN
Table Manners

Elliott spent the afternoon writing letters to inmates who had been proven innocent of the crimes they were convicted of and awaiting release from prison. He also reviewed a few cases the Innocence Project was considering. He was indebted to the Innocence Project for its work in gaining his freedom. And so, he was quick to speak at an event or to legislators or anyone who could be inspired by his story.

A nap from 4:30 p.m. until after 6 p.m. refreshed Elliott. It was too hot to sit outside, but he did endure the heat and humidity for a moment. He sat down and prayed. He knew God received prayers from wherever. But he often went to the balcony to pray when he was especially in need. He said being up there "brings me closer to God. He can hear me better."

His prayers seldom were for him. This one was. "Dear Lord, you have spared me of so much and brought me back from a living hell. What I need most now is the love and reconnection to my children. They are an extension of me, and yet we are disconnected. Please allow this evening to be the start of our being a close-knit, loving family again."

Those words settled Elliott, as prayer can do. He went back inside his place and showered and got dressed for the evening. He placed a photo he kept on a dresser in his room in the living room.

It was a studio shot of Elliott and his kids when they were fifteen. The smiles were broad and genuine. A happy time. He hoped seeing it would help advance the evening on his behalf.

Just before 8, Elliott pulled out the items he would be cooking. He cleaned the Cornish hens and chopped up the cheese into small blocks. He pulled out a chilled bottle of Zolo Sauvignon Blanc and opened and decanted a Meiomi Pinot Noir. He lit a candle on the coffee table in the living room and one in the kitchen, near the stove. He was ready.

Then 8 p.m. came…and 8:15 and 8:30…and no sign of his children. His emotions went from concerned to disappointed to angry. And just as he was about to become furious, the doorbell rang. He closed his eyes and took a deep breath.

Elliott made his way to the door and looked through the peephole. He could see Danielle smiling and Daniel expressionless. He opened it and smiled.

"You had me worried," he said. Danielle walked into his waiting arms. He hugged his little girl and closed his eyes. Her embrace felt so warm and was so comforting.

"Come on in," he said, and Danielle cleared the threshold. Elliott hugged his son, but Daniel did not hug him back.

"Good to see you, son," he said into his ear.

"Yeah, okay," Daniel said. Elliott let him go and Daniel walked over to his sister. Elliott took his key and locked the deadbolt, in case things got out of hand and they tried to abruptly leave. He was determined to settle things that night.

"Why couldn't you call your old man and tell me you'd be late?"

"I'm sorry, Daddy," Danielle said. "It was my fault. I went to the mall with Mom and she had me out there too late. I was hurrying up so we could get here when we did."

"I hope you're hungry; I'm about to throw down," he said.

"You haven't cooked already?" Daniel asked with frustration in his voice.

"I see someone is hungry," Elliott replied. "It won't take long; forty-five minutes. Everything is ready to go into the oven. Remember how I used to cook for you all?"

"Eat everything right out of the oven," Danielle said.

"That's right. How about a glass of wine?" he said.

"I see you still have to make a big production out of cooking," Danielle said. "Do you know I do the same thing now?"

Daniel gave his sister an angry look. Elliott ignored it.

"Aww, baby, you do?" he said. "That makes me feel good."

Danielle washed her hands in the kitchen sink and retrieved the wine out of the refrigerator. "Daniel, you like red, right? There's a Pinot over there and the decanter and glasses, too," Elliott said, pointing. He decided the best way to deal with Daniel was to act as if everything was fine and see where that took him.

With wine in hand, Elliott called them into the kitchen. "You know what comes now."

Instinctively, they placed their glasses on the counter and held hands. Daniel's grip on his father's hand was limp. Elliott ignored it and prayed.

"Gracious Lord, bless this food that is about to be prepared. And we especially ask that You bless this family and let the love You put into it stay with us and carry us through challenging times. In Jesus' precious name, we pray. Amen.

"Now, let's have a toast," Elliott added.

"Really?" Daniel said. "Is that really necessary?"

"You don't want to toast, don't toast," Danielle said. "Daddy, I'll toast with you."

Elliott stared at his son, who could feel his father's glare. "You do the toast, Danielle," Elliott said.

Raising her glass, she said, "To a wonderful evening with family."

Elliott and Danielle tapped glasses. They looked at Daniel. Without looking up, he raised his glass and his father and sister tapped it. Elliott smiled.

"Danielle, turn on some music and watch me work," Elliott said. "I'm making one of your favorite meals."

He stuffed the Cornish hens with Vidalia onions and seasoned them with Nature's Seasons, roasted garlic powder and crushed rosemary. He boiled and seasoned the elbow macaroni with Kosher salt and ground pepper, strained it in a colander and poured it into a pan. He added his secret ingredients: sugar and catsup and mixed it until the noodles were a darker color. He added the pieces of cheese and milk and placed it in the oven, alongside the Cornish hens.

Elliott turned around to see his kids laughing among themselves and flipping through old photo albums, and it all felt so normal, so wonderful. He sipped his wine and admired the vision.

"In about forty-five minutes, we'll eat," he said. "In the meantime, let's talk. Let's catch up."

"You start," Daniel said. There was sarcasm in his voice. Elliott ignored it.

"Sure, I'll start," Elliott said. He and Danielle sat on the lush couch and Daniel in a single leather chair. "I am good. My health is good, according to my last checkup. I'm walking almost every day. Still doing work for the Innocence Project; did some today, in fact. Been missing you guys a lot. So it does my heart good for us to be here like this."

"Would be better if Mom were here, wouldn't it?" Daniel said.

"Daniel…" Danielle whined.

"It's okay," Elliott said, tapping his daughter's leg. "Yes, it would be nice if your mom were here. But I really wanted it to be about us reconnecting."

"As if she would come," Daniel cracked.

"Actually, I spoke to her yesterday and she asked if she could come tonight," Elliott revealed.

"What?" Danielle said.

"Yes, but I told her it wasn't a good idea. I wanted to spend time with my children with no distractions."

"So, Mom would be a distraction?" Daniel said.

"She's not here and she's *still* a distraction," Elliott said. "Listen, I love Lucy—hey, I never thought about it being the name of the TV show—but anyway, I will always love your mom. But you and your mom have been good for the last few years. I, on the other hand, have not been able to spend much time with you."

"I understand," Danielle said.

"So what's been going on with you all?" Elliott said. "Daniel, how's your internship with *The Atlanta Journal-Constitution* going?"

"Fine," he said.

An awkward silence filled the room. Elliott refused to say anything. Danielle, too. Finally, after several seconds, Daniel said, "It was a little frustrating at first. They weren't giving me any real writing assignments. But I had to cover a major accident on Interstate 285 in Cobb County—a terrible scene—and they started to believe in me. So, I have been doing a lot since then."

"I've been reading your articles," Elliott said.

"You have?" his son asked.

"Yes. I liked the piece you did on Mayor Reed and his efforts to combat crime in certain areas of the city."

"You read that?" Daniel asked, sounding amazed.

"I read all your stories. Stopped buying the paper until you started your internship," Elliott said. "I see your name in the newspaper and I smile every time. Makes me very proud."

"Me, too, Daddy," Danielle said. "I can't believe this knucklehead is following his dream."

"And what about you? The London School of Economics?" Elliott said to his daughter. "That's pretty amazing. That means you're kind of smart."

"I'm excited about living in London, but a little nervous, too," she said. "I'm not worried about doing the work."

"What is it then?" Daniel asked.

"It's being away from you, Daniel," Elliott interjected. "You two have been together every step of your lives for twenty years—longer than that when you count your time in your mother's womb.

"I bet you all haven't even talked about it."

Neither of them said anything. "And you know why?" Elliott added, "because it's something you're both afraid of. I have been going to my therapist long enough to learn something, and the fear of the unknown is a powerful force. You both realized there would be a day when you'd separate. But for it to be a few months away, it's scary."

Again, his kids did not speak. "I'm going to go on with my psychoanalysis: I think—and this is all coming to me right at this moment—that you, Danielle, are ready to close our distance because you're going out of the country for a year. You have enough to deal with; you don't want not being close to the father you love being something hovering over you."

Danielle looked into her dad's eyes before taking a sip of wine.

"Daniel, you have problems with me, sure," Elliott continued.

"You believe I broke up our family. That was a reason to be upset with me. But now, since we've known Danielle is going to London for a year, you've been angry and directing it at me. You didn't know what to do with your feelings about being separated from your sister, so I was the easy target to take that anger."

Brother and sister looked at each other. Their father was right. They had not addressed being apart for the first time. Daniel was excited and proud that his sister was accepted into such a prestigious program. But he quickly considered the ramifications of being separated from his twin, and did not like them. Likewise, Danielle was proud when she received acceptance, but also terrified that her family would totally fracture while she was in England.

"Daddy, I...I don't know what to say," Danielle said.

"You don't have to say anything," Elliott said.

"But you're right," she said. "Daniel, how am I going to do this without you?"

"The selfish part of me wants you to stay—or for me to move to London, too," he said. "The selfish part of me is stronger than the other side of me. I don't know how this is going to work out, but we're going to make it work."

"You're going over there with me in September, right?" Danielle asked.

"I don't know," he said.

"What do you mean, you don't know?" his sister responded.

"It's the selfish side of me talking," Daniel answered. "It might be easier to say bye to you here than in London."

"No, I want you there with me for at least a few days, to help me get settled," she said.

"I was just thinking of making it easier for both of us," he said. "I don't know what I'm saying. I can be honest with you, right?"

"You've only been honest with me, so you'd better not stop now," Danielle said.

"I don't want you to go," Daniel said. "I've wanted to say that ever since you got accepted. I know it's selfish. I know it's not right. But it's the truth."

He rose from his seat and walked over to the wine and refilled his glass. Daniel stood there a few feet from his sister as she began to cry.

"I don't want to leave you," she said. "I don't know what I'm going to do without you. Maybe I shouldn't go."

"Don't cry," Daniel said. He put down his drink and sat on the couch between his sister and dad. He hugged her. "Don't cry. I know you have to go. If you had gotten accepted and told me you weren't going to go, I would have *made* you go. I'm just being selfish. If this is the reason for us to be apart, then it's a good one."

Elliott watched all of this in silence. Finally, hesitantly, he placed his hand on his son's back as Daniel held Danielle. "It's going to be all right," Elliott said. "What's that thing on the computer? Skype? You can do that as often as possible. Nothing can replace actually being there, but you can at least be in steady contact."

"Yeah, Dad's right," Daniel said. "We'll stay in touch, no matter the distance or the time difference or whatever. And after a while, we'll be so into our worlds that we'll be fine."

"But I don't want to be fine not being around you, Daniel," she said.

"I don't want it, either," he said. "But we knew it was going to happen at some point. This is our time to grow up, but not apart."

Elliott found himself getting emotional, seeing the love his kids expressed for each other. It was exactly what he and Lucy had hoped for their children and tried to instill in them. They hardly ever had conflict as small children, which was strange, and when they did Elliott made sure Daniel took the lead role in resolving the issue and protecting his sister. That upbringing served them well.

They double-dated when they went to their high-school prom. Once, when they were juniors in high school, Danielle had a stomachache and stayed home from school; Daniel stayed home to take care of her. And when Daniel sprained his ankle playing basketball and had to use crutches to get around, it was Danielle who carried his books. They decided on a college together; there was never a moment's thought of one going somewhere the other would not.

Elliott reminded them of those occasions and more over the following thirty minutes or so. "With love like that, how can you not feel funny or sad about not being in the same place," the father told his kids. "But, if you look at my life, you know that everything will be all right. Your separation from family is voluntary and will only make you both stronger, better people."

"You never talked much about being in prison to us," Daniel said. "We read about it, the old stories about when you were released. But why didn't you talk about it?"

"When you were really young I was trying to protect you from that. I didn't want you to be jaded about the world," Elliott said. "But when you got older, your mom and I decided you should know about it so you wouldn't be naïve to the world. In the end, we're a product of our experiences and that experience, as terrible as it was, helped shape me."

"But how, Dad?" Daniel said. "I asked you once about whether you had gotten over being locked up for something you did not do, and you said, 'I'm still getting over it.' Are you over it now?"

"It's been twenty-something, almost thirty years since I was exonerated," Elliott said, "and I still haven't gotten over it. I came to realize I'll never get over it. It was too much to ever let go. I saw people get killed, men get raped, lived in terrible conditions... Every day for almost twelve years was like a nightmare.

"I became a product of the environment. I did what I had to do to survive, which meant I stabbed a couple of guys with homemade knives. Thankfully, they didn't die, but they understood I wasn't going to be violated. It's a rough existence. There was a point where I never thought I would be a free man again. You can't know what that feels like, to have given up hope of being free.

"And then you can't know the feeling of pure joy to be free after so long. In between those times, it was crazy."

"Do you dream about it, Daddy?" Danielle said.

"All the time," Elliott said. "Remember, when I was put away, my father and my mother died before I got out. They never got to see me on the streets, where I was supposed to be. I finished college all those years later and got my degree, which they never got to see. That hurt me. So, I dream not only about being in prison, but also about stuff I missed out on while I was locked up.

"Think about this: The age you are right now is the age I was when they told me I raped and killed a woman and locked me up. All these years you have ahead—in London and writing for newspapers or websites, meeting new friends and traveling, having young romance, earning a living for the first time, starting a family—I missed all that. I was in prison with guys who deserved to be in prison, meaning they were hard-core criminals. And here I was, a kid at home working for the summer to have some money to go back to college and ended up in prison. I wish I had a better word, but I don't. It was crazy."

"Wow," Daniel said. "How did you do it? How do you overcome something like that?"

"God, first and foremost," Elliott said. "He held me together when I could have fallen apart. He gave me the words to talk myself out of potential danger. He kept me out of harm's way. He kept my head up when my spirits were down. He gave me courage when I was scared to death. And He led a friend to learn about the Innocence Project, the group of lawyers that free innocent men. They believed in my case and got the evidence and DNA testing to prove me innocent.

"When I got out, God carried me to many good people, including a woman named Danette. She's since passed away, but she hooked me up with my first job out of prison. Didn't even know me but believed in me. Did me a favor just because someone had done something like that to her years before. Great lady. And some years later I met your mother. Being in love gave me some normalcy. It removed me mentally from prison. I felt like I was living the life I was supposed to live—you know: fall in love, build a family.

"When you all were born, that's when I truly started to feel like a real person, like the person I always envisioned for myself. I had the American dream: a nice home, beautiful wife that I loved and kids that I adored. It was as close to perfect as I could visualize."

Elliott headed to the kitchen to prepare the vegetables. His children followed him. This was the most he had spoken of his prison experience and they were enthralled.

The kids watched as he put the cut broccoli in a steamer and drizzled olive oil over it and then Nature's Seasons and then shavings of garlic.

"Four or five minutes and we will be ready to eat," he announced. Elliott held his glass for Daniel to pour him more wine.

"So, Daddy, what did you do in there to entertain yourself?" Danielle asked. "How did you spend your days?"

"It wasn't entertaining, I can tell you that," he said, laughing. "There were three things to avoid: prison politics, homosexuality and drugs. I did that. There were a few guys in there who weren't maniacs and who you could talk to about life, sports, whatever. Betting on sports for packs of cigarettes is big in prison. In Lorton, where I was, in Northern Virginia, there were a lot of Redskin fans.

"Sundays during the NFL season would be crazy because nobody wanted their team to lose. It's hard for me to call any time fun in there because of where I was. But after so many years, most guys get used to it. Institutionalized. It's a way of life. And, to be honest, I fought it like crazy. I didn't want it to become a part of who I was. I fought it. But certain things were such a routine that it became a part of your life."

"Like what?" Daniel asked.

"Well, I'll give you one example," Elliott said. "I might have told you this before. We had to eat every day at a certain time and we only had fifteen minutes to do it. So, to eat all your food, you would rush, eat fast, stuff food in your mouth. It took me almost fifteen years to stop doing that. It drove your mother crazy."

"I remember her saying at the dinner table: 'Slow down,' but I always thought she was talking to me," Daniel said.

"No, it was me," Elliott said. "She noticed it the first time we went out to eat. I remember the look on her face. She was mortified. And she said, 'Uh, why are you eating like that? You're going to choke to death.' That was my opening to tell her my story. I was always hesitant to tell my story because I was afraid it could turn a woman off and she'd run and never look back."

"Knowing Mom, she probably wanted to know the whole story," Danielle said.

"You're right about that," Elliott said. "We finished dinner and talked right there in the restaurant until the place closed."

"In prison, you also become paranoid about your surroundings," Elliott added. "I'm always aware of who's around me, especially behind me. There's a paranoia about someone coming up from behind me to do me harm. I can't shake that feeling."

The dinner was ready and Danielle and Daniel marveled at their father's cooking. The food was delicious. But best for Elliott was that he sat at the dining room table with his children and had a nice meal and fun conversation. He felt like a full man.

"How's your cooking, Danielle?" he asked his daughter. His son answered.

"Terrible," Daniel said, laughing.

"Look who's talking," Danielle said. "He boiled eggs one morning and burned them. All the water evaporated and the eggs cracked open."

"What about that fish you cooked that was so dry that we choked on it?" Daniel said.

"So neither of you know what you're doing? That's what I get from this," Elliott said. "Well, you're going to London, where they say the food is bland. So, you should come here at least once a week and we can work on it. Same with you, Daniel. You'll be in your apartment. Can't eat out every night. And there's nothing more impressive to a woman than a man cooking a great meal for her."

"I don't have time for that," Daniel said. "It's easier to take them out."

"But all guys take women out," Elliott advised his son. "You want to stand out. You have a woman over for a meal that you prepared with your own hands…you're making a statement. That's not the norm of what they get from a man. That's a way to distinguish yourself.

"Plus, the money spent taking out women adds up. You can cook a great meal at home for less than half of a restaurant meal."

"That's true, because once they start adding on taxes and tip... that's why I don't tip much," Daniel said.

"Daniel, don't be cheap; leave a proper tip. Please," Elliott said. "Do right by people and it will come back to you. I truly believe that. And in the case of eating, learn how to cook so you don't have to worry about leaving a tip."

Daniel was too busy stuffing his mouth with mac and cheese to respond. So he nodded his head. Elliott glanced to his left at Danielle, and she was chomping down on the Cornish hen. Elliott was euphoric.

There was not much talking over the next ten minutes, as they all devoured the meal, with Daniel going back for seconds and thirds. "What?" he said, smiling. "Told you I was hungry. And this food is good."

"I miss eating your food, Daddy," Danielle said.

"I must admit," Daniel said, "I do, too."

"I miss spending time with you both," Elliott said. "If it has to be around dinner, so be it. But I'd like to see you more. Maybe we could go bowling next weekend. Or to a concert at Chastain Park. I believe Diana Ross is coming."

"Dad, we're here, but it's not like there isn't an issue between us," Daniel said as he cleared his plate and placed it in the sink. "We got to this place because you broke Mom's heart, which broke up the family. You want me to be honest, so I'm just saying. I've been angry about that for a long time. And I'm still angry. You're probably right about me feeling bad about Danielle moving to London. That does bother me. But before she got accepted it was you."

"Let's go in the living room and have some of this cheesecake," Elliott said. There, he refreshed everyone's drink. As they enjoyed the dessert, he made his case.

"I'm sorry you've been angry all that time and I'm sorry you feel like I broke up the family," he said. "I don't know how you could get that because I've never spoken to you about it, and neither has your mother. Anyway, my point is, your sister asked me what I did for entertainment when I was in prison. Probably the number one thing I did was read. I read more than two hundred books.

"Somewhere I read that 'Holding onto anger is like drinking poison and expecting the other person to die.' You get the point?"

"I get the point," Danielle said. "Being angry is poison—especially being angry with your father. You get that, Daniel?"

"I get it, but it's not that simple," Daniel said. "We had a perfect family. And then it wasn't. It's not like getting a beating and getting over it."

"I know more than you that it was a big deal," Elliott said. "I probably should have said this a long time ago. I love your mother. Your mother is the love of my friggin' life. I still love her. In a lot of ways she's still the only woman for me."

No one said anything. Finally, Elliott continued. "A marriage ending is never as simple as it seems," he said. "It's far more complicated than you could ever imagine. When your mom and I came to this decision, we cried about it. We cried about it because we thought of you and how it would impact you. Moving out of our house was the hardest thing I've ever done, and you know I have been through some stuff in my life."

"What happened, Daddy?" Danielle said. "If you loved Mommy so much, how could you…you know?"

"What I will say about that is this: It's more complicated than it seems," he said. "Infidelity sometimes happens, and it has nothing to do with love or how much you love your spouse or your family. That might sound crazy to you right now. It took me a while to come to grips with it, to understand how it could happen. Nevertheless, it's damaging.

"But if you ask your mother how she feels about me, three years later, she'll say she loves me."

"Well, if you love her and she loves you, then why does she live in Southwest Atlanta and you live here? Why aren't you together?" Daniel asked. "Why did our family break up?"

"The family doesn't have to be broken up," Elliott said. "Lots of couples divorce. Most marriages end in divorce. But it's how you stick together after a divorce that determines if the family breaks up. We don't have to be under one roof to be a family. Look at us right now. We've had dinner, finishing dessert, had some wine, some laughs, some disagreements, some revelations. We're a family."

"But how is Mom supposed to forgive you for what you did? How are we supposed to forgive you?" Daniel asked.

"How?" Elliott said. "If I can forgive a jury for sending me to prison for twelve years for crimes I didn't commit, you can certainly forgive your father who loves you and who has done all he could for you."

Neither of his kids said anything.

"Plus," he added, "to not forgive is a sin."

"A sin?" Daniel said, laughing.

"Yes," Elliott said, smiling. "It's in The Bible. John, chapter six, I think."

"Daddy!" Danielle yelled. "You need to stop."

"You want to go to hell?" Elliott said. "If you don't forgive your parent, who loves you more than anyone, then I'm sorry to say that you've punched an express ticket to hell while wearing gasoline drawers."

His kids did not want to, but they laughed. They were used to him making them crack up, and it felt good to them to feel that again.

But there was a major issue hovering above the occasion, one that Elliott actually wished was addressed earlier, to get it out of the way. He wondered why they had not raised the question. He also was somewhat relieved because he had not figured out a way to answer it without lying.

The evening went on without drama. Danielle placed the dishes in the dishwasher and cleaned up the kitchen. Daniel said, "Since Dad cooked and you cleaned up, the least I can do is drink some more wine."

Elliott laughed, but switched quickly to father mode. "I'm assuming you all rode together and that your sister is driving."

"Don't try to play daddy now," Daniel said.

Elliott did not ignore him. "I *am* your father and don't you ever think I won't play my role or that you're too big for me to put you in your place."

"Wait a minute," Danielle yelled from the kitchen. "We're having a nice time. Let's keep it that way."

"If you were around the last few years, then maybe it'd be okay for you to talk to me like that," Daniel said. "But let's keep it real: You haven't been a father to either of us lately."

"I haven't been a father or you haven't been a son?" Elliott asked. "Which is it? 'Cause from my view this is what I see: I see me always reaching out to check on you, to offer you whatever you need. I see me paying for your college room and board. I see me praying for you and for us to get past the anger. That's what I see.

"Oh, and I also see you accepting the money but not accepting my phone calls or returning them. I see you benefiting from all I—and your mother—have instilled in you. And I see you blaming me for breaking up the family when it doesn't have to be broken up. That's what I see. What do you see? What do *you* see, Danielle?"

"I see a family coming back together," Danielle said. "Daniel has been drinking wine all night, so his tongue is loose. We have talked about it—"

"Danielle, don't," her brother yelled.

"No, it's time to stop all this now," she said. "We have talked about it, Daddy, and we're sorry. From the beginning, you have tried to be there for us and we have been really mean to you. And disrespectful, too, which we are really sorry about. I don't want to miss my father anymore. Daniel doesn't either, whether he says it to you or not. Being mad about the divorce is not helping anyone, especially us. And you're right: Anything we've felt lately has been about me leaving for London. I don't want to leave my family, and especially Daniel. We're like each other's right hand. We've had trouble grasping the fact that we're going to be separated. And we've probably taken some of that out on you."

"I'm an easy target, I know," Elliott said. "But I'm about moving forward. Holding on to stuff does no one any good. You guys are my kids. There is no room for animosity or anger...not lingering animosity or anger. As your parent, I'm unconditional. I love you when you make me mad or disappoint me or make me happy and proud. There's no wavering."

"I want to hug you, Daddy," Danielle said, and they embraced.

"I don't have to go that far," Daniel said. "But...I do love you, Dad."

"That's enough for me," Elliott said. "I love you both. More than you could ever know."

Daniel excused himself and went into the bathroom. He ran the water and flushed the toilet to drown out his tears. He was a Momma's boy but Dad's pride and joy. The relief he experienced in telling his father that he loved him overflowed. To say the words released three years of anguish.

He gathered his emotions and wiped his face. After using the bathroom, he rejoined his sister and father.

"We should be leaving, right, Danielle?" he said.

"I guess so," she said. "We're supposed to go to a party on Peter Street."

Elliott was tempted to bring up Tamara. He was surprised they were about to leave without asking why he was at a club with their college friend. If he had an answer that would continue the good feelings they created, he would have. But Elliott was not silly.

"Well, I had hopes for tonight and it turned out better than I could have imagined," he told Danielle and Daniel before they headed out. "I feel so much better about everything."

"Me, too," Danielle said. "I can't wait to tell Mommy."

"Well," Daniel said, "I guess we have something to build on now."

Before Elliott could speak, his doorbell rang. Not once, but three times in succession.

"Who the hell is that?" he said.

"I thought you had to have a key to get up here," Daniel said.

"You do," Elliott responded. "Let me see who the hell this is."

His kids followed him to the door. *"Who is it?"* Elliott said in a booming, aggressive voice.

"Tamara," the voice came back. Danielle and Daniel looked at each other. Elliott's heart dropped.

CHAPTER TWELVE
Drama Breeds Drama

"What the hell?" Elliott said, looking back at his children.

"Did she say 'Tamara'?" Daniel said.

"What is she doing here?" Danielle wanted to know.

Elliott didn't answer. He unlocked the dead bolt and opened the door.

"What are you doing here?" he said in an angry tone to Tamara, who stood there wearing a cleavage-exposing top and an I-caught-you expression.

"I texted you that I was at a party downstairs at the Drink Shop," she said.

"So," Elliott responded. "You didn't hear back from me, did you? You don't come to my house like this."

"Why not? We're friends," Tamara said.

And that's when Daniel and Danielle stepped into her line of vision. They just looked at their friend.

"You need to go back to that party or wherever, " Elliott said. And he shut the door.

"Dad, what's going on with you and this girl?" Daniel said.

"Why would she show up at your door?" Danielle asked. "How does she even know where you live?"

Elliott had prided himself on always being truthful to his children. But there was nothing good to come out of truthfully sharing his relationship with Tamara.

"How well do you know this young lady?" he asked. "I think she has a problem."

"We know her from school," Danielle said. "But what's going on with you and her? First you're at a club with her and now she's at your front door? What's going on?"

"Nothing's going on," Elliott lied.

"Dad, something's gotta be going on," Daniel said. "I wanted to ask you about her, but Danielle made me promise to not bring it up. But here she is anyway, in living color."

"Look, come on, let's sit down," he said, leading them to the living area. He looked into the eyes of his kids, the kids with whom he had spent the evening rebuilding a relationship. He was not going to implode what was just built.

"I went to the movies by myself a few months ago up at CineBistro in Brookhaven," Elliott started. "I stopped at the bar there and she was there, too, with her date. We all started talking and exchanged numbers. I told them that I had a couple of small car dealerships and she contacted me about getting a vehicle.

"Evidently, she was looking for a car for her birthday. When we talked she asked me when I could meet with her. I told her I couldn't do it on Friday because I was going to Vanquish. She said, 'Wow, I'm having my birthday party at Vanquish Friday.' So I told her I would drive the car she was interested in and she could check it out. That's where we were going when I saw you that night. I wanted to talk to you but I was so shocked to see you... I didn't know what to say."

"Our other friends said you bought a bottle," Daniel said.

"I did; I can write it off as a business expense," Elliott said. "I weighed the difference between a three-hundred-fifty-dollar bottle of vodka or whatever it was over a twenty-one-thousand-dollar car she was interested in buying. It was a business decision."

"But how does she know where you live?" Daniel asked. He and Danielle were feeling better about the situation, but there were a few more questions that needed answering.

"I told her I live at the W," he said. "But I didn't tell her my unit number. I have no idea how she found out, but I'm going to get with the people downstairs and figure it out. We can't have people roaming the building. I pay too much for that when the place is supposed to be secure."

"Daddy, this is so crazy," Danielle said. "We wanted to talk about this, but I told Daniel to let it go for now."

"I wondered why it hadn't come up," Elliott said. "I was going to bring it up, but then you all said you had to go, so I was going to wait. But clearly something's going on with her. To ring my doorbell…that's crazy. I have to admit, though, that she asked me once if I dated younger women. I'm not arrogant enough to believe she was flirting with me. But she has called me more than once."

"What?" Danielle asked. "She asked if you dated younger women? You're old enough to be her father. Why would she think you'd be interested in her?"

"I can't account for that and I don't want you, either of you, to get into it with her," Elliott said. "I will handle it."

"How you gonna handle it, Dad?" Daniel said. "What you gonna do?"

"I'm gonna call her tomorrow and tell her she needs to back off, that I'm not interested in her and it was totally out of line to come to my home." He was trying his hardest to be convincing, but not go over the top.

"She's got some balls to show up at a man's house at almost eleven o'clock at night," Daniel said. "Why would she think that's cool?"

"She's crazy," Danielle said. "They said she used to date or sleep with Dr. Bainbridge. Something's not right about that."

"She dated a professor at Michigan State?" Elliott asked.

"Yeah, I did hear that," Daniel said. "Matter of fact, she also messed around with Grant, the assistant baseball coach. At least that was the rumor."

"Well, she's gonna stay away from me after I finish with her," Elliott said.

Quiet took over the room. Daniel and Danielle were confused. They wanted to believe their father, but it did not make sense that Tamara would show up at his door. It also did not make sense that a twenty-five-year-old would be interested in their sixty-one-year-old dad—or that he would be interested in a girl so young.

"I'm sorry this happened," he said. "But I'm glad you were here. I think seeing you embarrassed her and made her leave without acting up."

"I feel like I lost a friend," Danielle said.

"Well, you don't need a certain number of friends you have," Elliott said, "just friends you can be certain of."

"Well, that sounds good," Daniel said. "But I'm almost certain there is more to this situation."

"If there's more to it, then it's whatever is in her mind," Elliott said. He had to throw Tamara completely under the MARTA bus to ease his kids' minds. "From what you're telling me, she likes older men. But I was trying to sell a car to her. I had no idea she was this way."

Daniel studied his father's words. He sought an opening, a place where Elliott showed some ambivalence or empathy for Tamara. There was none.

"I really hate you all are in the middle of this," he said. "But it will go no further than this. I promise you that. Last thing I need is a stalker."

"So who are you dating these days, Dad?" Daniel said.

"No one in particular," he said. "I get my share of dates in, though. Nobody who would be your stepmother."

"Very funny," Danielle said. "You look great, so I wouldn't be surprised if there are women after you. I just don't want it to be someone we know."

"Neither do I," he said.

"Well, let's go, Danny," Daniel said to his sister. "I can't promise I won't say something to Tamara if I see her."

"I understand," Elliott said. "I just don't want it to get ugly. Be respectful, son. She *is* a woman."

Daniel nodded his head. The three of them exchanged hugs and his offspring left. Elliott went straight to the Pinot, only to find that he and Daniel had killed it. So he went to the Sauvignon Blanc, got a new glass and poured.

What the hell was she thinking? he said to himself. He was upset with Tamara that she would come to his house uninvited and especially perturbed that his kids were there to witness it. He felt like she forced him into lying about their relationship. Elliott could not bring himself to tell them the truth, that he pursued Tamara and had sex with her. Telling them that would blew up their relationship.

That thought made him feel pressure to speak to Tamara about how she would handle seeing Danielle and Daniel. She had to be embarrassed and hurt that he shut the door in her face and that her friends saw it. Elliott recalled that she said she had texted him earlier. So, he found his phone on top of the refrigerator and checked his messages.

There were four: one from Henry, asking about meeting for drinks; one from Nikki, letting him know that she found out that he was seeing Tamara and two from Tamara—one saying she was at the Drink Shop downstairs and wanted to see him, the other apologizing for coming to his house and asking him to come see her downstairs at the party.

The last text came in ten minutes earlier. Elliott sipped his wine and then ingested a big gulp of it. He believed he needed to do damage control. Daniel was subject to call Tamara to get some answers. He needed to get her to lie for him.

So he changed shirts, squirted on some John Varvatos Vintage cologne and headed down to the Drink Shop. He did not text her to let her know he was coming. He had a moment where he worried that Daniel and Danielle might be there, but figured he would smooth it over by telling them he went there to set Tamara straight.

To get to Drink Shop, Elliott had to catch the elevator down to the lobby level and then take the spiraling staircase near the hotel's front desk one flight up. At the top of the steps Elliott found the small space jammed with youngsters enjoying loud music and each other. Near the end of the bar sat Tamara, who perked up when she saw Elliott standing at the top of the staircase.

She excused herself from the young man who was in her face and made her way to Elliott. The young man followed.

"Hold up," he said to Tamara. "I bought you a drink. You gonna bounce on me like that?"

"I have to go," she said.

"Oh, shit. Is this your father here making you go home?" the guy said.

Elliott reached into his pocket and pulled out a twenty-dollar bill. "Here you go; I'm paying for her drink," he said to the guy. "Now you can leave her alone."

"Hey, listen, old school, don't disrespect me," he said.

"Not trying to disrespect you, *dog*," Elliott said, with what he called "prison anger" rising in him. "You got the money, now move on before you can't move on."

He gave the younger man a stare that was intense and threatening. "Yeah, okay, man. Whatever," the guy said before turning and walking away.

"See, I was mad at you and now you go do that and I'm completely turned on," Tamara said.

Elliott was not amused or flattered. "Let's go downstairs to the other bar." He turned and headed down the steps. Tamara hesitated for a moment, but followed him.

He did not look back, turning right at the bottom of the steps, past the front entrance of the hotel and into the bar, which was far quieter, with only a few pockets of people spread about. Elliot was sending a message to Tamara through his demeanor. Usually, he would make sure she made it down the steps, offering a hand. And he'd walk side-by-side. Walking ahead of her and not aiding her told Tamara that he was not happy—a psychological move that put her on the defensive.

Elliott flagged a server, ignoring Tamara as she approached and took a seat next to him. Angry as he was, he could not dispute that the woman had presence and oozed sexiness. But he would not give in to that part of his brain.

"Excuse my language, but what the fuck are you doing coming to my house?" he said calmly but sharply.

"Don't cuss at me," Tamara said.

"Oh, you want me to respect you and not cuss at you, but you want to disrespect me by showing up at my front door?" Elliott responded. "You get what you give."

Tamara said, "Elliott—"

He cut her off. "If the next words you say to me aren't 'I'm sorry,' I'm leaving."

"I'm sorry, Elliott. I am."

"You should be."

"Why are you so angry?"

"What? Are you serious?" Elliott answered. "First of all, you don't go to anyone's house uninvited. Period. That's just wrong. Secondly, I was there with my kids. You almost ruined a great night for us."

"How? By coming to your house?"

"Are you drunk?" Elliott asked.

"Yes."

"Well, that explains all the dumb questions," he said. "Let me make it easy for you to understand. I told you that my kids and I—your friends—have not really seen each other in a few years. I told you that bothered me. So, I was able to get them to come over for dinner and we made great progress into being what we used to be to each other. And then you show up. That was not good."

"I didn't know they were there; I didn't know you were there," she said. "I took a chance."

"That's not a chance you take, coming to my house," he snapped. "Even if I were alone, it's not the thing to do. You've got to know that. But, see, you thought I had a woman up there and you thought you'd be messing up something."

"I have the right to—"

"Stop it, Tamara," he said. "You're about to piss me off. You don't have the right to come to my house, unless invited. You don't have the right to see what I'm doing. You don't. And if you don't understand that, I misjudged you and how mature you are."

"You don't have to insult me, Elliott. I made a mistake."

"So own up to it and say you won't do it again," he said. "Anything else is bullshit. You could have destroyed everything that was gained tonight by doing that."

The server came over. "Can we have some water for her and I'll have a Macallan 15 Year. Neat," he said.

"Oh, I can't have a drink?" she asked.

"You said you're drunk. Why would you have another drink? You need to come down so you can drive home. Anyway, here's the thing, Tamara: Danielle and Daniel can't know about us."

"Why not? You're ashamed of me?" she asked.

"Not ashamed, but they wouldn't understand," he said. "Think about it. If your mother dated a guy your age, how would you feel?"

"I would feel that if it's okay with her, it's okay with me," Tamara said.

"That's a damned lie," Elliott shot back. "You're being silly now. You're telling me you wouldn't have any problem whatsoever? A twenty-five-year-old guy you know sleeping with your mother?"

"See, you didn't say I knew the guy. That makes a big difference," she said.

"Well, you know the point I was making," Elliott said.

"I was going by what you said. Anyway, yes, I see how that could be a problem," Tamara allowed. "So what did you tell them?"

"I told them I met you at the movies, that you wanted to buy a car from one of my lots and that I was taking you to see a car you were interested in when we were leaving Vanquish."

"What?" Tamara said, leaning back. "How the hell did you come up with *that* story?"

"I have no idea. I was panicked and it started coming out. I had to make it seem like it was strictly business."

"Well, how did I know where you live?" she inquired.

"I told them I mentioned that I lived in this building but I wasn't sure how you found out my unit number or how you got up there."

"Ran out of lies, huh?" She smiled.

"Ran out of good ones."

The drinks came.

"Why didn't you tell me you were going to be with Daniel and Danielle?" Tamara wanted to know.

"Because I don't have to tell you what I'm doing. I'm glad we met and I have enjoyed the time we've spent together. But I don't want either of us to get into thinking we have to be accountable to the other. That creates problems."

"But I'm not used to dealing with men like this," she said. "If you had just said, 'My children are coming over,' I wouldn't have knocked on your door. I wouldn't have felt like you were out with someone else. So, *you* created this problem."

"Yeah, that's one way to look at it." Elliott sipped his Scotch. "The other way is that you don't come over someone's house un-announced. Period."

Tamara laughed. "Okay, okay," she said. "You're being a chauvinist about this. You can come to my house anytime you want. You don't have to ask me. But you want to be in control because you have a dick."

Elliott smiled. "Not because I have a dick. Because I have a *big* dick."

CHAPTER THIRTEEN
Telephone Love

The morning came and Elliott asked Tamara, "Are you going to go with the program and lie to my kids for me?"

"You think you're slick, don't you?" she asked.

"What?"

"You ask me to do something for you after you've sexed me up. You know right now I'll do any damn thing you ask me."

Elliott smiled and pulled the covers over their naked bodies. They got beyond the talk of Daniel and Danielle. And when it was time for Tamara to go home, she said, "You can't send me out on the streets like this."

"Like what?"

"Tipsy and horny."

Elliott smiled. "That would be irresponsible of me, wouldn't it?"

And so he took her upstairs with him. "You socked it to me again," she said about their encounter. "Isn't that how people your age speak? 'Sock it to me'?"

"You'd be surprised. We also use terms like, 'Stomp it out' and 'Beat it up.' Aren't those phrases you twenty-somethings use?"

"Did you bring Nikki back here Friday night?"

"No, I didn't," Elliott said. "And how do you know her?"

"We're in the same sorority," Tamara said. "I don't know her that well, but we met in a chapter meeting and became friends on

Facebook. Glad we did. I wouldn't know you were dating her, too."

"There you go. Not dating her. We met out for a drink. That's it. And that's all I'm saying about it."

Tamara did not like it, but she accepted Elliott's position. He had her body feeling too good to argue with him. They lounged around until after 9 a.m. She wanted morning sex.

"I hate to disappoint you, but I don't like morning sex most of the time," he said. "I usually wake up not feeling sexy. My stomach is a little unsettled. My energy level isn't that high. Not all mornings, but most. That's why I try really hard to please you at night so in the morning you're still feeling it."

"I do still feel it, and I guess that's the issue," Tamara said. "I feel so good that I want some more."

Elliott shook his head as his cell phone rang. It was Lucy.

"My ex-wife," he said to Tamara. "I've got to take this."

He answered and put Lucy on hold. "I'm going to go," Tamara said. "Take your call. But you owe me some more. I'll call you later."

Tamara got dressed and Elliott walked her to the elevator before rejoining the phone call with his ex-wife.

"Hey, Lucy, what's going on? You don't call me, so something must be up."

"I wanted to talk to someone who knows me and can give me some honest insight. You're that one person."

"I am?" Elliott said. "Okay. Go."

"Well, I heard that you had a visitor last night who is our kids' age," Lucy said.

"Oh, boy. They told you about that?" Elliott said. "Why?"

"I'm their mother, that's why," she answered. "But that's not the point. They told me that she has an interest in you and seems to be attracted to older men. I get that, to some degree. I mean, you're twelve years older than me. But that's not why I called.

"I'll be fifty in four weeks…and I don't have anything to hold on to."

"What?" Elliott said. "You have your children, who are great, great kids. I'm sure you're referring to Danielle going to London and Daniel back to Michigan. But that's the way it's supposed to be: You do your job as a parent and the kids flourish and go on with their lives. You've got to look at the bigger picture."

"The picture I see is pint-sized," Lucy said.

"You have your health, right?" Elliott said. "That's a big one. You know how many people wish they felt like you feel and look like you look? Those are blessings. I'm not picking on you when I say this, but people's problems, I believe, stem from quickly identifying all that you *want* but not focusing on the great things that you *have*.

"And what is it exactly you want? The kids will be gone. What do you want?"

"I need someone in my life," she said.

"You mean you *want* a man in your life," Elliott asserted. "I'm guessing you don't *need* one."

"Want? Need? What's the difference? I don't have anyone," Lucy said, "and I'm about to be fifty years old."

"So why don't you get one?" Elliott asked.

"If it were that easy or that simple, I wouldn't feel as I do," she answered. "It's different for men, especially in Atlanta, than it is for women."

"I'm going to sit down for this one," Elliott said. "How is it different?"

"Are you kidding me? You don't know?" she said. "Well, I'm gonna tell you. First of all, for a man your age, you can still attract a woman in her twenties, thirties, forties and fifties. That's just about four decades of women. I know there aren't a lot of twenty-somethings interested in a sixty-one-year-old man. But the more you raise that age, the more the number of women you could have increases.

"And society is okay with a nice-looking man in his sixties with a twenty- or thirty-something-year-old woman. And men your age with women in their forties is the norm.

"Meanwhile, if I go out and meet a twenty-five-year-old kid, there's hardly any way he would be interested in me or interesting enough for me to be interested in him. Why would a young man want a fifty-year-old woman? And then the women who do date younger men are labeled as 'cougars.' So it's not set up for society to accept an older woman with a younger man.

"So there's that and then there are also so many single women in Atlanta that it's a competitive landscape," Lucy added. "Let's say the man is thirty-eight. That's still twelve years younger than me. What's the incentive to consider me when he has countless women his age and younger, all the way into the early twenties? It's just a tight situation for women my age."

"I wish I had an answer," Elliott said. "What I will say is that there may be a lot of women here, but not all of them are quality women. I can attest to that."

"How much dating have you been doing?" Lucy thought for a second about not going there, but she could not hold it in.

"As much as I like," he responded.

"Well, you're single so you can do what you want," she said, trying to sound unconcerned. "But for women here, not only are the numbers against us, but the quality of the men here is weak, too. Lots of professional men, educated men—but they either already have a woman or wife, are arrogant because they know they are in such demand or they are just weird."

"I tell you what's weird," Elliott said.

"What?"

"Me talking to my ex-wife about dating," Elliott said. "That's very weird."

"I guess it is, huh?" she said. "Well, through everything, you're the person who knows me the best. And, believe it or not, the person I trust the most."

"How ironic is that?" Elliott said. "Truth be told—since we're being transparent—I can say for sure no one knows me better than you. Since we've been divorced, it's been hard to fill the void. I can't even lie. But…I guess it is what it is."

"I am able to call you about this because I know you will be honest with me," Lucy said. "I need an honest perspective."

"We've been divorced about three years," Elliott said. "You telling me you haven't met anyone worth your time?"

"Let me tell you," she began, "it took me a while to get back out there. Then I met probably every kind of loser in this city. I met the liar who cannot tell the truth about anything, from where he lives to where he works to what he has done in his life. Pathetic. I met the married man who chases women as if he is single. I met the arrogant guy who believed the world spun on his axis. I met the good-looking guy who could not stay out of the mirror. I met an ugly guy who had money and thought that made him cute.

"I met a very nice guy who had no personality. I met a successful guy who was socially retarded. I met a guy who was ideal, except he was an alcoholic. I met a guy who was awaiting sentencing on armed robbery. I met the honest guy who was upfront about what he wanted from me: sex on the first date. I met the life of the party whose life was in shambles: no car, 'in between' jobs, living with his cousin. I met the guy with five kids by four women…with another child by another woman on the way. I met the guy who actually seemed really nice, but he had no manners; would not open the door for me, would talk with food in his mouth, would play with his cell phone at the dinner table.

"I'm not done. I met the guy who wanted to marry me after one conversation. Another guy said we should move in together, even though we didn't even know each other's last names. Still another guy asked me for a loan three days after meeting me…"

"Damn," Elliott said. "My first reaction is: You get around."

They both laughed.

"No, some of these guys I met in the same night," Lucy said. "You know how you go to an event and mingle. Well, I would meet three or four of these guys in one night and learn about them through conversation. It's crazy. And I know I pointed out that it's men in Atlanta like this. But I talked to my friend Cynthia in D.C., and she says the same thing about men there. And Candice says the same about men in Chicago and told me her sister, Tanya, says that about men in Houston. It's all over the place.

"But the one thing women in Atlanta complain about more than women anywhere else is the gay man who is undercover, Elliott. That's the one that makes us all comfortable staying home and watching *Scandal*, *The Newsroom* or *Breaking Bad*. You have any idea how many women I have met who have encountered this?"

"I've heard this from a few women, too," Elliott said. "It's crazy."

"And that's one of the reasons it's so lopsided here, women-to-men," Lucy added. "So many men are gay or bisexual or whatever. They use women to hide who they really are. And believe me when I tell you this: Many women here are petrified because of that."

Elliott wanted to tell her about Henry, but he could not muster the nerve. Not at that moment. There was venom in how Lucy spoke of the "down low brothers," and he did not want to set her afire with the news that someone she thought was straight actually was the kind of man of which she spoke. So, he kept it to himself, although he would eventually tell her the truth about Henry.

"Are you telling me there has not been one 'normal' guy you met in three years?" Elliott said.

"Well, it's been only about two years because I couldn't even think about being on the dating scene for a year after you moved out."

"After *you* insisted I move out, Lucy," Elliott asserted.

"Well, one of us had to move. I couldn't be around you. I—"

"Yeah, I know," he interrupted.

"So, in the two years or so, I met one guy who seemed like a man I could be interested in," she said. "He was fun and smart and a gentleman. Honestly, he reminded me of you. Maybe that's why I was interested in him."

"Hmmm," Elliott said. "What happened?"

"He lived in New York," she said. "That's too far away. I never understood how people could do long distance relationships. I don't know…I'm not built for it. I didn't like it when you went on speaking events for the Innocence Project. I guess I'm needy in that sense. But at least your trips were for a day or two. To be with someone you grow to care about, but he lives in another city? That's too much."

"You've got to have a trust in that person that is strong," Elliott said. "I have two guys I know whose wives live in separate cities. Three, in fact. One guy lives in Chicago and his wife lives in D.C. Another guy lives in Atlanta and his wife works for Disney in Orlando. And this other brother lives here and his wife in Dallas."

"How do they make that work?" Lucy asked. "I couldn't do it."

"Well, they trust, first of all," Elliott explained. "But one guy, the guy who lives in Chicago, he comes home almost every weekend. He's spending a lot of money on flights. But they don't have any kids and both are career people and so they have the money to do it.

"The others, I don't know how often they actually see each other. But here's the thing: They all say it's tough, but all say not being together every day keeps their marriage fresh. They miss each other, so when they get together there's no time or interest in the bullshit other marriages might go through. They are just about each other."

"Yeah, but what about the time when they aren't together?" Lucy asked.

"An idle mind, huh?" Elliott said.

"I don't want to even get into having too much freedom to see other people," she said. "I'm talking about plain missing them so much, doing something spontaneous during the week. Not being able to do that, having to plan everything, would eat me up."

"I'm sure they are conditioned to it to some degree," Elliot said. "You can get used to anything. After so many years, I got used to being in prison. And I got used to being sick with cancer. I got used to being hurt by our marriage breaking up."

Lucy did not respond. "Are you here?" Elliott said.

"Can I be totally honest with you?" she asked.

"No," he answered.

"Anyway," she said, dismissing his response, "I said all that I said—and I know it was a lot—to say that I miss you," Lucy revealed. She waited for Elliott to say something. When he didn't, she continued.

"I have to be honest with myself and say that, admit that. I'm alone because anyone I meet I compare to you, and they fall short.

Or I fall short of feeling about them as I do you. I know you've moved on. But I wanted you to know that I love you. I still love you and always will."

Elliott disbelieved what he heard. He and Lucy had not seen each other in more than a year and hardly spoke to each other. Their breakup was unique in that there were not the ugly fights that came with it. In fact, Elliott wanted to stay in the house and at least attempt to get beyond the deal-breaking issue. Lucy insisted he move out.

Moving on was another issue altogether. It was hard to do because he loved Lucy. He believed in the idea that an affair did not have to indicate a love interest, just something extra to do. Lucy believed in that notion as well, but she was unable to resolve it in her mind as an excuse to betray the marriage.

So, at her direction, Elliott moved from their home in Southwest Atlanta, stayed at the W hotel for a week and decided to purchase a place there.

"Lucy, I told you I loved you the day I moved out and I haven't stopped loving you," he said. "And I don't want to not love you. You're in my blood. But we've been through a lot, unfortunately. I would never had expected this for us, to be honest… But, anyway, I'm glad we're talking. We should talk more."

"Well, how about lunch one day?" she said.

"That can't hurt, can it?"

"I don't bite," Lucy said.

"I remember," Elliott answered.

CHAPTER FOURTEEN
SMH, OMG, LOL

Elliott spent much of Sunday at home alone, watching television, preparing a speech for an Innocence Project event and pondering his conversation with Lucy. Her interest in seeing him stunned Elliott. He had long since dismissed any hope of reconciling.

For three months he aggressively pursued Lucy, pleading with her to give their marriage another chance. She refused, even though every instinct in her told her to give in.

Finally, he told her, "You win. You're making a big mistake. And one day you will realize it."

That day, apparently, was Sunday morning. And it messed with his head. For all his dismissing of Lucy, she stayed in his heart. He was amazed that one phone call from her after three years shook his foundation.

Losing her was one of the low points of his life. Prison time as an innocent man was at the top, followed by his bout with cancer. But his failed marriage to the one woman that struck his chord beat him up. Lucy expressing an interest in seeing him conjured up all those emotions. The last time he saw her, a year or so earlier, she barely made eye contact at a mutual friend's wedding.

He was so disappointed that he did not attend the wedding reception. He could not bear enduring her dismissive nature toward him.

He recalled leaving with an empty feeling, as if it would have been better to not see her at all.

They had a few brief phone conversations since that day, but they all centered around their children and money. Emotionless. And yet, one call from her a year later moved him.

He was still in love with her.

He had planned to attend a Remy Martin tasting event near the King Plow Arts Center, but instead stayed home. He had left-overs from Saturday's dinner with Daniel and Danielle and was so overwhelmed by Lucy's conversation that he forgot to give Tamara the obligatory day-after-sex call.

So, she called him.

"See, this is what I'm talking about," she said when he answered the phone. "Niggas start taking you for granted when they know you really like them."

"Who? Nigga? That's what you called me?" he said. "What if I said, 'Bitches start making assumptions before they know what's going on?' How would you like that?"

"Oh, so I'm a bitch now?" she said.

"I'm a nigga now?" he asked. "Listen, there's a big age gap and, apparently, a communication gap, too. But I want to be clear about something so this isn't an issue again: Don't call me names, espe-cially that one. I treat you with the utmost respect. That's how you talk to your homeboys, fine—but not to me. You show your age when you jump to conclusions. You don't know what the hell is going on with me. First thing you do is ask a question before you start running off at the mouth. Make sense to you?"

Tamara was angry, but mostly humiliated. He made her feel like a chastised kid, which she really hated because of the age difference. She wanted to bridge the gap by being mature. That was important to her in dealing with Elliott and other older men of her past.

The way to make amends was to handle the situation maturely, she thought. And so she did. "I'm sorry, Elliott," Tamara began. "I was out of line. I hope everything is okay with you. I was expecting a call from you because I wanted to tell you how much I enjoyed being with you last night. And I wanted to invite you to an event next weekend. Oh, and I'm sorry I called you a…called you that name."

Elliott smiled. "Thank you for that, you little sexy bitch."

Tamara laughed and he laughed with her. "I'm sorry I didn't call you before now. A couple things had my attention. But the day isn't over and I don't want you to turn into this over-the-top, crazy woman when you think I have wronged you."

"Okay, okay. I get it," she said. "I just can't take no…no man disrespecting me."

"I wouldn't disrespect you," he said. "Long before you were born I learned the value of making that call the day after sex. That's the easiest thing to do, although many guys don't have the sense to make the call. But I got you."

They chatted for a few minutes before Tamara had to go. He was glad to hear her say that, and even laughed when she ended the call by saying, "I'll call you tomorrow…nigga."

Elliott contemplated calling Lucy, but thought better of it. If her attitude varied from earlier, he would be disappointed. He, in fact, was mad at himself for being hopeful of a chance to get her back. He had become an expert at giving up hope.

When he was locked up in Lorton and watched, however briefly, a man get raped, any hope for being free disintegrated in that moment. He became an inmate that morning. All his posturing and all his talk of not succumbing to being a criminal dissipated. The only way for him to survive was to let go of hope and accept his plight.

Although he had not committed a crime, he lived in prison among real-life criminals. The only way to make it was to adopt the same principles by which they lived, which was to be a savage when necessary. But to be that way required he give up all hope of ever being free.

He tried not to think about it, but when he looked at where he was in relation to where he had been, Elliott was proud of himself. The inhumanity of prison breaks men, whether they are criminals or not. In nearly twelve years, he was transformed into something different, someone different. He almost killed one man with a prison-made knife out of a toothbrush. Sent the guy to the infirmary for three weeks with multiple stab wounds. Why? Because the guy claimed Elliott had stolen a pack of cigarettes and challenged him in a gym full of inmates.

Elliott had to make the guy pay or he would have been considered weak and made a target by anyone looking for a patsy. So he did what he had to do. That was required. That was the culture.

That time in prison rotted a huge part of his soul, and he spent many nights crying silently in his prison cell. When the Innocence Project took his case and provided DNA test results that proved he was not a criminal, Elliott showed the kind of fortitude many men could not muster.

He overcame the lost twelve years, and Lucy was a major part of that gradual transformation back to solid citizen. She accepted him for the man she saw, not the perceived person who was wrongly accused and convicted. The women he encountered before Lucy were leery of Elliott, even as they read many accounts in *The Washington Post* and other credible news outlets not only about his innocence, but also about the apprehension of the confessed killer/rapist.

One woman told him, "You seem like a nice guy and I'm sorry about what happened to you. But I'm not comfortable dealing with someone who has spent that much time in prison. I'm not being insensitive. But I know how disease is transferred in prisons and how awful the environment is. I wish you the best, though."

Elliott could not be mad at her, but she and others deflated his spirit. He was a free man, exonerated of the ghastly crimes, and yet he remained a villain in some women's eyes. That hurt. He had to move from the D.C. area because his face had become familiar and the connotation was not all good.

He relocated to Atlanta and met Lucy, and his world changed. She was not judgmental. She empathized with what happened to him. She asked questions no else did, like "What did you take from your prison experience? How has it changed you? Do you dream of prison? Have you been institutionalized?"

The questions were asked with sensitivity and genuine curiosity and care, not prying, nosey inquiries. And with each answer, Lucy detected strength in Elliott that was almost overwhelming and increasingly attractive.

His interest in her heightened. She was a woman who did not predetermine who he was and did not judge him when he shared his story. His comfort level with her was high, allowing him to open up to her, and she, in turned, opened up to him.

Elliott knew in three conversations that his dating days—at least at that point—were over. He had found the one woman placed on earth for him. That's what he felt about Lucy.

And he said as much during the reciting of his vows during their wedding:

"I know God is good because He sent you to me, Lucy. The power of love is amazing. Your love validates that I am free. I know you were meant for me…"

Recalling his wedding day increased his desire to call Lucy. But he learned in prison to be patient, and so he instead worked on his Innocence Project presentation until he dozed off after watching *The Newsroom* on HBO. When he woke up to shower and go to bed, he had three text messages.

One was from Tamara, giving him details of the event she wanted him to accompany her to over the weekend. The second one was from Henry that read: "Listen, let's do lunch this week. I'm open." And the other was from Lucy: "I picked a day for lunch. How is Wednesday?"

Elliott froze. He knew Lucy as well as anyone. She would not reach out about lunch if she did not have an interest in trying to rekindle something with him. The text arrived six minutes before he read it. He waited another ten minutes before responding, an attempt to not seem anxious.

"Wednesday should work," he texted back. "Can I confirm tomorrow?"

Wednesday was open and he asked a question to get her to send him another message in an attempt to start an electronic dialogue. It worked.

"Sure, that's fine," Lucy texted back. "If that's not good, I understand. No pressure."

"I didn't even know you knew how to text," Elliott responded.

"I don't have any limitations," she fired back.

"Really? Since when? I recall your cooking skills being a little lacking."

"That was then, this is now," she answered.

"Gotta love progress," Elliott typed.

"And technology," she responded.

"And everlasting connections," he wrote. He hesitated before pushing *Send*. But he was nothing if not bold.

"We do have that, don't we?" Lucy wrote back. "No denying."

Elliott's heartbeat increased. He was as much excited as he was stunned to have substantive, pleasant communications with his former wife.

"I have not been the same without you," he wrote. Then he erased it before sending. He decided it was too strong of a declaration.

"You remain close to me over these last there years, even though we didn't see each other or talk much," he sent.

On the other end, Lucy sat in a yoga position, anticipating Elliott's responses. It took her two years to understand why infidelity ruined their marriage and another year to summon the courage to let Elliott know she wanted it back, wanted him back.

She deduced that the cheating was a cry for attention, not a declaration of misplaced love. It was meaningless, and not enough to detonate a family that was close and loving and thriving.

When the marriage came to a head and all the emotions poured out, Elliott apologized and told Lucy the family was bigger than the indiscretion. While she intuitively agreed with him, the hurt and disappointment ruled, and something in her believed the breach was too much to overcome. So, she insisted Elliott leave.

Upset, Lucy wanted to tell their kids why the family was splintering. Elliott pleaded long and hard for her to agree with him to never divulge the specifics of what had taken place. "Honor is at stake here," he said to Lucy. "I don't want that to be blemished."

Lucy reluctantly agreed, and despite Danielle's and Daniel's efforts to get details, the parents held to their promise.

"I know," Lucy texted Elliott. "It has been too long. It will be good to catch up with you."

"I feel the same way," he responded. He set down the phone and rushed to the bathroom to relieve himself. He thought of taking the phone with him, but he did that once and it slipped out of his hands and into the toilet. It was ruined.

When he returned, Lucy had sent another missive.

"I must warn you," it read. "I don't look the same."

Elliott said aloud. "Oh, no." He knew that meant she had gained weight.

"How so?" he texted.

"I don't use chemicals in my hair anymore," she responded. "I have been natural for about nine months and I love it. I feel free, in a sense."

Relieved, Elliott was prepared to respond. Before he could, Lucy sent another text.

"You thought I was gonna say I had gained weight, didn't you?" she wrote.

And Elliott laughed. *She knows me so well*, he thought.

"You set me up for that," he responded. "But you're right. You wearing an Afro now?"

"Like Pam Grier back in the day," she wrote. "No, just kidding. I wear locs now."

"Oh, wow," Elliott answered. "You wear dreads. Interesting."

"I don't wear 'dreads.' I wear locs," she insisted.

"Aren't they called 'dreadlocks'?" he wrote.

"Many people do. I say 'locs,'" Lucy answered. "Dread has a negative tone, don't you think?"

"I guess you're right," Elliott said. "Never really thought about it."

"What if I said you wear a dreadcut? How would that sound to you?"

He could not tell if she was offended or if she was being matter-of-fact. More than once his words in text messages were interpreted incorrectly, causing drama.

"I hear you," he responded. "I hear people with locs calling them dreadlocks. But I get your point. Locs it is."

"Thanks," she replied. "Dreaded weather. I dread going to work. The movie was dreadful. All negative."

He knew then it was a sensitive subject for her. So, he made sure to calm her.

"I can't wait to see them. I'm sure they are beautiful," he said.

"They are. I love them. I can swing them in the air if I want. LOL."

"Swing on," Elliott responded.

"Well, I'm going to read before I go to sleep," she wrote. "I will look to see if you can fit me in Wednesday.

"One question before we end this?" Elliott asked.

"Sure."

"Why do want to see me? You have avoided me for a long time, wouldn't even talk to me. Suddenly a phone call, long conversation, text messages and now lunch? That's a lot."

Lucy was expecting that question, but was hoping she would not have to address it until Wednesday. It was logical that he would go there.

"Well, I will give you the full story whenever I see you," she wrote. "But let's just say I realize it is important to embrace the people who really love you."

"I'm glad you know I'm among them," Elliott wrote back.

"Thank you," she texted.

"Thank YOU," Elliott responded.

CHAPTER FOURTEEN
Up High

The idea of the Monday blues never registered with Elliott. It was a new day, one to be thankful for and to savor. The start of the week was the day in which he visited the two car dealerships he owned: one in Cobb County and the other near Midtown Atlanta.

He enjoyed his summer experience when he was a kid at that Virginia dealership…until his arrest. When he won his $2.4 million civil suit, he put away $1 million in an interest-bearing account. He used some of the remaining money to purchase real estate and eventually two small auto dealerships, among other things.

Elliott had no financial concerns. He was debt-free after buying his place at the W Residences and paying off his Mercedes-Benz S550. But he was proof that financial freedom did not necessarily translate into complete happiness.

"Your need to date younger women and to keep yourself busy is an attempt to prevent yourself from focusing on the reality of your life," Dr. Nottingham told him during his session that afternoon.

"Which is?" Elliott asked.

"The reality of your life is that you are unfulfilled because you do not have the family life you expected to have, that you *need* to have," she said. "And that's normal. To not have what you once coveted can be difficult to face."

"But," Elliott said. "I know there's a 'but'."

Dr. Nottingham smiled. "But not facing it can be replaced by irrational behavior."

"What's my irrational behavior?"

"Irrational behavior is subjective," she answered. "For me, in your case, it's pursuing young women less than half your age. It's going out every chance you can get, to places your peers would not think of going."

"It doesn't feel irrational to me, Dr. Nottingham. It feels right. I feel like I'm getting back what was taken from me."

"Really? That's what you really think?"

"Okay, well, let me ask you something then," she said. "I was going to wait to ask this at another time, but this is the perfect time. If you believe dating young girls and frequenting places young people frequent is helping you get back what was taken from you when you were incarcerated, why aren't you developing friendships with twenty-something young men? Why don't you go to sports bars with twenty-somethings? Why don't you go to strip clubs with younger men? Why don't you dress like you're their age? That's what young men do and you missed out on that."

Elliott looked at her. Then looked away.

"See, Elliott, if you were truly trying to recapture your taken-away youth, why not recapture all of it?" she added. "If you did those other things men in their twenties did, then maybe it could be considered recapturing your lost youth. But you're only focusing on one aspect of life in your twenties: women. And that says to me that you're more about avoiding what's missing in your life than trying to fill it with what you didn't get to experience."

Elliott was speechless. What she said made so much sense. He never considered the other aspects of being in his twenties. He had no interest in gaining a friend among young men. There was nothing in common.

With younger women, the common thread was companionship. There was no age limit on companionship and how you get it or from whom you receive it.

"So," he finally said, "I'm just a dirty old man?"

"Well, I'm older than you, and I don't consider myself an old woman—so that's not it," Dr. Nottingham said. "What you are is a normal man who has been confused about how to move on after losing his family. Your love for your wife is evident. So, you have thought the best way to not think about her is to be involved with people who are not likely to remind you of her."

"Here's the thing, though," he said. "She called me yesterday. She eventually told me that she misses me, always loved me and wants to see me. She asked me to meet her for lunch on Wednesday."

"How do you feel about that?" the psychiatrist asked.

"I feel great about it," he said. "But, to be honest, I did think to myself: Why am I so accepting of her after she basically ignored me for three years?' What does that say?"

"What do you think it says?" Dr. Nottingham offered.

"I need you to figure this one out," Elliott said.

"You should try first, don't you think?"

"Well, maybe I was so accepting because I want her approval. When things got ugly at home, she insisted I leave. She rejected me. I want to get past that rejection."

"You should be sitting in my chair," she said, smiling. "Very good, Elliott. So, now that you know that, what do you do?"

"My instincts say to do what I need to do to remove feeling rejected."

"I see," Dr. Nottingham said. "And how do you do that? How far do you go? At what point is rejection rejected?"

"I don't know. I guess I'm going to have to feel that out. I will know when."

After his session, Elliott called Lucy, who did not answer. He left a message: "Hey there, how are you? This is Elliott. Do you notice that the kids never leave messages when they call? It must be an age thing. They tell me that I see that they called and that's enough. Anyway, Wednesday is good for lunch. Let me know when and where and I'm there."

He jumped in his car with intentions to head toward Midtown from Buckhead. He called Daniel.

"Got a question for you," he said. "First, how are you?"

"I'm good," Daniel said. "What's wrong?"

"Nothing. Where's your shadow—I mean, your sister," he said, laughing. Daniel laughed with him.

"I'm out on assignment for my internship. Danielle is taking a golf lesson at John A. White Park. What's going on?"

"First of all, I'm glad you answered the phone; that's a big deal. Thanks," Elliott said. "Second, I wasn't sure whom to call or if I should call you. But I'm going to lunch with your mom on Wednesday. Anything I should know?"

"You're going to lunch with Ma? Why?"

"I'm not sure. She called me yesterday and—"

"Ma called *you?* Are you serious?"

"Daniel, can you help me?"

"I don't know what to tell you," he said. "She never talks about you. She literally never talks about you."

"Well, what's been going on in her life? I'm trying to figure out why this is happening," Elliott said.

"I don't know what to tell you," Daniel said. "And, no disrespect, but you really expect me to help you if I did know something?"

"Yes, because I'm your father and I'm asking you. That's why," Elliott said.

"Dad, I'm sorry. I don't know what to tell you," Daniel said.

"She has been the same as far as I can tell. She hasn't been dating anyone. She's been the same."

"Okay," Elliott said. "Maybe she just wants to finally be friends after so long."

"Come to think of it, something did happen," Daniel said. "About two weeks ago, I didn't have to go to work until the afternoon. I came downstairs in the morning and she was dressed up, about to go out. It was a funeral. The mother of one of the families she covers on her job died. Don't know how, but it was sudden. She was sad. She said, 'I visited her home that morning. Talked to her. She seemed fine.'

"She was devastated, Dad. She said, 'I'm supposed to help people as a social worker.' Maybe she's thinking if something happened to you and you all didn't at least become friends again, she'd have regrets."

"Yeah," Elliott said. "That could be it."

"You didn't think it was a romantic thing, did you?" Daniel asked.

"I don't know what it could be," he said.

They hung up and Elliott returned Henry's call from Sunday. Turned out that he was at Lenox Square mall, and Elliott turned around and met him at Bloomingdale's. He was all right with going to that mall on a Monday, but the word was that Saturday was the day gay men used it as a meeting post.

"If you're straight, you do not want to go to Lenox on Saturday," a woman told him. "They are everywhere."

Elliott was not homophobic, but before Henry's revelation, he was as close as one could be without officially being one. So, he stayed away from the mall on Saturdays. When he caught up with Henry at the department store, they slapped hands and hugged like men do. Elliott, for all his accepting of Henry's lifestyle, was not completely comfortable being physically close to a gay man.

He, in fact, was uncomfortable as they walked the length of the mall toward the restaurant Prime. He noticed gay men walking together and straight people looking on as if offended. His mind played tricks on him; he thought people looked at him and Henry as a gay couple. And he started to sweat.

Henry did not notice and tried to carry on a conversation. "How did it go with your kids the other night?"

Elliott heard him but he was too busy trying to act like he was not with Henry.

"Hey, man, did you hear me?" Henry grabbed Elliott by the arm and he pulled away. "What's wrong?"

"Man, this is crazy."

"What?"

"Nothing. I mean, I'll talk about it when we sit down."

The five-minute walk down the mall and up the escalator to Prime seemed like a marathon to Elliott. He had accepted Henry as his friend, but they had not spent much time together beyond meeting out at a bar.

At the hostess stand, Elliott said, "Can we have a table in the back?"

"Why the back?" Henry asked.

"I don't know," Elliot said. "Never mind. I'm good wherever."

They were seated in a booth in the center of the restaurant, to Elliott's chagrin.

"What's up with you?" Henry asked.

"I have to be honest," Elliott said. "I almost panicked in the mall. I felt like people were looking at us as a couple."

"What?" Henry was appalled. "How did you get that?"

"I know what this mall is like on Saturdays," he said. "And I saw some gay men just now. It made me feel like people thought we were gay, too."

"You are trippin'," Henry said. "Do I look gay? Do you look gay? What does that even look like? Were we hugged up? So why would anyone think we're gay?"

"But you *are* gay," Elliott said.

"You only know that because I told you. I'm sure you know every gay man does not have feminine traits. Right?"

"Man, this is hard," Elliott said. "You know how I feel about you. But…"

"But what, Elliott?" Henry asked. "I'm not asking you for sex. I'm asking you to be my friend as we have been for about fifteen years."

"And I'm that; I want to be that," Elliott said. "But it's awkward. It is. I can't lie to you. You're the same person you have always been. And maybe we should talk about it now because after your son… passed, we never talked about it. We tried to carry on."

"What's there to talk about?" Henry asked.

The server came and they ordered sushi. Elliott ordered a French Connection: Courvoisier and Grand Marnier. The woman hung around, clearing place settings that would not be used, and Elliott waited for her to finish and leave before he continued.

"I'm sorry, man," he said. "Waiters eavesdrop. Last thing I want is for her to hear our conversation and tell people we're a gay couple."

"You have a problem with gays or a problem with your sexuality," Henry said.

"No, I don't. Or maybe I do have a problem with gays," he said. "I admit it. No, wait. Here's what I have a problem with—and I can say this to you because you're my boy and you want me to be honest, right?"

Henry looked at him.

"What I don't like about most or some gay men is that they fake like they're real men, dating women, fucking women, even marrying like you did and having kids…when they really want dick," he said. "I'm not trying to be crass or insensitive, but that's how I feel—and a whole lot of other people, too."

"Man, you're a piece of work," Henry said. "You go around at sixty-one fucking twenty-year-olds and you want to judge somebody?"

"Hold up, don't get on me and avoid my point," Elliott said. "I love you like a brother. But I don't have any respect for you messing with women and even having a child and you really are gay. What the hell is that about?"

Henry fumed. But he believed his friend deserved an answer, if only because Elliott was there to help him cope after his son's death.

"Listen, it's hard to explain," Henry said. "I'm not looking for sympathy when I say this. And it's no excuse, either. The reality is that I grew up in a family of men. Three brothers. All my first cousins were boys. We played sports and when we got older, chased girls and were basically regular boys. But I always had a different feeling about boys. It wasn't an attraction, at first. It was weird because I wasn't sure what was going on.

"Society, the way it is, told me to date girls; that's what boys or men do. So I did. Around high school, I started identifying the feelings I was having. I knew what was going on with me. It came to me, like the light bulb comes on. There was a guy named Art Procter. I liked him. He wasn't the best looking guy or the most muscular guy. But in the tenth grade, I felt attracted to him."

Elliott leaned back with a frown on his face.

"Don't get squeamish now. You asked. Anyway, it was like Art could read my mind. He knew I was attracted to him and he was attracted to me. One day, he told me as we were leaving the cafeteria: 'You like me, don't you?' And I punched him in the face. I was sent to the principal's office because a hall monitor saw it.

"The principal asked me why I hit him and I couldn't say. I wouldn't say. And he wouldn't tell what he said to me. I ended up apologizing to him and had some kind of punishment that I can't remember right now.

"But that was the beginning. But who could I tell? All of my friends were homophobic. They all used slurs and laughed at the guys who they thought were gay. I joined in with them because I was scared that they would think I was gay. Even though I didn't look it, I *felt* it, and I walked around feeling like people could see it on or in me, if you know what I mean. To be gay in my family was akin to signing up for a firing squad. My dad was an outright gay basher. We can start right there. And what do you think my brothers were and his brothers and my cousins? My dad passed down to us to be the manliest of men.

"To uphold that expectation, I did all the things straight men do. I had girlfriends. I played sports. I ridiculed gay people. I did every single thing I could to throw off anyone to ever think I could not be straight. I overcompensated. And Elliott, it was the worst thing in the world, the worst feeling. I was trapped inside my own body. You actually might be able to relate to it in this context: When you were in prison for, what, twelve years for a crime you didn't commit, you told me you had to adopt to the situation and act as a hardened criminal so hardened, crazy criminals would not bother you.

"So, you stabbed a guy and you talked shit and you postured for survival. It was like that for me, sort of."

"Wait, that's bullshit," Elliott said. "I was in prison for something I didn't do. I did what I had to do to stay alive and, ironically enough, prevent being fucked by a man. That's different from fooling women into thinking you're straight and, in one case, having a baby. See, that's the problem right there. Forget everything else. Forget that people believe it's unnatural and an act against God and whatever.

"To risk the health of a woman and to play with her feelings like that… Yeah, I have had sex with girls much younger than me. But it was straight up. No lies. No deceit. That's where you'll lose any discussion on this. This down-low shit is crazy and wrong. And we probably shouldn't have even started talking about this because it's pissing me off and making me feel differently about you."

"You want to talk about bullshit? That's bullshit," Henry said. "You are fishing for an excuse to run. It's cool. I'm really not surprised. You're totally insecure about who you are so you fuck around with young girls and you worry you'll be perceived as being gay by being seen with someone gay…even when nobody sees me as gay. How weak is that?

"Elliott, if you're my friend, then you're my friend. My sexuality should not matter. All the things we have done together over the years. The golf trips. The parties. The talks while you were going through your divorce. So much shit. And you're basically telling me that was all bullshit because I don't like women?"

"I'm telling you it was bullshit for you to not tell me you like men," Elliott said. "Look, I know it would have been hard to do, and—"

"And I would have gotten what I got from you when I did tell you: name-calling and disappointment."

"That was reactionary," Elliott said. "You gotta give me a pass on that. Not many men have experienced hearing that from their boy. It's a shock to the system, and, really, a slap in the face. Think about it, Henry: I fucking introduced you to women I knew. *Friends.* And unless you lied, you slept with at least two of them."

"I lied," Henry said. "Give me some credit. I could not, in good conscience, do that to people you knew."

"Thank God," Elliott said.

"They wanted me to sleep with them, but I kept coming up with excuses," Henry said.

"Like what?" Elliott wanted to know.

"With one girl—I believe it was Gloria—I was making tea before we were going to bed," Henry explained. "She was waiting for me in the bedroom. And then I screamed. She came running in. I was on the floor, holding my crotch, saying I spilled the hot water on myself. I poured water on the floor to make it look legitimate. So, I pretended I had scolded myself so I would be unable to have sex with her.

"And once I got through that situation, I faded away from her. It was the same trick with all of them; I had to do something to keep them away."

"That's pathetic," Elliott said. "Sad. And you didn't do that all the time because you got someone pregnant. Did your son know you were gay?"

"I was going to tell him," Henry said. "I was going to tell him to be proud of who he is and to stand tall, whatever his sexuality. We never had that conversation."

Elliott sipped his drink.

"Well, I don't know what to think of this conversation, Henry," Elliott said. "I will always be sorry about your son. No parent should ever have to bury his child. I would be devastated. I know inside you're still crushed."

"I will never be the same," Henry said.

"Does his mother know about your sexuality? Did you tell her?" Elliott asked.

"I told her right after I told you," Henry said. "She didn't take it so well. She doesn't talk to me to this day. Other than around the time of the funeral, I did not exist to her. She's worried about HIV, but I have been tested time and again. I'm good."

"Look, Henry, I'm not trying to make you feel bad," Elliott said. "I'm just saying that—and I'm sure you probably heard this—the perception of Atlanta as the 'San Francisco of the South' because of guys like you who hide your sexuality and bring other people— women—into the mix. That's just plain wrong.

"Yes, she's worried about HIV. But it's the deceit that hurts her the most. I'm sure of that."

"I apologized to her and that's all I can do," Henry said. "I didn't know what to do. I loved her. But we got to the point of sex because I had to continue the charade."

"Here's my public service announcement that you can turn into your own," Elliott said. "Now that you're sort of officially in the gay community, why don't you all call for transparency? Stop with the playing straight roles and getting women involved, getting married. That's sick.

"My friend, Nia, told me six weeks ago about meeting a guy who was not, you know, so-called 'gay-looking.' She's beautiful and he was a professional, a doctor or stockbroker or something. He invited her out a few times, but he didn't make a move. Some guy at the restaurant where they met told Nia that the man was gay. She was shocked because she said he didn't look gay.

"Anyway, she asks the guy and he says 'Yes.' And then he proceeds to tell her his boyfriend is a big-time lawyer who is married."

Henry jumped in. "I know where you're going with this."

"Let me finish," Elliott added. "So, the guy tells her he's interested in becoming her friend because he needs her to attend events with him and pose as his date around the city to prevent people from thinking he's gay. She would be his 'beard' and he'd pay her to play this role. If I didn't know her, I would have thought she was lying. That's some crazy shit.

"So that's the kind of thing you can be a leader in changing. If you're gay, be gay. Be proud of it. Nobody cares. Just don't fuck around with women to try to fool people into thinking you're not gay. That's all I'm saying."

"You make sense, but you're also being idealistic," Henry said. "You think men have been in the closet because we wanted to be there? Because it's fun? No. It's torture. It's sad. We live in a country where your sexuality means so much to *others* that you are not comfortable being who you truly are. You'd rather live in pain and deceit because you know the truth would lead to more pain and hurt to others. No one wants to sign up for that."

"Well, what happened with you?" Elliott asked. "You told me. What, your conscience got to you?"

"No, my friendship got to me," he answered. "I owed it to you as my friend. And I haven't told everyone. I believed you would not be judgmental. I didn't think you'd high-five me, but I thought you'd eventually appreciate that I was honest with you and even understand and empathize with why I was not up front from the beginning.

"There are a lot of men out here living in pain and fear, Elliott. Some will never come out. They'll live a married life as a father and love their family to their core. But their sexuality, which is a powerful thing, will drive them to men. It's not really a secret society anymore.

"You know what? I have a public service announcement job for you, Elliott. Why don't you announce that you have a good friend who is gay and you're heterosexual and still his friend? That could make other men feel strong enough to embrace their friend coming out because, trust me on this, almost every man out there has a friend or two who is secretly gay. You can believe that, Elliott."

That was enough for Elliott to suspend the debate. The sushi came and they enjoyed their food mostly in silence. Finally, Elliott said, "One more question, if I can. How differently do you feel about yourself having told someone?"

"E," Henry started, "when I say this I am not overdramatizing it, okay? I have never been more at peace in my life. I do my job better. I smile brighter. I feel solid. I miss my son; the anguish of knowing he's gone leaves a hole in my heart that simply cannot be filled. You know, I learned a lot about him at the funeral and since then. His peers have told me how he tutored them or encouraged them when down. A gay young man told me that my son was his only nongay friend, that he didn't care about his sexuality or what people would think of him. My son was strong in his convictions and his life hadn't even really started yet.

"Knowing how he was with people and being honest with myself and you and other people close to me has opened up my world. I lived in fear, Elliott. I was desperate to keep it a secret. I guarded it with everything I had. I know you have been going to therapy, well, I was, too. Talking to someone helped, definitely.

"But getting it off my chest to the people I care about, it was golden. Now, the flip side is the backlash. My brothers and cousins…they are not happy. They looked at me at the family reunion this summer and shook their heads and walked away. One of my country-ass cousins from Louisiana came up to me and said, 'You don't look gay.'

"I said, 'You don't look straight.' And his whole weekend was messed up."

The two friends shared a good laugh.

CHAPTER FIFTEEN
Beep... Beep... Beep...

By the time the evening rolled around, Elliott's conversation with Henry dissolved from his mind. That happened because he was at the opulent restaurant STK, attending an event called Magnum Mondays, and there was an overflow of distracting eye candy.

He rolled in around 8:30 and was astonished to see that the place was packed with beautiful, young people. It had the feel of Las Vegas, with showgirls and high fashion, oversized bottles of champagne served with sparkles sprouting, a deejay and elevated energy.

The week before, Elliott went to The Green Room, a coffee shop/ bookstore in Buckhead, to read and overheard two young ladies at the counter buying the caramel cake and talking about how much fun they had there the previous week.

"I'm sorry," he said to the young women, "I heard you talking about this event. Did you say at STK?"

They looked at him and wondered why it mattered; it was too young a crowd for him. But they answered anyway. "Yes, sir. STK in Midtown, by the Loews hotel," one of them said. "You know where that is?"

"Oh, yeah, I do," Elliott said. "Thanks. Maybe I'll see you there next week."

The girls glanced up and down at him, smiled an awkward smile. One said, "Okay then." Then she giggled.

So it was kismet that he ran into those two young ladies as soon as he entered the building. "Well, hello there," he said to them. It took them a second to place him. "We met briefly at the Green Room. You told me about this place."

"Oh, yeah," one said. She wore a puzzled expression that said, *What are you doing here?*

"Nice to see you," she said, and they walked off, snickering.

Elliott was used to the surprised looks and was unfazed by them. He was in his element.

This is happening on a Monday night? Wow, he said to himself. He made his way to the bar, which was long and up against an off-white-painted brick wall that was dramatically backlit with sweeping art of the same color hovering over it. It was three-deep to get to the actual bar, which did not bother Elliott because he had had that French Connection earlier with Henry. Besides, he was not there to drink.

In truth, he was not there to meet anyone, either. He loved the freedom that came with being out, the noise of conversation and music. It took him away from his existence. Sometimes he liked to be in the mix, feel the energy of the city. If a woman caught his eye, that would be a bonus. Because other women had fallen off as Tamara became somewhat of a fixture, he had room to add another prospect.

He noticed some people he had seen out over the last year or so, men and women. But no one there approached his age.

"I met you before," he said to a young woman who was sitting on a lounge chair with three friends.

"Don't all you men say that?" she responded from her seat, looking up at him.

"You don't remember? Now I'm offended," he said. "We were at Frank Ski's on a Wednesday night. Half off bottles of wine. Frank treated me to some good stuff, and you were there with a girl-friend. I told the bartender to get you a glass and I shared my bottle with you. You don't remember that?"

She perked up. "I remember," she said, rising from her seat. "You have a car dealership or something with cars, right?"

"Elliott," he said, extending his hand.

"Yvette," she said. "This is my friend, Brian."

The men locked eyes. They knew each other, too. But from where?

They shook hands, but stretched their brains to recall how they had met. After a few minutes of cordial conversation, Elliott excused himself. A moment later, Brian came up behind him and patted him on his lower back.

"I remember you now," he said to Elliott. "You were the guy who got smart with me at Compound that night."

Elliott looked away as if to visualize what Brian was referring to. And it hit him. They had had a contentious few minutes when Brian was talking to Nikki, when Elliott returned from the bar.

"Yeah, what's up?" he said. "I do remember meeting you briefly."

"You was talking shit," Brian said, with anger in his voice. Elliott could smell the alcohol on his breath. "You said you were her bodyguard. Well, you need a bodyguard tonight."

"Look, man, I don't know why you're all angry," Elliott said. "But I do know you'd better back up off me."

He surely did not want a fight, but he had been conditioned from prison to not allow someone to get the angle on him and to pro-tect himself by scoring the first punch, a knockout punch. So he positioned himself to do that. If Brian had said the wrong thing or moved the wrong way, he would have been decked.

"Yeah, okay, old man," Brian said. "I'll see you again."

He turned and walked away and Elliott kept his eyes on him until he was at a safe distance. He thought: *I guess I do need a drink.*

He returned to the bar area, but there was such a crush that ten minutes later he still had not made his way close enough to order. His night was blown by then anyway. He had reverted to prison mode in the moment he felt threatened by Brian. Instead of watching women, he watched out for Brian.

Every instinct in him told him to watch his back. And so he soon was uncomfortable among so many people. Many prison stabbings came in crowded conditions, where the attacker could emerge from the crowd from behind to make his assault. Elliott went to the bathroom, but waited at the door before going in to make sure he was not followed. He urinated as quickly as possible, fearing Brian would come in and attack him while he was vulnerable.

After finishing and washing his hands, he decided to leave. It had been a long day and he had a lot to consider. So he searched for Brian as he headed toward the door, but did not see him. Stepping outside into the warm night air gave him a sense of relief, and he let out a big sigh. He had not felt that kind of anxiety about his safety in some time.

His car was parked across the street in an open-air lot. He stood at the corner of Twelfth and Peachtree and watched two attractive ladies exit their car and walk into the spot. He shook his head, as much in response to his relentless interest in women as to their beauty.

He crossed Twelfth Street to his car, using the remote to unlock it as he heard a chime alerting him he had a text message. When he noticed it was from Lucy, he stopped in his tracks instead of entering the car to read it.

Things went dark after that. Brian came up from behind him

and smashed the right side of his head with a tire iron. Elliott crumpled to the ground, his phone and keys dropping a few feet from his body.

Brian stood over him for a moment, looking around to see if anyone witnessed the attack. He saw no one, and kicked Elliott several times in his midsection before the lot attendant noticed his movements from a distance.

"Hey, what are you doing?" he yelled, and Brian fled the scene to a car waiting for him on Twelfth Street. The attendant hurried over to tend to Elliott. He saw a gash on the side of his head and blood flowing down his face and neck. He was scared.

"Please hurry," he said to the 9-1-1 operator. "He's unconscious and bleeding a lot."

In minutes, the police arrived, retrieving Elliott's phone and keys and asking people nearby what they had seen, particularly the escape vehicle. Not long after, the ambulance pulled up, tended to Elliott and whisked him off to Piedmont Hospital, which was minutes away. En route, Elliott's eyes opened and he slowly regained consciousness. He was confused. He did not know where he was. Then he felt his head pounding, and that's when he became alarmed.

The EMS technician spoke to him. "Hey there. You're going to be fine. We're almost at the hospital."

Elliott remained confused. The blow was so exacting that his short-term memory was erased. He closed his eyes in the hope that the pain in his head would diminish as they hurried him out of the EMS truck and rolled him into emergency.

"Can you hear me?" the doctor asked when he arrived in an operating room.

Elliott nodded his head. "Good. I'm Dr. Roland. You have a gash in your head that we have to close up right now. It will be all right. We'll close it, get you some more blood, because you lost some, and get you all fixed up."

He asked Elliott questions about what he was allergic to, past surgeries, previous head injuries, if he were on medication, et al. A nurse looked through his wallet to find an emergency contact number, but there was none. The police provided his phone and she went through it and dialed the last numbers called. Those were numbers for Henry, Daniel and Tamara.

She reached them all and explained what happened. Before long, Elliott was in surgery, where he had ten staples in his skull to close the gash and three ribs tended to.

In the waiting room, Daniel, Danielle and Lucy arrived first and were directed to an area to wait. Danielle cried, even though she had no news about his condition. The police came to the visiting room and questioned the family.

They wanted to know if Elliott had any enemies, if he complained about someone threatening him. "I spoke to him today," Daniel said. "He was happy and hopeful."

One officer told them the parking lot attendant did not see the initial blow, but did see Brian kicking Elliott. He gave the cops a description of the car and one of the valet workers at STK caught some of the numbers off the license plate. Lucy took his business card and shared her information and was told she would be kept up-to-date on the investigation.

After more than an hour of waiting and worrying, Dr. Roland came over. "He's sleeping now. He took a really nasty blow to the head by an iron object, believed to be a tire iron. He's lucky. Maybe an inch lower and it would have struck his temple, and it could have been fatal."

Danielle cried more and Lucy put her hand over her mouth. Daniel listened intently. "But he's going to be fine. Mr. Thomas is in great shape, especially for a man his age, and that is serving him well. We closed the hole in his head with ten staples. Once his head heals, the scar will, too, and it will hardly be noticeable over time. But he does have a concussion, so his head will hurt for a while and he'll have to return for tests.

"He lost a lot of blood, but we're replenishing that. Also, he apparently was kicked several times and suffered three badly bruised ribs. So, he'll be sore for a few days and will be moving kind of gingerly. But we'll manage the pain with medication.

"We're going to keep him overnight to monitor his head and make sure no more damage was done that we believe. We have to be really careful with the brain. He should be discharged tomorrow afternoon if he tests out okay. I would say in the next thirty minutes we will have him moved into a room and you can go and see him."

"Wow, this is crazy," Daniel said as the doctor left. "I was just talking to him about your client, Mom, who you spoke to the day she died."

"That's exactly what I thought about," Lucy said, "because I texted him tonight around the time this happened."

They sat back down and looked up at the TV that was set on CNN. President Obama was speaking from earlier that day, but the sound was muted. There was relief that Elliott was okay.

Henry came hurriedly into the emergency room next. Lucy noticed him because he wore the same Atlanta Hawks red T-shirt he wore when she last ran into him, at Philips Arena the previous month at a playoff game.

He hugged Elliott's ex-wife and kids. "What the hell happened? I was just with him today. We had lunch."

They explained what the doctor had shared. But they were curious about a friend Henry had with him. It was an obviously gay man who stood off to the side. No one said anything, but Henry noticed them glancing over in the man's direction.

So, Henry waved him over. "This is Harold," he said, introducing him. "We were finishing dinner over at Einstein's, which isn't too far from here."

Daniel's attention rose and suspicions were confirmed. Einstein's was a restaurant in Midtown, the area of town where many homosexuals lived. That restaurant, on Juniper Street, was a favorite spot for gays in Atlanta.

They all sat down, with Harold, light-skinned and soft-spoken, leaving to find a men's room. When he got there, he sent Henry a text message that read: "This isn't the time to bring your personal stuff to this family. I will wait in the car."

Henry was relieved and appreciative of his friend's gesture. But Daniel had questions.

"So, Mr. Henry, I haven't seen you since, you know, the funeral. How have you been?"

"I was sitting here thinking about how much I hate hospitals," he said. "Really, I guess, you either hate hospitals or love them depending on when you come. When my son was born, it was a difficult delivery for his mother, but the doctors were great and he came out fine. I loved hospitals then.

"But to be in Grady that night, and for them to tell me that my son was gone... I hated hospitals then."

It was more of an answer than Daniel expected, and no one said anything. Then Henry went on. "I told your father today, ironically enough, that I would never be the same after losing him. There's a hole in my heart that cannot be filled."

Lucy moved over a seat and rubbed him on his back. "I know,

Henry. I don't even want to imagine. You're obviously a strong man to move on with your life."

"It hasn't been easy. But friends like Elliott and Harold have been very helpful."

Daniel got a little concerned then. He had seen the movie, *Waiting to Exhale*, and recalled the part where the son learned his estranged father was gay. Here was Elliott's friend using Daniel's father and this obviously gay man's name in the same sentence… Daniel wanted to know more. He *needed* to know more.

"So, how do you know—what did you say his name is—Harold, Mr. Henry?" Daniel asked.

Lucy looked at her son with an I-can't-believe-you-asked-that-question look. Danielle looked down at her feet.

"He's also into real estate. Mortgages," Henry said as casually as he could. "We send each other business all the time. He has clients that need homes. I have clients that need mortgages. So it has worked out."

Before they could dissect that answer, the nurse came out to let them know Elliott had been moved into a room. He could have two visitors at a time and for a few minutes each.

"Go ahead, Mom, you and Danielle," Daniel said. "Mr. Henry and I can go next."

They made their way to the third floor and Danielle and Lucy went into the room. The sight of him laid up with his head bandaged, his midsection wrapped and an IV in his arm—in addition to the heart monitor and other machines going "beep…beep… beep" —scared the women. Lucy's eyes welled up.

"Oh, my God," Danielle said when she walked in. "Daddy."

Elliott was awake but groggy and in pain. "There goes our lunch," he said to Lucy.

She smiled. "We just have to move it back a few days, that's all."

"Daddy," Danielle said. She couldn't say anything else; she was so emotional.

"Hey," Elliott said in a low voice. "I'm fine. Give me a week. We'll be on the golf course."

He was trying his best to minimize his condition while, at the same time, fending off immense pain to the head and ribs. So, he pushed the button in his right hand that delivered morphine into his bloodstream.

"I know you're sleepy and probably in pain," Lucy said. "But do you know who did this?"

He lied. "No."

There was only one possible culprit, he had deduced after officers explained what happened to him and where. Brian. He lied to police and Lucy because he had the contact info of the woman Brian was with, Yvette.

When he was told there was no attempt to steal his car, his wallet or even his iPhone, he knew it was all about hurting him, and that meant Brian. Having Yvette's business card was important because he was going to make sure the justice system played out on Brian. *His* justice system.

His time in prison at Lorton served him for this kind of payback. He had long been out of the prison system, but the prison system still resided in him. He became good at suppressing it. Elliot thought of getting Brian back as his ex-wife and daughter stood over him, and Danielle noticed his heart monitor rapidly increasing.

"Dad, what's going on? Your heart is beating so fast."

He lied again. "Was thinking about how lucky I am to see you both at the same time again."

"Just think about getting better," Lucy said. "Listen, we're going to go. The nurse said we shouldn't stay long and Henry and Daniel are down the hall and want to come in for a few minutes."

Elliott nodded his head, but he was fading. The medication and painkiller were taking effect. He dozed off and awoke to Daniel leaning over and talking into his ear.

"You're going to be all right," he said to his dad. "And we're going to find out who did this and get them."

He said the right thing; Elliott opened his eyes. "You goddamn right we are," he whispered to his son.

He looked over and noticed Henry. "How you get here?"

"Cops called me," Henry said. "My number was one of the last numbers you called, so they called me. You don't put a lock on your phone?"

Elliott said, "No need."

"Dad, this is messed up," Daniel said.

"Come here," Elliott said to his son. Daniel leaned his ear almost on Elliott's mouth. "I know who did this. We're going to get him."

Daniel leaned back to look at his father, who had fallen asleep. Daniel's heartbeat raced. But he questioned: *Did his father really know who did it or was it the drugs speaking?*

"What?" Henry said. "What did he say?"

Daniel did not know if he should trust Henry with his father's words. *If I tell him, he might tell the cops.*

So, the son lied. "Dad said he loved me and to not worry."

Henry knew of the strife between Elliott and his children, so he considered what Daniel said important and typical of someone in a traumatic position.

"This room is creeping me out," he said. "Come on. Dad is asleep."

As they took steps to rejoin Lucy and Danielle, Daniel told

Henry that he left his cell phone in his father's room and that he'd catch up to him.

Daniel went back in and woke his dad. When his eyes opened, Elliott said, "It takes me getting bashed to bring the family together."

"I see you're thinking just fine," Daniel said. He moved in closer and spoke in a lower voice. "Did you tell me you know who did this?"

"I said that?" Elliott said, speaking softly. "I thought...I was... dreaming. Yeah, I know the punk-bitch-ass fool who did it."

Daniel had not heard his father speak that way. It was like he had transformed into someone he did not recognize.

"Don't tell your sister or your mom. This is our project. They don't need to know."

What Daniel knew was that his father was serious about getting his payback.

"We gonna get this fool, Dad," he said. "Dad, Mr. Henry is here. His friend Harold is here, too." He wanted to know if his father knew who Harold was. It would give him some insight into who his father was.

"Who's Harold?" he asked.

"He said you met at the funeral," Daniel said.

Elliott nodded off without responding.

When they got back to the waiting room, Danielle was waiting; their mom was in the bathroom. "She said she'll meet us in the car," Danielle said, and they hugged Henry and headed to the parking lot.

In the bathroom, Lucy encountered a young woman who was in the mirror, applying lip gloss. They spoke. Both women looked distressed.

"You okay?" the young woman asked.

"I don't know," Lucy answered. "My ex-husband was admitted here. I think he's gonna be all right. But seeing him in that bed, hooked up to machines and in so much pain, it…"

"It scared you?" the woman asked.

"More than that, it confirmed that I'm still in love with him," Lucy said. She looked at herself in the mirror. "I can't believe I said that, can't believe I'm feeling this way."

"Wow," the young lady said. "Do you think he still loves you?"

"He hasn't said it, but I think he does," Lucy said. "I hope he does."

"Well, good luck. I've got to go see a friend upstairs myself," the woman said, extending her hand. "What's your name?"

"I'm Lucy Thomas," she said, surprising the woman. "And your name is…?"

"I'm Tamara. Nice to meet you."

CHAPTER SIXTEEN
Coming Clean

Tamara flirted with a male nurse who walked her to Elliott's room, even though visiting hours were over and she was not immediate family. "He's my mentor," she told the guy. "I won't be able to sleep if I don't see him… And maybe we could talk about it when you get off. When do you get off?"

"I'm just getting here, so I'm working through the night," he said. "But maybe we could do dinner this week. I'm pretty open."

"Me, too," Tamara said. "You can put your number in my phone after you walk me to his room."

Looking down at her breasts through the V-neck top she wore, the man said, "Definitely."

They got to the room and she stepped back when she saw how Elliott looked all bandaged up. "Here," she said, handing the guy her cell phone. He punched in his name and number.

"You can only stay about five minutes," he said. "I'll come back to get you and walk you out."

Tamara stared at Elliott and nodded her head. The guy left and she slowly approached his bed. She placed her purse in a chair and reached the railing of the bed.

As if he sensed her presence—or someone's presence—Elliott opened his eyes. Neither of them said anything for several seconds. Finally, Tamara said, "So you're not dead?"

"They let anyone in here, I guess," he said.

She smiled. "I'm so sorry this happened to you. The nurse said you have bruised ribs and a concussion."

"It could be worse."

"How did you get hurt? Chasing some young girl?" she joked.

"Cute," he said.

She looked down at his hand to see him pushing the button to provide morphine.

"You're in pain?"

"Take a guess," Elliott replied.

"I'm your only visitor? When are you getting out of here?" Tamara said.

"Maybe tomorrow," he answered. "My kids were here. And Lucy and—"

"Lucy?" Tamara said. "Who's Lucy?"

"Ex-wife."

Tamara knew right away that Lucy was the woman she had met in the bathroom, and she immediately became jealous. Her first instinct was to tell him that they had met. But she decided more could come out of holding back that information. Besides, Lucy told her that she still loved Elliott and wanted him back. That was not information she wanted Elliott to know.

"Okay, good," she said. "I can't stay long."

"I'm sleepy," Elliott said.

"Well, I won't come back since your family will be here tomorrow, I'm sure," she said. "Will you call me?"

"I will. Tamara. Thank you," he said before again dozing off.

She rubbed his hand and stared at him as he slept. It was in that moment that she believed she had feelings for Elliott. She wanted him to get better and was sorry he was in distress. She concluded that meant she cared for him, not just about him.

When he got better, she was going to profess her interests in being more than a fuck-buddy. Their age difference was significant and it was real. But she enjoyed her time with him and she learned something each time they were together and that's all she could ask for in a man.

Taking him around her family would be an issue. She knew that. So would introducing him around her coworkers and most of her friends. They would wonder if she had lost her mind. But she left the hospital saying to herself that she would figure that out later.

Elliott, meanwhile, woke up in the middle of the night scared. He dreamed he was back in prison, in the "hole," which was solitary confinement in a space that was small, dingy, filthy and lonely. He had done three months in the hole in Lorton, and was traumatized by the isolation.

He told Henry once, "Three months in the hole is torture. Not like water boarding or sliding bamboo sticks under your fingernails. It's mental. You lose some of who you are each day. You count the minutes, and the minutes move slower than any other time in your life. Getting out of the hole is like winning the prison lottery. A regular cell seems like a room at the Four Seasons."

Dreaming of being in the hole and waking up with a busted head and ribs in a hospital room messed with Elliott. He got cold to the point of shivers, but was too foolishly proud to call a nurse for more covers.

He wanted to go back to sleep, but feared his previous dream would resume. So he lay there thinking of fun events in his life, with the hope that they would influence his dreams.

Elliott thought about dancing with Lucy at a New Year's Eve party to bring in 2008. She wore a black dress accented with chiffon and he was distinguished in a tuxedo for the first time. The ballroom at the Mandarin Oriental in Buckhead was adorned with black and silver balloons. Champagne flowed. And around three hundred people—mostly couples—partied in high style.

He brought that night to the forefront of his mind because it was one of their most fun times together. The kids were at Lucy's sister's home, and he and Lucy had a room at the hotel, meaning they could get sloppy drunk if they wanted and stumble their way to the elevator and go to their room.

When midnight came, he kissed Lucy with such passion and love that she was astonished. "You either love me or you're glad it's a new year," she said.

"I love you," Elliott told her.

They shut down the party, dancing so hard that they both left the ballroom with their shoes in their hands. Before they hit the elevator button, he grabbed his wife by her arm and led her to the men's room.

"Are you serious?" she said. "Elliott. What are you doing?"

He made sure the room was empty and he turned Lucy around and pulled up her dress. She went with the flow and pulled down her thong and he unfastened his pants and let them fall to his ankles.

She leaned over so he could enter her and they had deep, passionate sex in the men's bathroom of the hotel. They could have waited another three minutes to do so in their room upstairs. But the adventure provided a sexy edge that was far more memorable.

He almost managed a smile while reminiscing, and then fell back to sleep. It would be nearly 7 a.m. when he awoke, as the nurse took his blood pressure and the doctor came in to examine him.

Elliott's head still hurt, but the pain was less intense. His ribs were really sore, making getting out of bed a chore.

"Doc, how long before the pain subsides in my ribs?" he said. "I'm scared to take a big breath."

"It's going to be that way for another day or so," he said. "You'll feel some gradual relief. But stay on top of the pain medicine to manage it as best you can."

The doctor told him he could go home in the afternoon.

"What?" he said. "Doc, I have insurance. I'm not feeling like I'm ready to go home just yet. This isn't a plush hotel, but with the pain I have, I'd rather be where I can be treated than at home."

"Never heard of someone wanting to stay in the hospital," he said. Elliott was taken aback…and angry.

"Doc, forgive my French, but I don't give a rat's ass what you ever heard of," he said. "I know I don't have to go home when I don't feel ready and you can't rush me out. I know that's what y'all do now. A woman has a baby at seven a.m. and you want her out of the hospital by seven p.m. Guy has hip replacement surgery and you try to get him out in two days. Bullshit like that.

"I ain't going for it."

"Calm down, Mr. Thomas," Dr. Roland said. "You're getting the wrong idea. Of course, if you're not ready to go, you shouldn't go. I wasn't trying to rush you out. With the injuries you sustained, the usual time of discharge is after one night."

"Hey, that's all well and good," Elliott said. His anger heightened the more he talked. "But—and maybe not you, but in general—these hospitals and insurance companies suck when it comes to customer service. You said it yourself: No one wants to stay in the hospital. So when someone says they're not ready to go, he should not hear the doctor talking about he never heard of someone who wants to stay."

Danielle stood in the doorway listening. She knocked on it before Dr. Roland could respond. "I see you're doing better, Daddy," she said. "What's going on?"

"Nothing," Dr. Roland said. "Your father wants to stay another day and we're going to accommodate him."

"I didn't say stay another day," Elliott jumped in. "I said I wasn't ready to go home today. That could mean tomorrow or it could mean next week. Either way, you're getting paid so what's the difference?"

"Daddy, I'm sure they don't want to rush you out," Danielle said. "If you're ready to go, you should go. Someone else might need the room."

"Well, there isn't even someone in the bed next to me," he said.

"That's going to change," Dr. Roland said. "Someone will be in here later this morning. Meanwhile, you seem to be doing much better. I will see you a little later."

When the doctor left, Danielle turned to her father. "I can't believe you went off on him like that. He's got to take care of you. It's like being mean to the waiter at a restaurant. You wait until *after* you have your food before you start talking trash."

Elliott laughed. Having his daughter there put him in a better mood. Their limited time over the years bothered him. Now here she was there first thing in the morning back at the hospital, looking after him.

"Why are you here so early?" he said.

"I don't know," Danielle said. "Well, partly because I remember when you were in the hospital before, dealing with cancer. You didn't like to be alone."

"I was scared to be alone then," Elliott said. "I felt like if I didn't feel well they might pull the plug on me. I needed someone there to say, 'No, don't give up on him.' This time, I have a headache like you wouldn't believe."

"You probably made it worse by lecturing the doctor," Danielle said.

"I'm hungry. Hospital food is one reason to go home," he said. "But my ribs are so tender that I'm almost afraid to swallow."

"Daddy, why did this happen?" Danielle asked. "This is crazy. And where were you going?"

"I was going home," he said. "I was at the restaurant, STK. Some guy came up behind and blasted me."

"I know, but why?" she asked. "The police said it was personal because he didn't take any money or your phone or anything. And he kicked you after you were already knocked out."

"You want me to explain why someone stupid does something?" Elliott said. "Why does someone rob a person with a gun, get the money or whatever it is they want, but still shoot the person? Who can explain that? No one. So I can't explain why someone would knock me out, much less kick me when I'm unconscious."

Danielle had not spent a lot of time with her father in recent years, but she remembered that he could become combative when pushed. She also knew that saying "Okay," would slow him down.

"Was your mom here last night?" he asked.

"Yes," Danielle said. "Mommy was here and Daniel and Mr. Henry. Do you remember anyone else?"

He remembered Tamara, too, and was worried that others had seen her. "That's it? No one else?" he asked.

"Were you expecting someone else?" Danielle asked.

"No. Just asking," he said.

"Mom is coming back this afternoon and then Daniel after he gets off work," she said. "We've got it all planned out. Shifts. We know how you can get when you're alone."

"How was your mom? I mean, I haven't seen her but just a few times since the divorce and she sees me like this?" he said. "I looked at myself in the mirror and I look like half a mummy."

"Only for a few days, Daddy," she said. "Mommy was upset, but the doctor made her feel better."

"Do you know we were supposed to have lunch tomorrow?"

"That was the first thing you said to her when we got here," Danielle said.

"What? Really? I don't remember that," Elliott said.

"I have a question: Why were you and Mommy going to lunch?" she asked. "I mean, I think it's great. But it's just a surprise. She doesn't even ask about you. Now you're going to lunch and she's coming to see you at the hospital? What's going on?"

"You're asking me?" he said. "I called Daniel to ask what he knew yesterday. And—"

"You called him, but not me?" she said.

"You were getting a golf lesson, honey," he said.

"Oh."

"Anyway, you don't know that she called me Sunday and texted me and asked me to lunch?" he said. "You didn't know that?"

"No, and I would tell you if I did," she said. "Maybe Mom is bored."

"Ouch," he said.

"I didn't mean it like that," Danielle said. "I should have just said I don't know."

"It's all right," Elliott said. "You know me. I'm tough as nails."

Danielle pulled up a chair and she and her dad talked and laughed and got along as if the time apart did not happen. Elliott's head throbbed and his ribs hurt, but his heart was full. He loved his children, but there was that tender spot reserved for a daughter in a father's heart.

"Daddy, I'm going to miss you when I go to London," she said.

"Well, guess what?" Elliott responded. "I don't know about anyone else, but I've always wanted to go to London. I just never had a reason. Now, I do."

Danielle smiled and her heart was full, too. She was the proverbial "Daddy's girl," and the family breakup had taken a significant toll on how she looked at him and their relationship. She witnessed how broken up her mother was, and decided she would help hold her up, that her father was strong enough to withstand the turmoil.

Daniel's influence was strong, too. But Danielle never fully gave in to shutting off her father as if he did not exist. She secretly sent him postcards from college and letters and generally stayed in touch without it being apparent that she was.

"You've been a light for me," Elliott said. "I know there was pressure to kick me to the curb. But you always did enough to let me know you're still my little girl."

"Always, Daddy," she said and leaned over the rail to hug Elliott.

"Why don't you get in the bed with him like you used to," came the words from Lucy as she entered the room.

"Mommy, don't hate," Danielle said.

"Hate? I don't want to be in the bed with him, okay?" she said. Mother and daughter hugged.

"How's the patient?" Lucy asked Danielle.

"He was a little grouchy at first," Danielle said. "Woke up on the wrong side of the IV, I guess."

"Very funny," Elliott said. "But I'm over it now."

Danielle explained to her mother Elliott's frustration with feeling rushed to go home.

"Well, since you're going to be here, you might as well enjoy it as much as you can," Lucy said.

"How am I gonna do that?" he said.

Lucy went into her bag and pulled out Mariah Carey's CD *The Emancipation of Mimi* and two movies: *Heat* with Robert De Niro and Al Pacino and *The Notebook*, which was one of her favorites that she believed Elliott would enjoy if she could get him to focus on it.

"Look at you, Lucy," Elliott said. "I love the natural hair, the locs.

Beautiful. It allows me to see your face better. In your face, I see what you're thinking, what you're feeling. Remember how I used to move the hair away from your face? I did that to see you but also to see what was on your mind."

"Well, that's my cue to leave," Danielle said. She got up, delicately hugged her dad and then her mom. "I will call later to find out if you're staying past tomorrow. Relax, Daddy. Don't get upset. Stay calm."

The second doctor came in as Danielle departed. "How are you feeling today? You're sitting up a little, which is a good sign. Head any better? How about your ribs? I'm sure they are still in bad shape."

"I feel better, definitely,' Elliott said. "The ribs, though."

"Yes, the ribs," the doctor said. "They are another thing altogether. Could be a few days before improvement. But you'll get there. Meanwhile, the technician will take you for another CT scan to make sure all is good there."

Lucy waited for about twenty minutes in his room as Elliott had the test done. She held her breath as she watched him gingerly get back into bed.

"I don't see you for what feels like years and it's under conditions like this," he said.

"It's fine," Lucy said. "I've seen you looking worse."

Elliott ate lunch with Mariah Carey playing as background noise. "Daniel called me," Lucy said. "He's all fired up about who did this to you. What did you tell him?"

"I told him I didn't know," Elliott said. "I've never been a fighter, and I'm even more mellow at my age. And you can't tell because of the bandages, but I look *good*."

"You were always more lenient about judging your appearance and I was always more honest," Lucy said, laughing. "But your kids said you looked good when they visited you."

"That dinner brought us a long way," he said. "I'm talking to my children again…To *you* again. Which leads to a question."

"The question is, 'What movie do we watch first? *Heat* or *The Notebook?*'" Lucy said.

Elliott was not sure why she wanted to avoid the question, but he went with it.

"You decide," he said. "I'm sure I'll be sleep in the next thirty minutes."

Lucy popped *The Notebook* into her laptop and sat it up on some pillows. Elliot had heard of the movie and knew it was the ultimate love story. *Why is she playing this movie for me to see?* he wondered to himself.

For several minutes, there was no divorce between them. They paused the movie to chat. Lucy made sure he was comfortable and helped him out of bed when he had to go to the bathroom about an hour into the movie. Elliott felt a connection with his ex, something he had given up hope on ever feeling again.

And yet, he would not allow himself to get optimistic. The scope of his personality forced him to look at the conditions under which Lucy was there. He was in pain in the hospital. They built a family together and spent almost twenty years as husband and wife…he was entitled to at least her care when he needed it. He was sure if the positions were reversed he would be there for her on the strength of their past alone, not in an attempt to get her back.

Still, there were moments that were tender. At times, he stared at her as she eyed the laptop. It was as if he needed to make sure she really was there.

"You look good, Lucy," he said at one point.

"Watch the movie, Elliott," she said without looking at him. He smiled and did as told. But the pain was overcome by joy.

The morphine and lack of sleep through the night took over, and

Elliott dozed off at the point in the movie when Ryan Gosling took Rachel McAdams on the canoe trip on the lake, amid what looked like hundreds of ducks. Lucy was disappointed because she really wanted him to see that part; it reminded her of a ride on the lake at Stone Mountain early in their marriage. Like in the movie, they got caught in the rain, but were unfazed by it because they were together.

Eventually, Lucy relaxed in her chair and fell asleep, too. About an hour later, Elliott woke up. The movie was over; the laptop screen was dark. He looked to his right to see Lucy asleep, her head resting on her left palm. The scene reminded him of the countless hours she had spent in his hospital room as he recovered from cancer.

In those times, he never envisioned or even entertained that they would not spend the rest of their lives together.

"Sleeping beauty," Elliott said, waking up Lucy. "I'm the one doped up on morphine. What's your excuse for sleeping?"

Lucy stretched and got her bearings. "Oh, boy, I guess I was asleep, too," she said. "I stayed up kind of late and got up early. But those power naps work. I feel good now. How you doing?"

"Okay, I guess," Elliott said. "The headache is more of a nagging thing than pounding like last night. The ribs? I don't know because I'm scared to move. That's how badly they hurt."

Lucy removed the laptop from the bed and went to the bathroom. When she returned, Elliott was determined to get some answers.

She stood next to his bed. "So, you think you want to go home tomorrow?"

"Yeah, I do," he said. "One more night should do it. Just didn't want to take a chance with a head injury. Could've been a clot or something."

"I can come by after work to make sure you're all right," Lucy said. "I have just two appointments in the morning. I could get there around one-thirty."

That was where Elliott had enough. He pushed the button to send morphine into his system and then came with it.

"All right, Lucy, what's going on?" he asked. "I have been trying to figure out what's on your mind."

Their eyes met and Lucy slowly shook her head. "I don't know what you mean."

Elliott looked at her.

"Let me say that despite everything—divorce, not speaking to you, avoiding you—I never stopped loving you," she said.

Elliott had longed to hear something like that from her for years. He gave her a half-smile and she continued.

"I really didn't want a divorce," she went on. "I felt like that's what you wanted and you would not say it."

"Lucy, that's bull," Elliott asserted.

"No, it's not," she said. "It's what I believed."

"Since when was I unable to communicate exactly what I wanted?" he asked.

"Always," she said. "You're a great communicator about most things. With me, you always hedged toward what I wanted."

"Can I get an example?" he asked.

"When we got together and before we were married, you said you didn't want children," she said. "After we got married, the thought of a family hit me strong. When I told you I thought I wanted kids, you immediately said, 'Okay.' It made me feel like you wanted kids because I wanted kids.

"Then, when we bought our house, you went with my choice. Schools for the kids, furniture, vacation destinations."

"You ever think that I agreed to those things because I actually agreed with you," Elliott said. "I wanted children for the same reason you did: To build a family with you. What do I know about furniture? I trusted you with that. We both liked the same house; that's strange? And if you think about the schools, I expressed my favor to them before you did.

"Still, all that is something different. I told you I didn't want a divorce. You said you did. Totally different from what you're talking about."

"I felt like you wanted it but wouldn't say it," Lucy said.

"Why are we even talking about this?" Elliott asked. "We're divorced because you wanted a divorce, and, to your point, I gave you what you wanted. But my question is: why are you here now?"

"Because, Elliott, I don't think we shouldn't be married," she said.

"That was an awkward sentence," he said. "Edit yourself."

"We should be together," she blurted out.

Before Elliott could respond, the male nurse came in. "I have to check your blood pressure real quick."

Elliott and Lucy looked at each other as the nurse did his business. When he was done, they nodded to him and continued their conversation.

"Lucy, I don't know how to take all this," he said. "I never wanted a divorce. Never. I wanted to work it out. But you didn't. Now, almost three years later, you come back with this, out of the blue. What do you want me to say to that?"

"I know it's out of left field," she said. "But I'm tired of not being honest with myself."

"I hear you and I'm glad you're making that step," Elliott said. "It's important and you should. But as much as I agree with you that we should be together, it's not that simple."

"It can be, Elliott," she said.

"I have seen you about three times now in three years, and because you want to get back together, I should drop everything and forget everything, too?" he asked. "It's not even fair to ask me that."

Frustrated, Lucy packed up her things. "Well, I guess I feel like a fool."

"A fool for being honest about your feelings?" Elliott said.

"That's what I feel like."

"You shouldn't go."

"I can't stay," she said, and walked out. Down the hall, coming toward her was Tamara. They smiled at each other.

Tamara said, "Good to see you again."

"You, too," Lucy offered.

Tamara kept walking. Lucy turned around and watched her walk into Elliott's room.

CHAPTER SEVENTEEN
Bedside Manners

"Tamara, you shouldn't be here, not now," Elliott said as she walked in.

"I had to come by and see how you were," she said.

"You told me you'd call me."

"You remember that? You were in and out."

"My son is going to be up here any minute. I really don't need him to see you here."

"Why are you trying to hide me?"

"Really? I've got to go through this right now, in the hospital? You know damn well what the problem is. You're my kids' friend. They have a problem with that. I'm trying to rebuild our relationship. I can't have you in the middle of that. You shouldn't want to be in the middle of that."

"I don't want to be, but I don't want to be some secret side chick, either."

"I understand and you're not a side chick, whatever that is. Please, Tamara, come visit me tomorrow when I'm home. I can't have any drama in this hospital."

"Well, can I leave these?" she said of the bouquet of flowers she held.

"Put them right there," Elliott said, pointing. "I will call you tonight."

Tamara begrudgingly left the flowers and departed the room without looking back at Elliott. She was perturbed that she had been dismissed. Elliott was relieved. He also was frustrated.

He had grown to enjoy his single life. In fact, the first thought he had after realizing he was so badly hurt was that he would miss the day party Sunday at Shout. Being the old man in the club had become a badge of honor in a sense. He pulled it off. And he was living the life he decided he wanted to live when his marriage ended.

It would help him recapture the years he missed while in prison and fulfill the fantasies of men his age. And as for Lucy, as much as he loved her, she had insisted on divorce and neglected him for years, and he did not feel good about that, no matter how much she meant to him.

"How does Lucy think I'm gonna come back because she said 'Come back?'" Elliott said to Henry over the phone. He blocked out that Henry was gay and focused on the fact that he was his friend.

"Women want what they want," Henry said. "Why do you think some of the ones who seem to be the most upstanding still have affairs? I was in the middle of some crazy stuff with women you would never guess would be scandalous."

"Let me ask you something," Elliott said. "Let me know if I'm going too far."

Henry knew then the discussion would be about his sexuality. "Go ahead."

"Do you miss dating women?" he asked. "I mean, you dated women all your life as you tried to keep your sexuality a secret. Now you don't deal with women anymore. How does that feel?"

"It feels right," he said. "I love women as people. I love their sensitivity and their kindness and softness. But I don't miss the physical part—I'm sure that's what you were talking about."

"So, here's another question then," Elliott said. "What's the difference between dating men and women?"

"You know what? In the end," Henry said, "there isn't any difference. It's all about the person and how you and he or she get along. Simple as that. The values in people don't change based on their sex. It's about the individual.

"Some men are as bitchy as women. And some women are as petty as men."

"So, as soon as I notice a bitchy, petty woman, I know I'm dealing with a lesbian," Elliott joked.

"Man," he continued, "I'm in a situation here. My ex-wife who I love wants to get back together. The young girl I'm dating is cool, but she knows my kids. My kids are coming around, but how will they handle it if I refuse their mom or if I admit to being involved with their friend?

"And how will Tamara handle me basically dumping her for my ex? And how would Lucy receive me dealing with a twenty-five-year-old, a twenty-five-year-old who is a friend of our kids?"

"I can't even keep up with all that," Henry said. "You know what my advice is: Be true to yourself."

They chatted some more, but when Elliott hung up, he could not decide what being true to himself meant. Daniel knocked on the door before coming in, giving Elliott a chance to let that thought go, at least temporarily.

"So what's happening, Dad?" Daniel asked. "How you feeling?"

"I feel like it's great to have family," he said. "Your sister was up here bright and early and your mom left a little while ago. Now you. I feel good about that.

"As for everything else, getting better. Gonna sleep here tonight and go home tomorrow to really heal."

Daniel pulled a chair near the bed. "I saw your doctor down the hall and he told me things are coming along good. You remember what you said to me last night?"

"Perfectly," Elliott said.

"So who was it?" Daniel asked.

"Some guy named Brian," Elliott said. "He's obviously crazy. At Compound one night—"

"Compound? The club?" Daniel interrupted. "You were at Compound? Doing what?"

"Just hanging out."

"Dad, that's crazy. You're sixty-something years old."

"You want to hear about this or not?" Elliott said.

"I do, but…"

"I was at Compound because I was invited to a party," Elliott said. "I met a woman and we started talking. I went to the bar to get us a drink, and when I came back this guy, Brian, was talking to her.

"He acted like he was offended when I came back with the drinks. I told him I was her bodyguard. That was it. He finally left, but he looked at me like he had a problem. But once he left, I never gave him a second thought.

"So, the other night at STK, I saw someone I knew and he was with her. She introduced us and he looked familiar, but I couldn't place him. After I walked away, he came up behind me and reminded me that we met at Compound. Then he threatened me. I told him to back up off me or he'd be sorry.

"After that, I started feeling paranoid because the place was packed and I started to feel like I did in prison, like something bad could happen at any time. So, I left. When I got to my car, a text from your mother came in. I stopped to read it. And that's when he came up from behind me and hit me."

"Dad, what's going on?" Daniel said. "You having a mid-life crisis or something? Compound? STK? I saw you with my own eyes at Vanquish. What are you doing?"

"I'm exercising my rights as a free man to do what I want to do," Elliott said.

"But hanging out at young people's spots is a fail for you," Daniel said.

"A fail?" Elliott asked.

"Yes, a fail, messed up, wrong. We should not be hanging out at the same clubs. That's crazy."

"That's beside the point," Elliott said. "This guy tried to kill me— and for no reason."

"The police said it had to be personal because whoever did it kicked you when you were unconscious. And he didn't take anything."

"Exactly," Elliott said.

"So, how we gonna find him before the police find him?"

"Well, I'm alive, which means the police won't put as much effort into it as they would if it was a murder case," Elliott said. "Plus, they don't know who they're looking for. I do. And I have the contact information of the woman he was with."

"How'd you get that?"

"I met her at Frank Ski's one night when I was drinking wine and she gave me her card," Elliott explained. "I never called her, but I saw her card in a kitchen drawer last week."

"So how do you want to do this?" Daniel asked. "I mean, we find him and I can take care of him the right way."

He stood up and looked to make sure no one was entering the room. Then he raised his T-shirt to expose a gun in his waistband.

"Daniel, why do you have a gun?" Elliott said. He was shocked and concerned. "Why? What's going on?"

"I've got to protect myself and Danielle," he said. "These days, you better be carrying or you're ready to get carried out in a body bag."

"What are you, a tough guy now?" Elliott asked. He had heard it phrased that way in *The Sopranos* and other movies featuring the Mafia and it just came out that way.

"Now?" Daniel said. "You taught me to be tough a long time ago."

"Tough means being able to handle any situation with your mind first and then with your hands, if necessary," Elliott said. "I never, not once, said anything about getting a gun."

"Times change," Daniel said. "You see what happened to Trayvon Martin. That punk George Zimmerman wouldn't have been so eager to get in Trayvon's face if he didn't have a gun. The gun gave him confidence. He started the fight, Trayvon fought back and was kicking his butt and Zimmerman shot him to end the fight.

"That was enough for me. You're not gonna have an advantage over me when we start fighting. You said being tough is using your head. I looked at what happened to Trayvon—and how Zimmerman was found innocent—and I used my head. I got a gun."

"Listen, I hear you on that," Elliott said. "You know where I was when the verdict was handed down last month? At a Hooters. It was a mixed crowd, but mostly white. Black people were angry, white people were happy. That was sad; a kid was dead and they were happy that the guy responsible for his death got off.

"I never looked at it like if Trayvon had a gun, it would have been a fair fight. I looked at it like if George Zimmerman did *not* have a gun, not only would it have been a fair fight—a teenager would be alive."

"So what do you want to do to this guy, Dad?" Daniel asked. "Break his legs?"

"I'm not trying to kill him, I can tell you that," Elliott said. "I'm not a killer. And neither are you. What's this all about? And you're not old enough to purchase a gun. So where did you get it?"

"I know people," he said.

"So I ask again: You're a tough guy now?"

"I do what I have to do."

"And what did you have to do?"

"Dad, you haven't been around the last few years."

"Wait, don't put that out there like it's the truth," Elliott said. "I was always here. You didn't make yourself available."

"I'll give you that," he said. "But things have changed. You left and I had to protect my sister and my mother. By any means necessary."

"Protect them from what? Who?" Elliott asked. "And how were you going to do this? You're not a roughneck. You're not a thug. You grew up in the suburbs and you probably never had a fight in your life."

"You don't know, do you?" Daniel said. "I asked Mom not to tell you, and I guess she didn't."

"Don't play coy," Elliott said.

"I got kicked out of school for fighting," Daniel said.

Elliott's expression told of his shock.

"Buddy said something to Danielle, threatened her," he explained. "I wasn't gonna let that go. So I caught him when he didn't have a bunch of friends around and got with him. After that, every time we saw each other, we fought. So, I got sick of it. Went into East Lansing and found a guy who knew a guy and got me some protection."

"So carrying a gun makes you feel like you're a big man?" Elliott asked.

"I don't just carry it," he answered.

"You used it?"

"I was gonna," he said. "I pulled it out, had it pointed at him. Turned my head to see if someone was watching and he ran. He told the campus police…Eventually, I got kicked out."

"Goddamn, Daniel," Elliott yelled.

"No, no. Don't you start lecturing me on what I should be doing or shouldn't be doing," he said. "If you were around, maybe I wouldn't be so angry… At least that's what the therapist says."

"Damn, everyone is seeing a therapist?" Elliott said. "And if yours told you I'm the reason you're walking around like you're some gangster, then he's a quack."

"Yeah, you don't want no responsibility, right?" Daniel said. "Nothing's your fault? You think it was all good that our family broke up? I guess it was for you since you did exactly what you wanted and said fuck everyone else."

"Listen, I don't care how grown you think you are, you don't use profanity around me, boy," Elliott said.

"I ain't no boy; I'm a man," Daniel said defiantly.

"Boy, watch how you speak to me. I don't care what the situation is, you don't disrespect me."

"See, you're ready to beat me up over disrespecting you, just like you want to get back at that guy who hit you. But you have a problem with me doing what I need to do to protect my sister? That's some bull."

"I think you'd better leave."

"What?"

"If you don't have something to say that makes sense, that shows you were raised properly, then I don't want to hear it, not today."

"I don't even know why I'm here. Ain't seen you but a few times in over two years anyway."

"You're here because you're supposed to be here. But you have anger that has to be dealt with. And, please, get rid of that gun. Nothing good can come from you having it."

Daniel sat down in the chair to the right of Elliott's bed. "How are you on this internship if you've been kicked out of school?" his father asked.

"I didn't tell them and so they don't know," he answered.

"What are you going to do about school? You're going to finish, right?"

"I am, I guess," Daniel said. "Probably go to Georgia State. I will figure it out."

Elliott tried to advance the conversation, but his mind was consumed with seeing a scary side of his son he did not know existed. He had seen young men with baby faces in prison that had the nerve of a killer. He also had met inmates, after listening to their stories, who'd made one mistake that had turned their lives into a mess. He was desperate for that to not happen to Daniel. He believed healing Daniel would heal his family.

"So how has Danielle handled you being kicked out of school?" Elliott asked.

"She was very upset," Daniel admitted. "I didn't come home, though. I stayed there to be with her. She's the only reason I didn't shoot that guy when I really had the chance. I could feel her telling me not to do it."

"Well, keep that voice in your head," Elliott said. "Come here, son."

He extended his hand for Daniel to clutch. His son looked down at it and finally grasped it. "Forget about this guy who hit me," Elliott said. "It's not worth it. I'm not a criminal. You're not a criminal. Whatever role I played in you feeling as you do, I'm sorry.

I certainly never wanted this for you. And whatever is broken, we're going to fix."

"How we gonna do that, Dad? I appreciate what you're saying. I do. But we know what divorce does. It breaks up families. Danielle and I used to feel sorry for our friends that had divorced parents. Then it was us, and it was…it was messed up."

"I know it was tough; that's why I continually tried to reach you and your sister and wrote you letters and e-mails when I didn't hear back," Elliott said. "I thought we could help each other get through it.

"Here's the thing: It's not too late," he added. "Maybe getting my head cracked open was the best thing to happen to us."

"What? How you figure?" Daniel asked.

"Well, I saw you and Danielle and your mother for two days in a row for the first time in a long time. I talked to all of you like we used to talk. I saw through you all being here that you care. I didn't know it, but I needed that."

"Yeah," Daniel said, looking distracted.

"What's wrong?" Elliott asked.

"I don't know how you can let that guy do that to you and let it go," Daniel wanted to know. "You said you know who he is, right? We should at least give him a beat down."

"Let me think about it," Elliott said. He had already made up his mind to not seek retribution. The fear of returning to prison was deterrent enough. He would get the guy's information from Yvette and share it with the police. But he wanted to keep Daniel engaged, so he hedged on what he would do about Brian.

He hedged on what he was going to do with the other major decisions in his life, too.

CHAPTER SEVENTEEN
Home Sour Home

E lliott spent an uneventful second night in the hospital; he did not call anyone or have any more visitors. He read and rested after receiving some good news from the doctors: His bruised ribs were already healing, so the pain he endured was likely to subside quicker.

The headaches Elliott suffered finally stopped being a perpetual nuisance. They would come and go, which gave him long periods of relief.

"See what I mean?" he said to the doctor Monday morning. "I feel almost a hundred percent better than I did yesterday. And staying that extra night here did it."

"Well, I'm glad," he said. "As long as you're progressing, I'm happy."

He had Danielle pick him up and take him home. "You need anything before I go?" she said. She had cooked his dinner—baked salmon, rice pilaf and roasted beets—and gotten him comfortable.

"No, daughter, I'm good. Thank you for you help. As you can see, I'm getting around fine now, so I'll be all right," he said. "But I would like to talk to you for a minute."

She sat on the couch next to Elliott. He said, "I believe getting my head smashed was the best thing for all of us."

"How can you say that, Daddy? You could have died."

"But I didn't, and that's the point," he said. "Because I was in the hospital, I got to see you three days in a row now and your mom and Daniel two days straight. I got to spend most of that time with each of you alone, so we got to talk and be together. I've missed that. I need it. I really need it. I have been functioning without it, but it's not the same as having it."

Danielle nodded her head in agreement. "I've missed you, too, Daddy," she said. "I feel like for the last two years—or whatever it has been—that I have been torn. I communicated with you more than Mommy and Daniel did, but I didn't get to see you, and that hurt. But that's my fault. They made me make a choice. And since I saw how hurt Mommy was and how angry Daniel was—and I knew how strong you were—I tried to help them by being loyal to them."

"It's okay, sweetheart," Elliott said. "Daniel said the same thing. I understand. And you said something that I found out yesterday, which is Daniel's anger issues."

"He blames a lot of it on you, Daddy," she said.

"Yes, we talked about it. He also told me that he got kicked out of college. I know you and he are tight like Krazy Glue. But you've got to tell me when something like that happens. Don't you think?"

"I know. I know," Danielle said in a low voice. "It really ate me up. But he made me promise and Mommy said you would overreact and I don't think we believed it, but we went with it because it was easy."

"Did you know he has a gun on him most of the time?"

"No, I didn't. He told you that?"

"No. He didn't tell me. He *showed* me the gun yesterday."

"At the hospital?"

"Yes. But I'm dealing with it. I'm going to handle it. I had no idea. I had no idea that the divorce would hit him as it did. But like I told him yesterday, it's not too late.

"But what about you, Danielle? How has all this affected you?"

Usually quick to respond, Danielle did not say anything. She looked away, a sign to Elliott that all was not well.

"Well, it has worn on me, to be honest," she said. "It's been three years and I thought for sure we all would have adjusted. But I have tried to help Daniel calm down and Mommy pick her head up. It's been a lot.

"I remember one day last year or earlier this year—I can't remember which—when Daniel and I were at dinner at The Pecan restaurant in College Park. It was our birthday. Some girl wanted to take him out, but he wanted to spend it with me. So we get there and you know it's wonderful, but not that big.

"Everything is fine, until at this table there is a family there— mother and father and two kids—and someone brings a slice of cake over. Well, it was the parents' wedding anniversary. They seemed so happy. But Daniel got so mad.

"He stopped talking to me. And then when he did start again, he said, 'See, this pisses me off. That should be us. Instead, it's you and me here, Mom somewhere and Dad somewhere else. That's not how it's supposed to be.'

"I didn't know what to say. I finally told him, 'Divorce doesn't mean we don't love each other. You know we do.' And he said, 'If Dad loved Mom, he wouldn't have done what he did and he wouldn't have left us. Period.' Needless to say, it wasn't a very good birthday for him—or me.

"Then, maybe two days later, I'm at home with Mommy. We're doing whatever around the house. Daniel was with us, but he took a phone call and went into his bedroom. I said something to her and she didn't answer. So I repeated it and got nothing. So, I turned around and she was leaning over on a counter in the kitchen, crying.

"I didn't know what was going on. I put my arm around her. She said, 'I'm sorry our family is broken up like this.' I was like, 'Mommy, it's been about two years. Everyone is moving on. We're fine.'

"But she wasn't fine. I think Mommy went out on some dates; she really kind of hid that from me. But whoever she went out with wasn't you. She missed you and the life we had."

"I'm feeling like the jerk over here now," Elliott said. "I never got over what we had, but I tried to get over it. I have gone on and lived my life the best way I know how. I had to do something, or else I would have been angry and sad, too.

"But I get it. You have dealt with a lot."

"Too much, Daddy," Danielle said. "That's one of the reasons I even applied to the London School of Economics. I needed to get away and do my own thing, work on me. That might sound selfish, but the same guy Daniel kept fighting is the person who told me, 'We always have to look out for ourselves.' He said, 'That's not selfish. It's important.'

"And that's why Daniel was so mad at him—because I told him Keyon said I should create my own happiness. When I told Daniel I was going to London, he went off. And he blamed Keyon.

"You know how close Daniel and I are. I really don't know what I'm going to do not being with him all the time. But I'm ready to find out."

"Oh, boy. This is something else, learning all I have learned in the last few days," he said.

"I'm not glad you got hurt, Daddy," she said. "But being in the hospital has helped bring us together again. We're not together, but we're all talking, even you and Mommy."

"I know you have to go, but one more question," Elliott said to

Danielle. "What's really going on with your mother? I ask because I hardly heard from her, but then she called me one morning asking advice about men."

"Mommy?"

"Yes, your mom," Elliott said. "It turned out to be a really nice conversation. Then she texted me that night and we ended up setting up a lunch date that was supposed to happen tomorrow."

"Mommy is depressed, Daddy. That's the only thing I can think of. She's still all into her work. But I don't see her enjoying life that much. She's kind of in a rut. And she wants you to help her get out of it."

"Well, there's something else I want to share with you, but we'll do that later," Elliott said. "I won't keep you from where you have to go."

They hugged and Danielle kissed her dad on his face. He melted. "I miss that, girl," he said, smiling as she headed for the door. "I need more."

Elliott retreated to his bedroom after taking a dose of medication and gently lay across the bed. His ribs continued to heal, but a headache came on, and he made his place as dark as he could and lay there in quiet. He figured he brought on the discomfort in trying to process all that was going on around his family.

But as he rested, he thought of Tamara for a while, too. Having a twenty-five-year-old seriously interested in him massaged his ego. He enjoyed the fact that he could attract a younger woman's interest. The other two much younger women he dealt with were more of a passing thing, something to do to see if he could do it.

He saw more in Tamara, and it made him feel youthful and accomplished to have her feel something for him. It was the type of feeling he had hoped for but did not really expect when he decided he would try to recapture the years he missed.

The other young women he met gave him the confidence to continue his old man in the club ways. But Tamara confirmed that he had arrived. She was a catch for any man, and to beat out the much-younger competition was something he did not take lightly.

He smiled to himself that he had so sexually pleased her that she was coming back for more. *I put it down*, he said to himself.

After dozing off, he discovered a text message from Tamara that read: "See, this is what I'm talking about. Ignoring me. That's not cool. Call me soon. Or I will be over there."

He rested his head back on the pillow and thought: *She's bringing too much drama*. He wondered how long he could take her insecurity and threats. And he faced the reality that they had little in common. What could he have with her? By the time she was thirty-five, he'd be seventy-one, and surely of a different mindset of chasing a young woman around Atlanta.

His soul-searching went on for another hour or so—until Tamara called.

"Why can't you call me?" she said when he answered the phone.

"That's some greeting," he said. "And hello to you, too."

"This is not about pleasantries," Tamara said. "This is about showing me respect. You can screw me when it's convenient for you. But you can't do me the common courtesy when I'm looking to check up on you, make sure you're all right?"

For all Elliott had hoped for in Tamara, that rant gave him serious pause. Everything was about her. He was the one who suffered a serious blow to the head. He was the one in the hospital for two days. He was the one recovering. And yet she made it about her.

He quickly prayed his prayer of peace, and she even interrupted that. "I see you don't have anything to say to all that," Tamara interjected. "This is what I'm talking about with men. Whether you're twenty or sixty, you all are all the same."

And that was the tipping point for Elliot. "What the fuck are you talking about?" he started. "I have tried to be patient with you, but you think the world revolves around you? I'm over here in pain trying to get settled, and you calling me up with this bullshit. I ain't got time for it."

Tamara was taken aback. Elliott had not erupted on her, had not shown any signs of the potential for an explosion, so she was thrown off.

"This is why you don't have anyone," she said. "You can't handle when someone cares about you."

Elliott laughed, angering Tamara.

"There's nothing funny," she said.

"No, actually, it is hilarious that you believe you know me and can tell me about myself," he said. "All you know is I fucked you good."

Elliott regretted the words as they flew out of his mouth. "I'm sorry—"

"Why are you sorry?" Tamara said. "You said what you mean. Yeah, you did fuck me good. You fucked me over, that's what you did. I'm sure you're happy. I'm sure you go to the senior citizens home, take out your dentures and laugh with the other old farts about your conquest. I'm glad I gave you a good memory before you keel over, you old fart."

Elliott laughed loudly. "What's so funny?" she said.

"You," he admitted. "That was funny as hell. And I deserved it. I see you're witty when you're angry."

Tamara's fury declined rapidly. "I shouldn't have said all that," she said. "I…"

"It's okay," Elliott said. "I shouldn't have cursed at you. But I do think we probably should back up a little."

"We're just getting started," she said. "I went to the airport today and paid the express rate of three-hundred dollars to get my passport. We have a trip to take, remember?"

"Yeah, I remember," he said. "We have to talk about that—and everything else. I'm pretty much gonna stay in the house much of the week. Maybe you can come over after work tomorrow."

"I was supposed to go to a fundraiser at Bar One. I can come over after that, around nine."

They agreed, and Elliott dozed off to sleep. He dreamed of Tamara coming to visit him. In the dream, she rang the doorbell, and he opened the door to find her in a long, flowing white gown. He opened the door wider and she entered a house that was not his. It was lit with dozens of candles, with wax overflowing.

She walked through the house with Elliott following her, a breeze blowing up her dress. In that moment, he felt attached to her, attracted to her, in love with her.

"Wait, come here," he said. She stopped and slowly turned around. But she was in darkness and he could not see her face. "Come here," he repeated.

She walked slowly forward and into the light. When she became visible, he was startled to see Lucy.

Elliott woke up then and wondered what his dream meant. He had not had a dream about Lucy in more than a year, and all of those were confrontational dreams about their breakup.

He was hungry, so he got himself together and ate some of the meal Danielle prepared for him. His home was quiet: no TV, no music, no conversation. He did not have many times like that, and it allowed him to clear his head.

Problem was, he did not know what to do, but after he ate he sat out on the balcony with a glass of sweet tea and was honest with himself. Dr. Nottingham had told him he'd come to a crossroad in his life, and the way to get beyond it would be by being honest.

"I say this knowing that being honest with yourself is among the hardest things to do," she said. "Our tendency is to justify our behavior. We want to believe what we have done or said or even think is right. We need that. We're comfortable with that. To be honest, we have to face some discomfort. Who wants to be uncomfortable?

"But when you are ready to be uncomfortable, to speak the truth, then you can clear that crossroads and come out on the other side renewed."

And so, Elliott Thomas decided he needed to be honest with himself before he could be honest with his family. He hoped, when all the discussion was done, he would find the person he should be at this juncture of his life.

CHAPTER EIGHTEEN
Mirror, Mirror

His life had been something far different from what he imagined when he was twenty. As he sipped his tea and looked out at the Atlanta skyline, Elliott assessed his life as challenging instead of fulfilled.

Less than four hundred men knew what it was to be imprisoned for crimes they did not commit and eventually be exonerated. His world of hopelessness became one of access. The remnants of that dozen years in prison remained in him, though, no matter how far removed he was from it—in time or space.

Moving to Atlanta separated him from where he was wrongly convicted and the passing years made the memories of prison less clear. But whether innocent of the crimes he was convicted or not, Elliott had been an inmate, and with that came trauma that seeped into his soul.

He discussed with Lucy and his therapist and, to a lesser degree, Henry, how it all impacted him. But as transparent as he tried to be, he could not fully convey the pain and suffering and heartache and misery he endured. There were no good days in his life for nearly twelve years. There were days that were better than others, but none of them rewarding.

And as adjusted as he became over the years—completing his degree, serving as somewhat of an ambassador for the Innocence

Project, finding the love of his life in Lucy and raising a family—he could not escape his past.

When cancer invaded his prostate, he concluded that his life was destined to be lived in distress. He even questioned God. *How can I go to prison for crimes I did not commit, survive that and then get cancer? Why am I being punished this way?*

What he learned was that he had a zest for life, and giving up without giving his best was not an option. He beat cancer. And he admitted while sitting on the balcony that beating prison and beating cancer gave him a feeling of invincibility.

Although he survived his divorce, it was devastating. He had beaten prison and beaten cancer and thought he had life made. The divorce, though, was something else for the depth of the disappointment and because it came when he had relaxed and believed only joy was in front of him. And that was the driving force behind living the life he decided he wanted—he needed to distract himself from his pain.

Trying to recapture years gone by seemed to be the sensible way to do it…at that time.

Battered and bruised and alone with his honest thoughts, he regretted so much, starting with not fighting for his marriage. Lucy bullied him into divorce when the decision should have been theirs to make, not hers. But he had an urgent need to support her, to give her what she wanted. He also concluded that he did not want to be married to someone who insisted she did not want to be married to him.

So he chased young women under the guise of catching up on years missed in prison. The reality was that dating younger women was a safe way of not meeting someone who might remind him of Lucy. Elliott admitted that the years after his divorce were full of pain: pain at how the marriage dissolved and pain that it *had* dissolved.

He and Lucy connected in a spiritual way, a sort of kindred spirits who endured life-altering events when they both were twenty…and came out on the other side scarred, but sane and ready to take on the world.

Many a night he cried with her when she dreamed of being raped or when it became a heavy thought. She could sense any angst in his demeanor and would hug and comfort him before he would express any distress. That's how connected they were.

Trying to fill the void Lucy left was futile, an attempt by a desperate, disconsolate man to distract himself enough to get over it. It didn't work.

He forced himself to dismiss ever reconciling, but now there was his life's only love expressing her desire for him. Elliott could not help but be resistant, though. She took him through hell, refusing to consider not divorcing and limiting her contact with him over the years. He got over being angry with her, but he considered her treatment of him some kind of warped punishment that he did not deserve.

So, while he loved her still, he wondered if he could trust her. He made it through prison, survived cancer and kept his head up after divorce. But to have her lure him back only to shun him again was a prospect that scared him. *That's big*, he thought. *I admit that I'm scared.*

His head began to hurt, and he swore it was about the thoughts running through it and not the concussion. He finished his tea and slid into bed, hoping sleep would alleviate the pain and fear.

It did not work. His head felt okay—and his ribs were better, too—but rejection from Lucy still scared him. He got up and brushed his teeth, and it occurred to him to call on what he felt in prison. He used his fear to become brave. He was so scared of what might happen to him that he became braver than he ever had been to protect himself.

In this case, his bravery led him to call Lucy.

"So how are you feeling?" she asked.

"Not so good."

"Really? What's wrong?"

"Physically, I feel fine. But with you, I don't know."

"What do you mean?"

"I mean we need to talk. But not over the phone. We were supposed to have lunch tomorrow. We should have lunch tomorrow."

"But your head is wrapped up; you want to go somewhere like that?"

"You can come here or I can come to you."

They decided on Lucy coming to Elliot. "You shouldn't be driving or doing much at all," she said.

They hung up, agreeing to see each other the next day, which seemed like a long time for Elliott since he was stuck in the house. He could not go for his daily walk, could not go to Sutra, a club on Crescent Avenue that was popular on Tuesday nights.

The day picked up when Henry came by for a visit. Elliott was glad he did, for in his quest to get to the other side of the crossroads, resolving his feelings about his friend's sexuality became a priority.

Henry brought lunch with him from Mango's Caribbean Restaurant: curry chicken, rice and peas, cabbage and plantains. They sat at his dining room table and chatted about sports. When they were done, Elliott elevated the conversation.

"So, who was this you brought with you to the hospital the other day?"

"Why?"

"Why? Because my son asked me about him. It raised some questions in him that he presented to me."

"Questions like what?"

"Questions like, 'Why is Mr. Henry hanging out with a guy who is obviously gay?' Not exactly like that, but something like that."

"Look, I don't have to get your approval for who I spend my time with, Elliott. But for your information, that was a friend and business associate, Harold. You met him before."

"Yeah, I did. And I recall saying to you that he was suspect. I also recall you blowing it off."

"That was then, this is now, Elliott," Henry said. "What's the problem?"

"The problem is my son now questions your sexuality because no straight man would hang out with a gay man," he answered. "So, since he questions your sexuality, that means he questions mine. And I can't have that."

"I can't believe we're back at this," Henry said. "You can tell your son that I'm gay. That's fine. Or I can tell him. My point is, I don't care if he knows. Now, as far as him associating you with being gay because I'm gay, that's something you have to address.

"Look, I'm not trying to be flippant or insensitive. And I definitely don't want to get into another debate with you about this. Either you're my friend or you're not. I would understand if you said you couldn't handle the association. I wouldn't like it and I would be hurt by it. But I would get it. You would be like every other guy who was my friend but now isn't. You'd be too weak to stand by friendship over perception."

"Dude, you're here, aren't you?" Elliott said. "If I was weak and didn't value your friendship, you wouldn't be in my house. But if we're gonna be straight up, let's be straight up. Maybe it's not meant for me to understand, but I don't get the whole gay thing. Two men having sex—I hope I can say this to you because we're friends—but two men having sex just ain't right. It ain't right, Henry. It says so in The Bible and it says so on the street."

"I can't and won't try to justify anything to you," Henry said. "You're back to judging me when you have no room to be judgmental. Sex with girls your daughter's age…something seems really wrong with that to me."

"I won't try to say that there's nothing wrong with that. When you say it out loud, it doesn't sound so good," Elliott said. "But they were adults, consenting adults. And it's not a sin."

"I can't believe you're trying to call on The Bible as moral high ground," Henry said. "I have to deal with my Maker at that time and He will judge me. Not you. Until then, though, you let me live my life and you live yours."

Elliott wanted to end the talk, but needed to be clear about something. "This isn't easy for me. Henry, I'm not worried about people's assumptions."

Henry gave him a side-eye look.

"Okay, well, I'm not worried anymore," Elliott said. "Either I'm in or I'm out. And I'm in. But I can't promise it will always be comfortable. This conversation isn't comfortable. But to be honest with myself, I have to go to some uncomfortable places to eventually get comfortable."

Henry nodded his head.

Then Elliott added, "But I don't know if I'll ever get comfortable with this." He smiled at Henry and Henry smiled back.

"Yeah, I bet you can't get comfortable with it since you're probably fighting your own sexuality demons," Henry said. "You were in prison for twelve years. I'm sure someone got to you."

"It's time for you to leave, talking that crazy shit," Elliott said, laughing.

The men exchanged handshakes and a delicate hug to protect Elliott's ribs. "Come here, let me squeeze your butt. I bet it's tight," Henry said, laughing as he ran toward the door.

"You better get out of here," Elliott yelled. He and Henry had a tough conversation and were able to joke about it in the end. He hoped the other conversations he had would end the same way.

CHAPTER NINETEEN
Age Is More Than A Number

Elliott rested after Henry left and tried to figure out what he was going to say to Tamara. He was torn. Ending the relationship would likely result in ending the friendship, too.

She called around nine-thirty, saying she was on her way. By the time she arrived, near ten, Elliott had steadied his mind on how to approach her. But Tamara showed up borderline drunk and definitely tipsy.

"I hate to see you like this," she said. "I'm glad you're up and moving better, but I'm sure you're still hurting."

Elliott sat down gingerly on the couch and elevated his feet on an ottoman. "I'm doing better. What's up with you?"

"I'm good. I wish you were with me tonight."

"Girl, if we were out at an event like that, people would think I'm your father. We don't look like the average couple."

"So what? You living for them or for yourself?"

Elliott wanted to respond, but Tamara continued. "Look, look at this. How cute am I?"

It was her passport. "So where we going? You said you'd tell me once I got my passport. Well, as you can see, I didn't waste any time."

"No, you didn't," Elliott said. "That's good that you handled that."

"So, where we going?"

"I don't know," Elliott said. "I hadn't bought any tickets. I wanted you to have your passport and then we could decide. But…"

"But what?" Tamara said. "But your ex-wife, Lucy, wants you back?"

Elliott was surprised by that remark. "She wants you back, right?" she went on.

"Why would you say that?"

"Because she told me," Tamara said.

Elliott was really surprised and only halfway believed her. "What are you talking about?"

"I met her in the bathroom at the hospital one night. She didn't know who I was and we started talking. She told me she was in love with you and you were in love with her. At least that's what she hoped."

He still was not sure if she was telling the truth. "You don't believe me, do you?" she said. "Ask her if she met a woman in the bathroom that night. She said she had just left your room.

"But I didn't know it was your ex-wife until the next day, when I came up to your room and you told me to leave. I ran into her in the hallway. We both knew who each other was then."

Elliott did not know what to think then. But the timeline of when he saw Lucy and when he saw Tamara jibed with how she said things unfolded.

"Your ex is a good-looking woman," Tamara said. "She's not me, but for her age, she looks good… So, what did you tell her when she told you how she felt?"

"Tamara, I can't—no, I *won't*—get into my conversation with Lucy," he said.

"Why not?" she said, raising her voice. "I'm tired of you playing games. You're damn near a senior citizen and you're playing games with me. I ain't having it."

"You need to calm down; what are you upset about?" Elliott said. "I'm not telling her about my conversations with you and vice versa. So you can get all upset if you want, but that's it."

"Look, Elliott, I have to tell you; I'm in love with you," she said.

"What? Come on, Tamara," he said.

"So you're dismissing my feelings like that? I'm serious. I feel like we can be good together."

"I'm not dismissing your feelings because you don't have any for me," he said. "My ego told me you did. You want me to be honest and that's what I have to be with you. I like young women, or I convinced myself that I do. So I met you and pursued you because you were the right age for what I was into at that point in my life."

"So now you're not into me anymore, just like that?" she asked. "Your wife comes crawling back and you're not into me anymore? That's fucked up."

"What I'm saying is that I was never into you," Elliott confessed. "That doesn't mean I never liked you because I did. I do. I would never have spent any time with you or even have you at my house if I didn't. But I wasn't into you. I was into distracting myself so I wouldn't think about my ex-wife.

"And you have to be honest, too. You only claimed you had feelings for me only after knowing Lucy said she loved me."

"Don't act like I can't identify my own feelings," she said. "I wouldn't have slept with you if I didn't have feelings for you."

"Sleeping together was a mistake," he said. "Look at me; I'm sixty-one years old. I'm old enough to be your father and damn near your grandfather. We're not supposed to be together.

"If you saw a couple with our age difference together, you'd think something was wrong with her. I don't want people to think that about you."

"You know what I'd think?" Tamara asked. "I'd think that old dude must be putting it down. He either has some money or he was tapping that ass right."

"So why would I think that you think differently about me?"

"You don't have to. You obviously have money to be living here. But I never asked about your money; I have my own. But you surely did tap that ass right. I'm not even gonna front. That's enough reason to be with your old ass right now."

"And when you turn thirty-five and I'm seventy-one, then what?"

"We'll worry about that at that time. Let me tell you something. You don't understand how terrible it is out here for women. That's probably why your ex-wife wants you back. She's saying, 'Fuck what he did to end the marriage. It's better to have someone I know and love cheat on me than someone I don't know and don't love who will probably cheat, too.'"

"Look, I shared a little about my life with you," Elliott said. "You know about what I went through. I missed my twenties. So having relationships with young women was my way of trying to live a part of my life that I missed. That's what it boils down to. If I wasn't doing that, we would never be here right now. That doesn't take away from really liking you and enjoying our time together. But we can't have a relationship. This is where it should end."

"How in the hell is a sixty-one-year-old man gonna dump a twenty-five-year-old woman?" Tamara said. "I could see if I was fat and ugly or dumb and crazy. But I'm none of that. Guys are after me all day every day, and the one man I want to be with doesn't want to be with me? This is crazy."

"I don't know what to say beyond what I told you," Elliott said. "I'm still in love with my ex-wife."

"Were you in love with her those times we had sex?" she asked.

"Yes," Elliott said.

"Don't you want me now?" Tamara slid closer to him on the couch and reached for his crotch. "Let me have some more of that."

Elliott wanted to push her away, but he was tentative because of his injured ribs. "Cut it out, Tamara."

"I will. But let me suck you off first."

The man in Elliott gave that a consideration for a quick second. And he admitted it. "That sounds good and I probably need that, Tamara. But no. Probably, you should go now."

She moved forward instead of toward the door...until the doorbell rang. "Who's that?"

"I have no idea," Elliott said. "I don't get how people come up here without my knowledge. This is the second time in a week."

"Want me to answer it?" she asked.

"Hell, no. I got it," he said, pulling himself off the couch.

"Who is it?" he yelled with attitude.

"Sorry, Daddy, it's me," Danielle said.

"Oh, shit," Elliott said. "This isn't good. You've got to hide."

"Are you crazy? I'm not hiding," Tamara said. "You'd better let her in and face this or let her stay out there."

Elliott's head spun. This was the last thing he expected—or needed. "Hold on, Danielle," he said toward the door. He turned to Tamara. "Sit down. And please don't blow this whole thing up."

He opened the door. "Hey, honey, how are you?" They hugged at the door. "Look who's here."

Danielle stepped in and stopped in her tracks when she saw Tamara.

"What the hell is she doing here? What are you doing here?" Danielle wanted to know.

"Danny, come on in," Elliott said. "She came to see how I'm doing."

"Why do you care how he's doing?" Danielle said. "What's going on?"

"Your father is my friend," Tamara said. "I know he told you some story about trying to buy a car from him. But in reality, we're friends."

"Dad…" Danielle said, turning to Elliott.

He smiled and shook his head. This moment was one he feared would not happen. It was awkward. And it made Elliott nervous. All the ground gained over the previous week could be ruined.

"Yes, Tamara and I are friends," Elliot said.

"But what's that mean?" Danielle asked.

"It means—" Tamara started, but was cut off by Elliott.

"It means," he said, "that we met and have seen each other a few times since then."

"You're dating her?" his daughter asked.

"I was," Elliott said.

"What do you mean you were?" Tamara interjected.

"What did I tell you a few minutes ago?" Elliott said.

"Wait a minute," Danielle said. "I want to make sure I'm hearing this right. Tamara, you're dating my sixty-one-year-old father?"

"Yes, Danielle," she said. "I didn't know he was your father until we saw you at Vanquish."

"And that wasn't enough for you to stop seeing him?" Danielle said. She turned to her father. "That wasn't enough for you to stop seeing her?"

Neither of them answered because Danielle already knew the answer. "Danielle, I want to talk to you in private, after Tamara leaves," he said.

"Yeah, and I want to talk to you, too," she said. Then she turned to Tamara. "It's time for you to leave."

"You don't say when I leave," Tamara shot back.

"Oh, yes, she does," Elliott said. He was determined to leave no ambiguity with Danielle.

"I met your mother on Monday night at the hospital," Tamara said.

"So what? What does that have to do with anything?" Danielle asked.

"She seems like a nice woman," Tamara said. "She told me she's in love with Elliott. She told me that in the bathroom. She sounded kind of desperate to me."

"Desperate?" Danielle said. "My mother isn't desperate for anything. And you shouldn't be talking about my mother anyway. Just leave."

"I'm leaving," she said. "I came over to check on Elliott and let him know I got my passport so we can take my birthday trip he has planned."

Elliott shook his head. Tamara was trying to bury him in his daughter's eyes.

"I can go anytime other than next week, Elliott," she said before leaving. "No hug and a goodbye kiss? I understand. See you tomorrow."

"Dad, I can't believe you," Danielle said. She was close to crying but was too angry for tears to flow. "What are you doing running around with her?"

Elliott was busted. There was no wiggle room, no way to finesse the reality. So, he came with it. Danielle took a seat and listened intently.

"I met her and we went out a few times," he said. "I didn't stop seeing her after I knew you all were friends. I don't know why, but I didn't. I know the age difference is crazy, and, to be honest, that's what the whole thing was about for me.

"I love your mother and I never stopped loving her. I dated women who were as far away from your mom as possible. I didn't want to be reminded of her. That's the truth."

"What about all this passport stuff and taking her on a trip?" Danielle said.

"No, that was before I found out you and she were friends," Elliott said. "She did show me her passport tonight, but I had already told her that it was over."

"Dad, I heard what you said, but come on," she said. "You dated a girl how many years younger than you? Thirty-six years younger than you? I'm so embarrassed."

"Why are you embarrassed?"

"Why? She went to school with me, Dad. She knows some of my friends. How embarrassing it will be with her running her mouth about this. And wait until Daniel finds out. You think he's angry now. He'll be here any minute. He stopped at the bar at Drinkshop downstairs first."

"What are you all doing here?" Elliott asked.

"Dad, you were just discharged from the hospital," she said. "I called you and texted you that we were on our way. You didn't get it?"

Elliott found his cell on the dresser in his bedroom. "Oh, man, I didn't even know where my phone was," he said, scanning his missed calls. "I see Daniel called, too. And Henry."

"Yeah, Mr. Henry is another thing," Danielle said. "What's going on with him? Is he gay? You're hanging with a girl a little older than me, and a gay man? I don't know what to think."

She pulled out her cell phone and called her brother.

"You're not going to believe who was here," Danielle said into the phone.

She told her father that Daniel ran into Tamara. Elliott yelled, "Tell Daniel not to do anything crazy."

She nodded to her father and listened. "What? Do I need to come down there?"

On the lobby level, Daniel and Tamara were sparring. "So you're trying to get money out of my father?" he charged. "You know what that makes you?"

"You're just mad because I wasn't checking for you," she fired back.

"What? I never liked you," Daniel said. "You trippin'."

"No, I ain't. We went to the Michigan game in Ann Arbor and were at that party that night at the Alpha fraternity house," she said. "You asked me to dance and I said 'Later.' Ever since then you've tried me."

"I asked you to dance because I felt sorry for you," Daniel said.

"And don't think I didn't catch you calling me a ho," she said. "I don't appreciate that."

"Hey, if the street corner fits…" he cracked. And even Tamara had to laugh.

"I should smack you, but that was funny," she said. They looked at each other, and their eyes calmed them.

"Seriously, don't be mad at me. And don't be mad at your father," Tamara said. Her buzz was fading and her true self stepped forward. "We are two adults who met and liked each other. Obviously, there's a big age difference, but we both knew that."

"What would you want to do with an old man?" Daniel said. "He's my father and he's cool, but he's old."

"He is old in age, but not in spirit," she said. "Did you notice that I never dated anyone at school? I didn't because they were too young for me. I've always liked much older men, even when I was in middle school and first started liking boys. It was the assistant principal, Mr. Hunter, that I felt drawn to."

"So what's my dad's excuse?" Daniel said.

"To be honest, he was trying to fill a void," she answered. "That's what he told me and that's what I believe. The problem is that I really like him and care about him."

"Tamara, come on," Daniel said. "Are you serious?"

"I am," she said. "You don't see all there is in your father?"

"What I see is someone who betrayed his wife—my mother—and broke up our family," he said. "That's why we haven't really been in his life the last few years. He turned our world upside down."

"But he's your father," she said. "You mean to tell me that you're going to have this beef with your father the rest of your life? Remember my last year at school, when we went to Selena Saunders' father's funeral and how broken up she was? Well, I found out later that she was doing all that crying and carrying on because she felt guilty. She got into an argument with her father and had not spoken to him in six months. Then he died suddenly and she realized how petty it was to be that way with her dad.

"And you know why she stopped speaking to him? Because he wouldn't let her take her car back to school after she crashed for the second time in one semester."

Tamara got through to Daniel. They ended their conversation with nothing resolved, but with Daniel feeling like he had to harness his anger and contempt for Elliott. When he arrived upstairs, Danielle was at the door, on her way out.

"Let me ask you both this before you go," Elliott said. "Are you upset that I have seen a twenty-five-year-old or because I have seen a twenty-five-year-old that you know?"

The brother and sister looked at each other. "For me, it's the fact that she's twenty-five," Daniel said. "She's too old for me, but not too young for you, and you're sixty?"

"Sixty-one," Danielle pointed out. "For me, it's knowing her, too.

I mean, she knows a lot of our friends in school. Think of how that makes us look."

"Why does it have to make you look negative?" Elliott said.

"Ah, come on, Dad," Daniel said. "It doesn't make us look good. Our father is running around with a former classmate? Really? Seriously? We have to explain how bad that looks?"

"No, you don't and I shouldn't have asked that," Elliott said. "It was a reflex. Well, obviously, like I told Danielle, I did not know she was your friend until that night at Vanquish. We could have ended it there, but we chose not to, and I take responsibility for that. My position at the time was I needed to live my life the way I want to live it. I needed to be distracted from how I feel about your mother.

"But the reality is that my actions, you know, impacted your life, too. And that's where I should have drawn the line…and I didn't."

His kids looked at him with sad expressions, looks that sunk his spirits. They left without saying "goodbye." They simply turned and walked away.

Elliott closed the door and wondered if he would see his children again. He hardly slept that night. And when the next day came and went with neither Daniel nor Danielle calling, he was devastated. Lucy was supposed to come by, but did not. Tamara did not call.

His escape usually was to go out to be around people. But this old man was bruised—more emotionally than physically—and unable to go anywhere. He was stuck at home alone with his thoughts and regrets.

CHAPTER TWENTY
Dawn Of A New Day

The morning came and Elliott felt no symptoms of a concussion. His ribs were much less tender. He felt fine... physically. Emotionally, he was drained and abandoned, like all the progress made to reconnect his family diminished into vapor.

It was a similar feeling to what he had when he was in prison. Lonely. Hopeless. Pitiful. Those feelings were only fleeting while locked up, though. He knew he could not survive carrying vulnerable emotions. So he would start each day with a prayer that he stopped reciting once he was freed.

He stopped praying the prayer because it was a reminder of his dozen years of hell. But that morning, as he showered, he realized the prayer was what helped him get through that hell. And so, he dropped to his knees right there in the shower, with the water funneling down his back.

"God, you know my heart, and that I am not supposed to be in this place. I ask You to bless and protect me through this day. Direct me away from danger. Keep my spirits up. And lead me on the path to redemption. In Jesus' precious name, I pray, Amen."

Afterward, he was mad at himself for a moment. He abandoned that prayer because it would remind him of prison, but it was just as needed in the free world. And in the case of his family, he was in a figurative place he did not belong and he needed direction for redemption. The prayer set him on that course.

He called Tamara. She was at her office, but stepped outside to take the call. "I'm sorry that I misled you," he said. "You're a special young lady. You deserve someone who can be there for you for the long haul."

"If you liked me, how did you mislead me?" she asked.

"I needed you. I used you to fill a void in my life," he said.

"Elliott, we all need someone to fill a void," Tamara said. "That's just how it is. But thank you for saying that. I had fun with you. I feel like I learned a lot and I got my passport. So I'm better for the experience."

Elliott laughed. "You're ahead of your time," he said. "I will stay in touch."

"You better," she said. "Gotta get back to work. Take care."

"You, too," he said, smiling. There was relief that he and Tamara had ended their relationship, but mostly because it was amicable. He wanted her to feel good about him and their time together.

Still, making inroads with his children and ex-wife would be more difficult. He, in fact, hoped only that they would listen to him and in the end, be willing to start over, fresh, with open hearts and minds.

He called Lucy, who reluctantly answered. "Yes, Elliott."

"This evening, I want to come over," he said. "You and our kids are the most important people in my life. Period. Somehow I have allowed this to get out of hand. We might be divorced, but we still should be a family. So I want to call a family meeting."

"A family meeting. Really, Elliott?"

"Call it whatever you like, Lucy. I'll be there at seven. Can you make sure the kids are there, too?"

"They'll be there," she said. "I had already planned to cook dinner."

"Good. I'll come hungry," he said.

"Who said there'll be enough for you?"

"Bye, Lucy."

He took a deep breath. His spirits soared. He next called Henry. He realized that it was the anniversary of the death of his son.

"I wanted to check on you," he said. "Have you been to the cemetery yet?"

"Ah, man, you remembered?" Henry said, his voice low. "Yes, I was there pretty much at sunrise. It's so quiet there, Elliott. The cemetery is the most peaceful place on earth. I was the only one there. I go about every week as it is. But, you know, today…I still miss him, man."

"Of course, you do," Elliott said.

"No, I mean like almost every day I wake up and I think he's still with me. It takes me a few seconds, sometimes several seconds, to realize…to realize I had to bury my son. It's still so crazy to me."

Elliott did not know what to say, so he did not say anything.

"Before I left the cemetery this morning, Jarrod's mother showed up. You know how our relationship has been. She was alone. LaWanda brought flowers, too. I waited on her to have her private time with him. The pain we have for losing our son is beyond description.

"When she was done, she came over. We didn't say a word to each other. She walked right into my arms and we hugged and cried together.

"We stood for about two minutes. I walked her to her car. We looked at each other through the tears, hugged again, and then she left. I'm telling you this, Elliott, because you still have two children, and you've got to make peace with them."

If Elliott was not inspired to do so before calling Henry, he was then. Elliott had intended on telling Henry that he would be a better friend to him, that his sexual preference would not be a subject of debate or a deterrent to how they functioned. Instead, he decided that the action would be more powerful than words.

"Next time you go to the cemetery, please let me know," he told his friend. "I want to go with you. In the meantime, when these staples come out of my head, see if Harold wants to roll out with us and let's get some drinks."

Elliott spent the rest of the day reading. Prison turned him into a bibliophile. He was so afraid his mind would rot if he did not read continuously. At one point, he went two years without a television in his cell.

After a late breakfast, he lay in bed and dug into DeVon Franklin's *Produced By Faith*. One passage resonated with him. *"There are times when I get fearful or upset about something that does not work out in my favor, and in those moments, I have to remind myself that God is working. He will ultimately provide..."*

Elliott had failed to honor God by consistently going to church after he was released from prison, even though he believed God protected him and saw him through. His reason: God did not have to allow him to go to prison in the first place.

Clarity can be fleeting. In the storm, vision gets obstructed. That passage in Franklin's book resonated with Elliott and gave him clarity to see what he could not see or was not prepared to see. But in those words, he believed God governed his life and would not allow his family to remain fractured.

So when he pulled up that evening at seven to the house he once called home, the fear he once had about what would transpire was not with him.

Remarkably, he had not been back to the house since Lucy demanded he leave; Daniel and his cousin had collected his remaining property and delivered it to him. So he felt awkward at the door, waiting for someone to answer his knocks.

But nothing could move him off his base. He was at peace with whatever the outcome of the night, which relieved him of the pressure of trying to convince anyone of anything.

"Hi," Danielle said when she opened the door. The fact that she did not say "Daddy" let him know where her emotions were. But he didn't care.

"Hi, honey." He hugged her and kissed her on the side of her face.

She walked ahead of him, through the living room and dining room and into the kitchen. Elliott walked slowly and took in his old home. He saw art on the walls he had forgotten and noticed that new carpet was under his feet.

He handed bottles of red and white wine to Daniel, who gave him a faint greeting. "Wasn't sure what your mom cooked, so I bought one of each."

Lucy came out of the downstairs bathroom, smiling and bubbly. "Hi, Elliott. Haven't seen you in this house in a long time."

"I know," he said. "Good to be here again."

Daniel went to the family room, where an NBA game was playing on the television. The sound was down while Ronnie Jordan's *The Antidote* played from the iPod dock. Elliott looked around and it felt like home, with Danielle and Lucy in the kitchen and he in the family room with Daniel watching sports.

"Thanks for having me over," he said to Lucy from the family room.

"Can we talk after dinner?" she said. Dinner was important to Lucy. When married, she insisted they eat together, as a family, most every night. She was lenient on Fridays and Saturdays, but

Sunday through Thursday was dinner at the dining room table. It was where they stayed in touch with each other.

"If nothing else, I want to have a nice dinner," she added.

Elliott did not respond. He turned to Daniel. "Hey, listen, you mind opening that bottle of Syrah? I could use a glass of wine. You could, too, right?"

Daniel did not answer, but he opened the wine and brought his father a glass.

"You know what my last memory of you is in this house—other than leaving that night?" Daniel said. "We were playing Scrabble—me, you and Danielle. And you put down the word, 'proud.' It was a triple-word score for you. And you said, 'That's a great word because I'm proud of you. And I'll make sure you're always proud of me.' And the next day you were gone. And I can't say I've been that proud of you since then."

"I'm sorry you feel that way, son. I am," Elliott said. "The good news is that I'm still alive, which means there is a chance to turn it around."

Daniel looked at his father for a second or two and turned to watch the game. They sat in silence for a few minutes before Danielle announced, "You can wash your hands. It's ready."

Elliott looked around the house some more and it did not feel like home as much. The look of it changed with the paint colors. There were new art pieces and no family photos that included him. He looked at himself in the mirror as he washed his hands, and his task seemed more daunting.

They got through dinner with lighthearted banter and even a few jokes. "Daddy," Danielle said, "I never realized how big your head is. Having that wrapping around it outlines it. It's shaped like a tea kettle."

He was fine with being the target and was glad to see that the tension was minimized. "The staples come out next week, I think," he said. "I want to see how this thing heals, what kind of mark it leaves."

The meal of sautéed shrimp with stir-fried vegetables and rice pilaf went down nicely. They consumed both bottles of wine.

"Can I help clean up?" he asked.

"Yes, you can do the dishes," Lucy said. "No, don't worry about it. I'll get them later. Let's talk. You came over her for the first time in three years for a reason."

They moved to the family room, where Daniel turned off the music, but kept the game on the television.

"Can you turn that off?" Elliott asked.

"The sound is down; what's the difference?" Daniel snapped.

"Turn it off," Lucy said, and he did.

Then Elliott got right to it. "First of all, I'm doing better," he said. "It's disappointing no one asked, so I thought I'd tell you. Secondly, I want to say I'm sorry."

"Sorry for what?" Danielle said.

"To you and Daniel, I'm sorry for embarrassing you with Tamara," Elliott answered. "I'll explain to you as I explained to her. I used her as a way to try to fill a void in my life, the void I have felt ever since the day I walked out of that door.

"The void was big because there was the void of not having the three most important people in my life. You kids are an extension of your mother and me and I would stand in front of a firing squad for you. When you would barely communicate with me, I felt helpless and hopeless and that's a very tough place to be for someone who loves his kids as much as I love you.

"Listen, I spoke to Henry this morning. Do you know today is the one-year anniversary of when Jarrod was killed? It was heart-breaking to hear him talk about how much he misses his son. Last thing he told me was to make it right with you. He helped me understand that our relationship is too important to let it flounder like it has."

He blinked away tears. "I love you and I need you to be my kids again. I need that relationship. One reason why I enjoyed talking to Tamara so much was because she reminded me of you: the youthfulness, the energy.

"At the same time, I needed her to not make me think of your mother."

Daniel was calm and it was evident that Elliott's heartfelt words got to him. But he and Danielle remained puzzled by one thing.

"Dad, that sounds good," he said. "It does and I'll be honest and say I feel better, a little better."

"Me, too," Danielle chimed in.

"But," Daniel continued, "if you loved Mom and us so much, how could you leave? How could you do what you did to break up this family? That's important because it's been traumatic. Danielle and I talk about it all the time."

"You do?" Lucy asked.

"Yes, we do, Mom," Danielle said. "And we think we're doing well and then something happens that makes us get upset and angry all over again. Angry at you, Dad."

"Angry also because you shut us out of everything," Daniel added. "We wanted to know what happened, why you cheated on Mom—shoot, cheated on all of us—to cause all this mess."

"You all aren't kids, but the children should not be in the middle of something their parents go through," Elliott said.

"You've been saying that for three years, Dad," Daniel said. "Give it a rest. How can we ever let go of our anger if you treat us like we don't matter? We *are* in the middle of it. You put us there when you cheated."

"Stop it," Lucy said.

"Lucy, don't," Elliott interjected. "Don't."

"It's time," she said.

"What, Mommy?" Danielle asked.

"Lucy, we had an agreement," Elliott said.

"See, you're still trying to stop her from telling the truth," Daniel said. "Why won't you just admit it, Dad?"

"There's nothing for him to admit," Lucy said. "It wasn't him. It was me. I cheated."

Elliott dropped his head.

"What?" Danielle said. "Mommy…"

"It's true," Lucy said. "I can't live with this eating away at me anymore. Your father was good to me. I cheated on him. I broke up the family."

Elliott sat with his head in his hands. Tears slid down Danielle's face. Daniel's mouth was open. Lucy broke the silence.

"I was going through something and—"

"Lucy," Elliott jumped in. "You don't have to do this."

"Thank you, Elliott, but I do," she said. "You have protected me for three years. And I'm ashamed that I let your kids think the worst of you when I was the one who caused all this mess."

"Mom, you had an affair? I can't believe it," Daniel said.

"Baby, it's true," she said. "I was in a bad place, even though we had a wonderful family. And I broke our vows."

"Lucy, that's enough," Elliott said.

She had told her ex-husband the story at the time. "You were a good husband and a good father," she said back, then added, "I was needy and insecure. You notice that whenever you spoke at an Innocence Project event I was trying to go? I wanted to see you and support you, yes. But I needed constant attention that showed I was loved and needed.

"You probably didn't notice it because you were always there. We spent more time together than most married couples. But there was a stretch of about a month when you were gone a lot and I couldn't go because of work. Three weekends in a row. I met my sister and her friend at the St. Regis for dinner one night and when we were leaving, they jumped into their cars from the valet and I had them hold mine. I had to go to the bathroom.

"Well, it was upstairs and when I came out, I decided I wanted a drink at the bar. I get there, end up meeting a man and woman who were in town on business. She left me and the guy there and I got to drinking and he invited me to his room and…That was the only time I saw him."

"But he called the house, Lucy," Elliott responded. "That's how I found out."

"I had given him our number before I even finished my first drink," she said. "There's no excuse. I'm not gonna say it just happened. That would be an insult to you. It happened because I felt lonely but mostly because I was stupid."

The details hurt Elliott even more, but he needed to hear them to assure it was not his fault.

"But why did you make Dad leave then?" Daniel said to his mother. "I was here. I heard you repeatedly tell him to leave."

"Because I couldn't face him," Lucy said. "Because I didn't deserve him. Seeing him would remind me of how awful a person I was."

"I left at the time because I believed she needed to clear her head," Elliott said.

"You were going to stay, knowing she—knowing what happened?" Daniel said.

"I'm not going to act like it was okay; it wasn't," Elliott said. "I was hurt and damaged. But we were a family, and if there was a way to get beyond it, I wanted to try."

"I can't believe this," Danielle said. "Dad, you took all our shit—excuse my language—for all this time when you didn't do anything? To protect Mom?"

"That's your mother," he said. "I made her promise that we'd not talk to you about it. Not lie to you, just not talk about it. I know how much your mom loves you and how much respect she deserves from you. I didn't…I didn't want that tarnished."

"But you'd allow us to look at you in that way?" Daniel said.

"That's love," he said. "When you're in love, truly in love, you're programmed to protect."

"I'm so sorry, first to Elliott; I never should have let you take that burden," Lucy said. Then she sobbed. "Kids, I love you very much. I'm so sorry. I…I'm so ashamed. I'm so embarrassed."

Her children hugged her. "I'm so glad to see this," Elliott said. "This family has been through enough pain. We need to comfort each other."

Elliott was not going to expose Lucy, no matter how the evening went. But Lucy admitting her infidelity lifted a burden off of him.

"Dad, I'm sorry, man," Daniel said. "I have been so mad at you and treated you so crazy. I'm sorry."

"Me, too, Daddy," Danielle said, wiping away her tears. She moved over to Elliott and hugged him, resting her head on his chest. "I love you so much."

Elliott closed his eyes and tears seeped through. He felt reconnected to his family again. Finally.

CHAPTER TWENTY-ONE
We Be Clubbin'

The emotion of the revelation poured out for the next hour. Lucy did not face the wrath Elliott endured, mostly because the family could not transition more ill feelings to someone it loved so much. The kids were depleted of negative energy and overcome with love.

"Where does this leave us, Elliott?" Lucy said. "I mean, as I told you in the hospital, I do love you."

"We should leave," Daniel said. "We're going upstairs."

They left the room, but did not go to their rooms. They eavesdropped from the kitchen.

"Why are you telling me this now?" Elliott asked.

"Just like I couldn't take not telling the kids the truth, I couldn't take not letting you know how I feel," she said. "I'm aware that what I did was unforgivable. But I can't live any longer not telling the truth. Whatever you feel or say, I will deal with it. I feel so relieved just to say what's on my heart."

"Me, too," Elliott said. "I hoped the kids would stop asking. It was hard phrasing my answers so I wasn't lying to them."

"This whole thing has been a nightmare," Lucy said. "I'm sorry, Elliott. If you could find it in your heart to forgive me, it would mean the world to me."

"I forgave you a long time ago," Elliott said. "But I'm not different from most men. We have a double standard about cheating. We want you to forgive us, but if you cheat on us, well, it's the end of the world. I went through that stage. As much as I was trying to save the marriage, I was torn up inside and I felt stupid, too. And maybe if my life before you was different, I would never have forgiven you. But I needed to let go of that burden to be able to live any kind of life, and I have.

"Also, I'm not crazy; I knew you very well and I knew—maybe from being sexually assaulted—that you needed to feel loved. That's why there were times when I blamed myself because I knew, and yet I still glossed over it, thinking you'd be fine.

"I don't blame myself anymore. But I do know that I could have been better about that part of it."

"I'm so much better now," Lucy said. "I have been in therapy and addressed it. Just so you know, I would never, ever hurt you again. My punishment is that I have to live with knowing I betrayed the love of my life."

Lucy was losing her composure when Elliott slid next to her on the couch. He put his hand on her left knee. Touching her warmed his body.

"We've been through a lot," he said. "All of it self-inflicted. I don't know where this will go, but I know where it has the potential to go. We've cleared a big hurdle—my kids don't hate me anymore."

Danielle and Daniel could not take it anymore. They came from around the corner.

"Can we be a family again?" Danielle asked.

"I'll say this," Elliott began. "I never stopped loving your mother."

"And I never stopped loving your father," Lucy added.

"And so, we have a chance to at least do family things to try to build back what was lost," Elliott said.

"I can't ask for any more than that," Lucy said. She hugged Elliott, and he felt at home again.

"I have an idea for our first family outing," he said.

"What?" the three of them said in unison.

"There's a party on Saturday at Bottle Bar in Buckhead," Elliott interjected.

"Dad, no way," Daniel said.

"A party, Daddy?" Danielle said. "Really?"

"What can I say?" Elliott cracked. "Once the old man in the club, always the old man in the club."

He was only half-joking.

Ω

The Craft

I was fifty-two at the conclusion of writing this book—not quite old enough in theory to be an old man in the club. Still, I stopped clubbing several years ago. I liked to dance as much as the next guy. But it was just too loud in there, which may be a sign that I was too old for the club scene.

My preference for lounges and relative quiet took over in my early-40s. But, like you, I always wondered why the guy who was obviously two or three generations older than me would roam the nightclub as if he were hanging with his peers. That curiosity spawned this book.

As an author, I like to address situations—and confront questions—that we all consider, but sometimes never receive an answer. In many cases, there is no answer. It is what it is. In the case of the old man in the club, I created a multi-level answer in Elliott Thomas.

Without even trying, we pass judgment on someone in a nanosecond. Almost instantly we assess a person's values, motives and character. We do this without even saying a word to the person. Most of the time it is an involuntary reaction. We just do it.

But is it fair?

To my way of thinking, a man sixty-one years old who hangs out with young adults his children's age does it for reasons beyond being the proverbial "dirty old man," although those characters certainly exist. In the case of this book, Elliott was more complex. He had his reasons—real and imagined—and that's what made writing this book so much fun and so challenging.

To explore his psyche, address his demons, examine his hang-ups and dive into his heart took me on a literary journey that was fulfilling. I did not always agree with Elliott on this journey. But I empathized with him. I admired his strength, his commitment—to himself, his ex-wife, his kids and his friend, Henry.

And by the time I was done, I understood his actions, even if I did not agree with all of them. Above all, I came to a conclusion about myself: No more judging of people from a distance.

We have no idea what has happened in people's lives that impact how they act, what they do, who they are. After Elliott Thomas, I look at the old man in the club differently. He *could* be there because he's a pervert. I choose to believe he's there for reasons far more complicated than I could imagine. And since this is a free country, why not do the things that make you feel your best?

I do not expect to be the old man in the club one day. But if you see me out there in a decade or so, don't judge me. I would have my reasons. Just offer me a drink and point me toward the exit.

Curtis Bunn

Discussion Questions

1) What was your impression of "old men in the club" before the book and did it change after reading it?

2) What would make a young woman attracted to a man her father's age and did you understand Tamara's interest in Elliott?

3) Did you approve/understand Danielle's and Daniel's disenchantment with and treatment of their father? Why?

4) What did you think of Elliott's commitment to keeping the secret he kept, even though it impacted the way his children felt about him?

5) What did you make of Lucy's confession? Should she have said something earlier?

6) How did you take Elliott remaining friends with Henry after learning about his lifestyle?

7) Did you have any empathy for Henry or were you mortified by his actions? Is there any room to forgive him?

8) Can relationships with a thirty-five-year age difference work?

9) Did Elliott's past justify his desires to pursue younger women?

10) What are your thoughts on the book's cover? Was it effective? Did it match the book's content?

About the Author

Curtis Bunn is an award-winning sports journalist who transitioned into a best-selling and critically acclaimed author of novels that provide one-of-a-kind insight into the psyche of men. A graduate of Norfolk State University, he is a book club favorite who founded the National Book Club Conference, which hosts an annual event described as "Literary Bliss." Visit him at curtisbunn.com and on Facebook and Twitter @curtisbunn.

SEIZE THE DAY

BY CURTIS BUNN
COMING SOON FROM STREBOR BOOKS

CHAPTER 1: LIFE

I'm about to die. Doctor said so. Maybe not today. Perhaps to-morrow. Whenever it's coming, it's coming soon.

Cancer.

But I'm not scared. I'm a little anxious, a little curious, to be honest. Curious about how it will happen. Where I will be at that moment—the place and where will I be in my head, my mind. Will I get scared when I feel it coming? *Will* I feel it coming?

Well, those are thoughts for another day, a day that, truth be told, should not come for a few months or so. That's how long it will take the cancer to totally ravage and deplete my body and put me to sleep. Forever. That's what the doctors say. And they know everything.

So, here I am. In the prime of my life…waiting on death.

Can't cry about it. Not anymore. When I said I wasn't scared, I was talking about now. Three weeks ago, when Dr. Wamer gave me the news, I was scared as shit.

Do you have any idea what it's like to be told you're at the end of your life's journey? At forty-five? With a young daughter? With so much more to do? With so much not done?

I was so overwhelmed that it took me two days to pull myself out of bed, to turn on the lights in my house, to eat an apple. Then it took me another two days to tell my father, who took it as if cancer were eating away at his existence.

"Why can't it be me, Calvin?" he said. "Why you? You've lived a good life. The best thing I ever did was marry your momma—God rest her soul—and contribute to your birth. The rest of my life, I can't say I'm that proud of. Except you. You've made me proud."

And why did he say that? I bawled like a freshly spanked new-born, and my sixty-eight-year-old dad and I hugged each other at the kitchen table at his house for what seemed like an hour, two men afraid out of their wits.

Since then, I have pulled myself together—what's left of me, that is. Doctors say they can't do surgery, but I can try radiation and perhaps chemo. But there are no guarantees. That's code for: "it won't work." And I have seen how debilitating those treatments can be.

It never made sense to me that you go to the doctor for a check-up feeling fine. Then he tells you that you have cancer or some hideous disease and starts firing chemicals into your bloodstream like you shoot up a turkey you're about to fry on Thanksgiving. Almost immediately you feel like shit and before long, you start looking like shit. You lose your hair, you lose your energy…you lose who you are. And eventually you lose your will to live.

For some, for most, that's the route they choose and I don't begrudge them that. That's their choice.

Me, I would rather live whatever time I have left instead of having my insides burned out and become so drained that I could not live, only exist…until I die.

Maybe it's me, but that doesn't seem like fun. Haven't had much fun since I went to the hospital for my annual checkup, feeling good and looking forward to a date that night with a nice lady I had met. Next thing I know, they tell me I have some form of cancer I can't pronounce, much/less spell. "Sarcoma" something or other. Attacks the blood cells, organs, bones…you name it. When they said it was fatal, I lost interest in any more specifics.

I will be forty-six in four months…if I make it that long. I have a twenty-year-old daughter and a zest for life that is as strong as a weightlifter on steroids. Staying laid up in a hospital, withdrawn and diminished after chemotherapy does not qualify as living to me.

When I finally was up to eating, I ended up at this spot in midtown Atlanta called Carpe Diem in the plaza across from Grady High School. It was an interesting spot with good sandwiches and nice desserts, which fulfilled my sweet teeth. Yes, I enjoy cakes and pies too much to limit my attraction to "sweet tooth." That's why I said "sweet *teeth*."

Anyway, I sat alone, at a high-top table near the bar—a dying man with a plate of food and his thoughts. Ever since the doctors told me I would die, I haven't been able to slow down my thinking. Everything is on express.

People walk right by me, many of them speak to me or smile at me. None of them realize they were in contact with a dead man.

That's how I see myself—Walking Dead. I'm like a zombie, a creature walking around the earth but already departed. I just don't look like one…yet.

I see everything differently now, too. Like, it does not matter if my favorite football team, the Washington Redskins, wins another Super Bowl. I don't care much anymore about my wardrobe or purchasing that Mercedes 500 I had been eyeing or even if my 401(k) flattens out. It all seems so meaningless to me now.

Still, I'm not sure what I'm inspired to do or how to live out my life, other than to *not* let doctors turn me into a bed-ridden slob before my time. That, again, did not appeal to me and I didn't ask anyone else's opinion on it. I just went with it.

My daughter, Maya…I couldn't tell her. I can't even say her name without getting choked up. That's how daughters are to their dads; we live to their heartbeat.

My father told her. "She deserves to know," he reasoned. "Maybe not everything going on with you. But this? She deserved to know this."

Maya did not even call me about it. She just showed up at my house one Saturday afternoon, right before I was about to get in a round of golf. The garage door went up and there she was, pain and sadness all over her soft, lovely face. I know my daughter and that look made me cry, without her saying a word.

"Daddy," she said, hugging me so tightly. Every time we embraced, I smelled baby powder, like I did when she was an infant. It was my imagination or my desire for my little girl to remain my little girl.

"I'm OK, Maya," I said. "It's going to be all right."

She sobbed and sobbed and I held her as tightly as I could without making her uncomfortable. It broke my heart. We're here as parents to protect our children. It crushed me that I was the cause of her anguish.

"You didn't have to come here, sweetheart," I managed to get out when I finally composed myself. "See, this is why I didn't want to tell you right away. You are all upset over something you can't control. It's out of both our hands right now."

Maya wiped her face and looked up at me with those eyes that were the replica of mine: brown and piercing.

"Daddy, we can't control it, but you've got to let the doctors try," she said. "I spoke to an oncologist from Johns Hopkins on my way over here. He said nothing good will come out of doing nothing."

I had to break it down for her so—as, Isaiah Washington said in the movie *Love Jones*—"It will forever be broke."

"Let's go inside," I said. I wiped away her tears and kissed both sides of her precious face. She turned me into mush. We both were.

I called my friend, Thornell, and told him I had to renege on golf. I hadn't told him the news, either. That would be another tough call. But nothing compared to that talk with Maya.

"Sweetheart, about two months before I went to the doctor, I spoke to an old high school classmate at Ballou. His name was Kevin Hill. Yes, your godfather. Great guy, as you know. Do you know how we met? We played basketball against each other in junior high and became friends when we ended up at Ballou High together. When Kevin got sick with MS, it slowly but surely ravaged his nervous system over the years until he was unable to do anything but lie in bed to die.

"I visited him at Washington Hospital Center. We reminisced and I was able to make him laugh and take his mind away from his plight, at least for a few moments. But the whole time I was looking at him and feeling so sorry for him; there was so much more for him to do in life. I thought I didn't convey that, but he sensed it. And he wrote a letter to me that means more to me now than ever."

I pulled out the folded sheet of paper with the letterhead that read: "Kevin Hill…Remember Me."

And then I read it to Maya: "Calvin, don't feel sorry for me. The things I did in my life, I enjoyed them. I could have done more, but I learned and accepted that God's plan was different. But all this time laying around in bed, I have had a lot of time to think. And I have a lot of regrets. I regret not traveling and not mending my relationship with my sister and not learning Spanish and so many other things. You know what I should have done, but makes no sense to do now? Cut off all my hair. I saw how some bald guys looked so cool with a shaved head. Even Samuel Jackson looked cool with a bald head in *Shaft*. I should have done that a long time ago. Now, if I do it, no one will see it.

"Anyway, my point is: Don't live with regrets. Live your life. *Carpe diem*. You know what that means? It means: seize the day. Seize it. Take it. Own it. Make it yours and get the most out of it.

"Nothing is promised. Yeah, you've heard this before. We all have. But we go about a day as if it's no big deal to make the most of it because we can do it the next day. Or the next. That's not the right approach. I'm thirty-six. I got this disease from bad luck. If I knew it was coming, I would have done a lot of things I planned to do later. You and I have done a lot together and been as close as two friends could be, so I can say this to you without you getting offended: Get off your ass and live your life."

Maya got it then. The fear and hope left her. Reality settled in. She knew, at that point, I was done. No amount of radiation, chemo, surgery, Tylenol or anything else could help me. My days had been finalized. It had to be about what I did with those days that mattered.

"Daddy, what can I do to help you?" she asked.

"Love me, baby," I said. "Your love means everything to me. And pray for me. Pray that I'm able to make my last days here meaningful and fun and that I live them as if I'm alive, not waiting for death."

My daughter cried. "I can do that, Daddy," she said softly while hugging me.

We corralled our emotions after a while and I walked her to her car. "I feel so much better," I told her, and it was the truth. I didn't realize how much of a burden it was not having had that conversation with her. I finally was prepared to live my final days, to "seize" them as my friend Kevin said I should.

Problem was, I didn't know how or where to begin. I actually did not have lofty dreams of travel or glory. I didn't have a "Bucket List." I was an ordinary man with few extraordinary ambitions. I didn't like to travel much because I didn't like to fly and riding too long in a vehicle made me car sick.

I ate when necessary, but did not have exotic tastes. I had plenty of friends, but only Kevin whom I spent much time enjoying. I had but one vice: golf.

My first thought was just to play golf every day…until I collapsed on a lush fairway. Kevin would appreciate that. He and I were so close that we had become like brothers. For sure, we had a connection that is rare among people: I carried his kidney in my body.

When one of mine was damaged in a bad car crash and I needed a new one to avoid a life of dialysis, I was amazed by two things: Kevin was willing, without hesitation, to go through tests to see if we were compatible; and that he *was* a match. I had no siblings and my father's kidneys were not healthy enough to share.

If Kevin had any reservations about doing it, I never saw them. If there was any fear, I never felt it. And he never expressed any ambivalence about donating an organ to his friend.

For all I had done with and for him in the twenty-eight years we had known each other, there was nothing I could do to repay Kevin for his deed to me. And as I read his letter as I had each day, something occurred to me the way an idea comes to a prolific author: As a way of honoring Kevin, I would live out some of the things he never got to do based on what he wrote me in that letter and shared with me in conversations.

That was the least I could do, considering the kidney transplant allowed me to live fifteen years past when I was told I would die without a new one. Kevin saved my life. Doing things he wanted to do would extend my life, even if just for a little while.